Wahida Clark Presents

STREET TALES

A STREET LIT COLLABORATION

Shannon Holmes

Wahida Clark

Sa'id Salaam

Reds Johnson

Hood Chronicles

Wahida Clark Presents Publishing
60 Evergreen Place
Suite 904A
East Orange, New Jersey 07018
1(866) 910-6920
www.wclarkpublishing.com

Library of Congress Cataloging-In-Publication Data:
Shannon Holmes, Wahida Clark, Hood Chronicles, Reds Johnson, Sa'id Salaam
Street Tales: A Street Lit Anthology
ISBN 13-digit 9781947732483 (paper)
ISBN 13-digit 9781947732490 (ebook)
LCCN: 2019943686

1. Sex - 2. Domestic violence - 3. Washington DC - 4. African American- HIV - 5.Homosexuality - 6. Violence - 7. Relationships - 8. New Jersey –

Cover design and layout by Nuance Art, LLC
Book design by $weet & Tasty Visual Arts
www.artdiggs.com

WHO'S READY?

Wanna Sneak Peek?

STREET TALES FOREWORD

I was a little over a year into my 10½ -year federal prison sentence when I called home to tell them to send me some money. My niece, Kisha, said, "Wahida, we will see what we can do. Your money is gone. You are losing the house; we can't make the payments. All the vehicles have been repossessed; your businesses have been shut down. As a matter of fact, we are packing up now and heading back to Jersey."

My arrest left my two teenage daughters on the outside, and my husband, Yah Yah, was also locked up. Even though I was in a federal prison camp, I had to buy my own soap powder, pay to wash clothes, pay to eat fresh fruits and vegetables from the kitchen, pay to get my hair braided, etc. I quickly learned that it cost money to live in prison.

I was used to keeping money on my husband's books, and thanks to my Allah, my children never wanted for anything. But now here I was at my job inside of a federal prison camp fulfilling my duty as the prison librarian.

No money! What was I going to do? I needed to survive *now*! I needed to take care of my family *NOW*! I needed to be building up some sort of nest egg for when I got out of prison in 9½ years. Yes, I was thinking that far ahead. And having no money, and no means to make money was gnawing away at me.

I prayed for guidance. Now, here I was sitting alone in the prison library; I picked up the *XXL* magazine and opened it. There was a sidebar, and at the top was a small picture of Shannon Holmes. The article said he was in prison and had written a book, *B-More Careful.*

I said, "What! He's in prison and wrote a book?" That was huge to me. I said, "I'm in prison." I leaned back into my chair and my eyes roamed the spines of all the books surrounding me. "He's in prison. I'm in prison." I began to visualize my name, *Wahida Clark*, on the spines of all the books on the shelves. I had just shed a few tears the night before and prayed for guidance. Then it hit me. "I'm going to write a book."

I didn't know what I was going to write. I didn't know how to write, but I knew I had to make it happen. I knew I had to write a book, get it published and make some money. Right then, right there I was on the path to writing the first Street Lit book to become a series: *Thugs and the Women Who Love Them*. Thank you, Shannon Holmes, this anthology is dedicated to you, first and foremost.

Now here we are, collaborating on this *Street Tales* project with some of the finest, most motivated authors in the game. They are dedicated to the craft of writing, the *business* of writing and to this genre . . . Street Lit. I salute you and I respect your hustle; we are honored to have your brilliant minds on this project. A super big shout-out goes to all those who are incarcerated but still making it happen.

Ladies first: Reds Johnson, a young sister always on her grind; I'm looking forward to our project together. Hood Chronicles and Sa'id Salaam, this book felt like a mixtape. Lol. Authors were hitting me up, "Yo, Wahida, let me get on that." Lol. To one of the OGs in the game, Victor L. Martin, your story *My Reason* will be in *Street Tales Vol. 2* along with the mighty Joe Awsum's *Thots and Robbers* and the longer version of *In The Shadow of Darkness* by Vance Phillips.

To the readers, thank you for your support now, in advance and definitely in the future! Enjoy these tales from the streets, spun by unique voices and styles. We write the same stories, but like a wise man named Uncle Yah Yah told me, "There are as many ways to see a thing as there are people to see it."

Wahida Clark
The Official Queen of Street Lit ™

DEDICATION

TO THE MEN AND WOMEN LOCKED DOWN

WASTE NO TIME

MONEY HUNGRY

LET'S GO . . . .

WAHIDA CLARK PRESENTS

Money Hungry

A SHORT STORY BY

SHANNON HOLMES

MONEY HUNGRY

By Shannon Holmes

What you do for money is unimportant when money is more important . . .

Keke sat on her bed in her South Bronx apartment building, scanning through her Instagram feed as she waited for her driver to pull up. Her eyes traveled from one Instagram to the next as she peered into each person's social media world. Like most kids in their late teens and early twenties, Keke thought with her eyes. She judged success or failure by what a person posted to their perspective page. Growing up in this Internet age, it was obvious why. However, social media was all a façade, but to Keke, her perception had become her reality.

"Oh, this nigga is litty," she commented, excited by the sight of the money. "He runnin' it up!"

Intensely, she studied a picture of a table full of money, nothing but blue-faced hundreds. It was a post from a credit card scammer, Young Haze-turned-aspiring rapper, who was using his ill-begotten gains to attain popularity in the music industry.

The hash tags read:

#differentkindofbag #wearenotthesame #youniggasbroke

"I know that's right, bro," Keke exclaimed. "Let these niggas and bitches know."

Keke made a mental note to get next to him ASAP. Even if he didn't give her a dime, she was assured of a good time while in his company—all the high-grade weed, like Gorilla Glue, she could smoke, and all the Hennessey she could drink. Plus, a picture with him would boast her online status, as well as add to her followers.

1

"All you bum-ass niggas, stop dick-ridin' my brozay and step ya fuckin' game up," Keke commented under the picture, leaving crying-faced emojis.

Doing things like this excited Keke. She had a host of addictions, which she hadn't been able to master yet—everything from designer clothes, to eating out at expensive restaurants, popping Percocet's to partying on a nightly basis. Her way of life made her a slave to her trade.

She continued to scroll down her Instagram feed before she began trolling her friends and a chick she disliked but followed.

"This bitch is a bird!" she said looking at another female's post. "I wouldn't be caught dead in that outfit. Bitch, that's the best you could do for ya b-day? Maybe you need to be sellin' pussy."

After seeing all these weak posts, Keke decided to post a picture of herself. She angled the iPhone X lens on herself for a close-up selfie pose. Her face was a compilation of perfect angles. The filters she selected made her skin look smooth, soft, and flawless.

"You bitches ain't got nuttin' on me," Keke wrote in a caption. #Baddie. #feelingmyself. #spicy.

Keke had social media down to a science; she knew the best times to post and what to say to get the most interactions. She laughed as she posted the pictures, captions, and hash tags to all her social media accounts: Facebook, Instagram, and Snapchat. She felt a sense of satisfaction in what she did. Now, she just watched and waited for the "likes" to come rolling in.

Her good feeling only lasted for a moment. Suddenly, her phone rang, breaking her weird form of entertainment.

"Come downstairs," her driver spoke into the phone. "I'm outside."

"Comin' down now," Keke responded.

Keke got up off the bed, snatched her phone charger out of the wall, and proceeded to exit her bedroom. It was impossible for her not to glance in the mirror next to the door and check out her image. She made sure every strand of hair in her cornrows was in place, and her makeup was holding up fine. She had to be looking her best. Keke didn't know if this was going to be a long night or what. No matter what, she had to be prepared.

Keke's curvaceous body belied her nineteen years on this earth. Her measurements didn't lie at 34-28-38. She crammed her phat ass into every nook and cranny of her thousand-dollar, low-rise Balmain-designer blue jeans. Her black Born Fly sweatshirt could hardly contain her breasts. To her, appearance was everything. She wasn't born beautiful, so clothes were a big part of her appeal. So what she wasn't all that attractive in the face? At least, she was fly as hell.

Within a few seconds, her self-analysis was over. Keke was satisfied that her hair, lipstick, and makeup were on point. She closed the social media application on her smartphone. It was time to work.

When it came to money, she was about her business. If it didn't make dollars, it didn't make sense. Her hunger for money is what separated Keke from other chicks in the hood. She was willing to do everything and anything to get it—including sell her body.

Keke exited her apartment building with an air of confidence that made the boys that stood around stop and stare.

"Yo, Keke, what's good?" someone yelled out. "Can I come?"

"Nah, nigga," she replied. "First, get ya money right; then holla."

At a young age, she learned that grown men and hormone-raging boys had their own idea of beauty, and she would let their lustful words define her. However, these kids were too young for Keke to take seriously. She entered the car with a smile on her face, knowing that all eyes were on her body.

"What's good, ole man?" she announced. "First address is the Jet Set Hotel on Third Avenue."

Keke's phone had constantly been ringing from a third-party phone application that she used to conceal her real telephone number. She had clients lined up, waiting for her arrival to perform her sexual services. Keke would take them—not in the order in which they had come—but according to the highest bidder—or whomever she determined was the easiest to deal with.

"Yeah, I know where that is," her driver responded. "Be there ina minute."

As the neighborhood cabdriver, Larry had made driving his legal hustle. He would take anyone, anywhere, in and around New York City, even out of state if the money were right. He was an ex-con who found a way to hustle the hustlers and play the players. He was a good, reliable driver with a valid driver's license and registration . . . Someone who was indispensable in the hood. Another plus was that he was one of a select few drivers who actually let his passengers smoke weed in his car.

Small in stature, Larry wasn't the argumentative type. Usually, anything offensive Keke said to him went in one ear and out the other. He was there for the money—nothing more, nothing less. This was a job to him just like any other. He had to get his passenger to her destination on time.

As he took off from the curb, Larry's dark, leathery, skinned hands gripped the steering wheel ever so tightly. He glanced over at Keke, who busied herself putting her phone charger into the cigarette lighter.

"Put on your seat belt," he said. "I ain't tryin'a get a ticket."

Instinctively, Keke responded, reaching over and grabbing the seat belt, placing it across her breast until it clicked into a locking mechanism. She did so to avoid hearing Larry's mouth. She wasn't in a talkative mood. Her body language made that very clear.

As usual, Keke was nonverbally responsive to him. She chose once again to bury her head into the phone, checking her dates on her sideline app she had lined up for the night. She used the third-party app for privacy reasons so that the dates wouldn't have her personal phone number. Naturally, that's how she wanted it. She didn't want these sex-starved weirdos calling her phone all hours of the day and night. She didn't want anyone in her family to know how she was secretly earning her money.

Her eyes lit up when she saw her first date of the night. It was her regular, José.

Yes, easy money, she thought.

Larry didn't need to use the navigation for this one. He knew exactly where this location was. He trained his eyes on the streets as he made his way toward the destination.

"Yo, I'm here. Could you please come to the door," Keke spoke confidently into her smartphone to the trick.

Keke exited the car, still on the phone. She was cool, calm, and collected as she entered the hotel. This was regular shit for her, so there was no reason to be afraid. She knew exactly what she was getting herself into. The sex act would be over soon. Most of her clients came extremely fast. In fact, she counted on it.

She inspected her facial features one last time on her camera phone. The most unflattering part of her body was indeed her face. She shook off the feeling of disappointment. Keke had learned to live with it. She had been screwed in that department. One part of her face, in particular, seemed to jump out at whoever was in close proximity to her. She always caught people staring at her fat, mushed-in nose whenever she held a casual conversation.

Behind her back—and sometimes to her face—they said it made her resemble a certain breed of dog called a "pug." She was insulted more times in her life than she cared to remember over her nose. The kids in her neighborhood used to tease her, calling her "Poochie." She hated it. In fact, Keke had promised herself if she could ever save up enough money turning tricks or run into a trick that had some real money, she was going to get herself a nose job. That would make her feel so much better about herself and less self-conscious. It would raise her stock in the looks department quite a bit, as well.

Her big bubble lips were something that she used to get harassed about too. But as soon as she came of age sexually, that stigma became one of her most valuable assets. Every boy in the neighborhood wanted her pillow-soft lips wrapped around their penis. And for good reason. Keke had actually been performing fellatio on older boys before she allowed anyone to penetrate her. But it wouldn't be long before she allowed some older boy to sweet-talk her out of that too.

From the neck up, Keke was below average. But her body was another story unto itself.

"Damn, girl! Ya body is bangin', yo! She thick!" Their words validated her in ways that the mirror couldn't. The sudden showering of her body with attention built up her self-esteem. She loved the idea of being wanted, no matter how degrading the remarks got. It was just the idea that she was the object of the opposite sex's desires that stimulated her.

Keke arrived at the hotel, and the first word that came to mind was "sleazy." Besides a few couples that occupied the rooms, a lot of in-calls were taking place there. The pimps and hoes that gathered in the hotel had combined to turn the honest establishment into a traphouse atmosphere.

The second floor was where the room was located. Once Keke reached the door, she knocked softly. There was no need to alarm the man. He had been expecting her. Instantly, the door opened, revealing a skinny, weird-looking Hispanic man. His eyes moved past Keke but then doubled back once he scanned the hallway and made sure she was alone.

Keke was about to ask him what he was looking at when she realized that he was probably high.

"José, you gon' let me in or what?" she snapped. "I don't have time to waste."

"Oh, I'm sorry, baby." He apologized. "Come in."

José stuck his head out the door to make sure Keke wasn't followed, or the police weren't trying to set him up. He scanned up and down the hall expecting to find someone, but no one was there. Satisfied, he closed the door.

José was one of Keke's regulars every Friday night after work. He liked to get high and have her come over and jerk him off. Keke didn't care what kind of sexual deviant the man was just as long as she got paid.

She walked over to the TV where the hotel porn channel was on and scooped up her money. She counted it silently, making sure every dollar was there. Pleased with what she counted, Keke mentally prepared herself to perform the sex act.

Next thing she knew, José was ass naked lying on the bed with his private parts exposed. She took one look at his limp dick and knew this was going to be easy money. Walking over to him, she sat on the edge of the bed and took hold of his penis. She proceeded to pull hard on it, not taking into account what type of discomfort she might be putting him in. All Keke cared about was the money, which she already had in her possession. If he came, he came. She didn't care. That was on him.

Keke beat his dick so hard and fast that she swore that the man would have blue balls once she finished jerking him off. José seemed to like the treatment he was receiving. He gyrated his hips as if he were having intercourse, never losing sight of the pornography that was on TV.

José was physically stimulated; now, he needed to control his mind and focus himself on the task at hand. The harder he tried to ignore Keke, the more easily it became to concentrate. He closed his eyes, and all of those pornographic images began to flash through his mind. He was doing the nasty with some of his favorite porn stars. His mind was in a sexual frenzy. Without Keke really being aware, he came. A small trickle of semen was released from the head of his dick onto her hand.

José was physically spent as he lay on the bed recuperating.

"About fuckin' time," Keke announced as she headed to the bathroom to wash her hands.

Despite her nasty attitude, José liked the fact that she didn't treat him like the sucker he was. She made him feel good about paying her, and that was the difference between her and the other girls on backpage.com. It was the sole reason he kept seeing her every week.

Keke got back into the car and handed Larry a small percentage of her pay. They would repeat this process every time Keke got a call to turn a trick.

****

"In fifty feet, you will have arrived at your destination," the automated computer voice announced. They arrived on Allerton Avenue.

"Yo, stop right here. Fuck it, keep drivin'," she suddenly said to her driver. "I don't want you to pull up directly in front of the house. How many times I gotta tell you that? You know how much bread you blew for me doin' that shit? Niggas be thinkin' you my pimp. And these scary-ass niggas don't wanna spend no money on no bitch wit' a pimp."

"How many times you goin' to tell me that, Keke? You said that a million times. You not talkin' to a kid," Larry replied, shaking his head. "Sometimes, I think you like talkin' just to be talkin'. I heard you the first."

"See, that's ya problem. You too caught in ya feelings. You blowin' mine! You hear me, but you not listenin'. 'Cause if you were, you would have been stopped somewhere back there by now," she snapped. "You old niggas is hardheaded as fuck. And y'all think y'all know every muthafuckin' thing. Just 'cause you been on this earth longer than me don't make you smarter than me. I been doin' this shit longer than you been drivin' me, my nigga."

You can't ever make me feel bad about my age, Larry thought. *I know a lot of dead young motherfuckers.*

Unwilling to escalate the situation, Larry remained silent. Mentally, he shook his head in disgust. He just reminded himself that this was a different time, and he was dealing with a different generation. Nowadays, these kids didn't believe that shit stunk. These pill-popping, plastic surgery-having, poor decision-making youngins had no idea of what the consequences would be of their choices. Sadly, Keke routinely ignored much of Larry's sound advice.

For her, there was something about the way Larry disregarded her instructions and injected the wisdom that he had amassed after sixty years on this earth that rubbed her wrong. Keke had her own mind and her own opinions about life and the dirt that she did. Wasn't no old man going to tell her any different, at least not one she was employing.

"Right here, good?" he said while smoothly maneuvering the vehicle into a parking space just out of sight of the row house.

"Yeah!" Keke spat. "Don't pull off yet either. Wait until I get inside."

Larry watched intently while Keke made her way to the front door. With each step, his eyes seemed to be mesmerized by her voluptuous ass. Truth be told, Larry would love to sip from her fountain of youth, which was one of the reasons he tolerated Keke's foul mouth so much. He was hoping to hang around long enough to get a shot of that pussy. Although Keke sold her body on the Internet, she wasn't with mixing business with pleasure. Quietly, Larry was too reliable in his role as her driver to lose him over some sex, despite anything he said. She had turned Larry down in not so uncertain terms more times than she could count. Still, that hadn't stopped him from cracking on her every now and then.

In her mind, it wasn't going to happen. On the contrary, in his mind, it just might. Nothing was certain, yet anything was possible, especially if he caught Keke on a bad night.

Their relationship was one of convenience; she needed a ride to and fro to her dates, and he needed the extra money. Although they had two different personalities, they found a way to make it work. Keke ignored his sexual advances, while he ignored her disrespectful rants.

As soon as Keke stepped into the house, the stench of beer assaulted her nostrils. She followed the short Mexican man to his room.

"Money, first!" Keke demanded. "I'm not doin' shit until you put some money in my hand, yo. Yo comprende?"

Keke stared defiantly at the lick. This icy look accompanied by her nasty attitude was usually enough for her to get her point across. Her sharp tongue intimidated most men of her own race, let alone some short Mexican immigrant who understood very little English.

"Sí, señorita," he replied sheepishly as he handed her his hard-earned cash.

Since arriving in America, the man had acquired a sexual fetish for African American women. In his culture, they were a forbidden fruit; off-limits. Mexicans tended to date within their own race, hardly ever outside of it, unless it was a Caucasian.

"I pay for one hour. One hour," the man said in broken English with a heavy Spanish accent.

"Listen, Papi," Keke began before even engaging in sex with the man. "I forgot my condoms in the car. I have to go to the car and get them. I'll be right back."

Keke almost laughed in his face. The idea of ripping the man off was so ridiculous; it was almost too easy.

"Now, you wait right here. I'll be right back in five minutes," she promised. "When I get back, I'm goin' to fuck the shit outta yo. OK?"

The Mexican man nodded his head in agreement. It was clear he intended to act on the lustful look in in his eye. Quickly, Keke flashed a seductive smile back at him.

With that said, she quietly exited the house, giving the man a reassuring smile all the way out the door. Once she got outside, Keke laughed all the way to the curb. She pictured a confused foreigner waiting for her to return. She couldn't believe how gullible men were. White and Mexican men were the easiest to manipulate. Black guys always gave her the most trouble. They always seemed to want a whole lot of sexual acts performed on them for the least amount of money. Keke tried to avoid them whenever she could. Most times, they just weren't worth the hassle.

Whenever Keke saw the opportunity to get paid for nothing, she took advantage of it, even if that meant lying, robbing, and stealing. A come-up was a come-up in her book. She saw nothing wrong with victimizing these strangers she had met on the Internet. A great majority of them she would never see again anyway. With all the lewd sexual acts she was asked to perform, Keke felt like she was owed a little extra. Virtue seemed to be the last thing she was worried about in this line of work.

"Where is this nigga at?" Keke mumbled to herself. She wanted to get out of there before the trick discovered that he had been got.

Her eyes widened as she looked up and down the street in an effort to spot her ride, a late-model black Honda Accord. Unfortunately for her, she had no such luck spotting it. Every car she laid her eyes on appeared to be it. The vehicles were mirages—false alarm after false alarm. However, none actually were her ride, which annoyed her even more.

Frustrated, Keke dialed his number. He picked up on the first ring.

"Where you at?" she shouted into the phone.

"Right around the corner," he told her. His answer barely registered with Keke.

With all the crazy things that this girl was into, Larry felt like the last thing she should be doing is worrying about him. He was as reliable as they come.

"Nigga, I need you right here, right now!" she snapped. "Hurry up. I'm tryin'a get the fuck up outta here."

She had no idea, where "right around the corner" was, and she wasn't trying to find out. Larry had better come to her since that what's she was paying him for. Not long after she hung up the phone, Larry pulled up right in front of her, and Keke hopped into the car.

"Where we headed now?" he asked.

"Just drive, motherfucker; just drive!" she ordered as she inserted the USB charger back into her phone.

Keke busied herself on her phone checking her app for messages. From time to time, she'd catch Larry looking over at her, trying to mind her business.

"Take me to McDonald's," she blurted out. "I'm hungry as hell."

Quickly, Larry found a nearby McDonald's. He pulled into the drive-thru, and Keke ordered some food.

"Lemme get a quarter pounder wit' cheese, large fries, hold the mayo . . ." she said into the speaker, ". . . and lemme get a supersize Sprite, a four-piece chicken McNugget wit' sweet and sour sauce."

"Will that complete your order, ma'am?" The cashier working the drive-thru asked.

Keke turned to Larry. "You want somethin', old man?"

"Nah, you know I don't eat this shit. It ain't no good," he remarked.

"That's not what I asked you," Keke said, shaking her head. "Why everything gotta be a fuckin' debate wit' you? You know what, forget it. You ain't gettin' shit now. Yeah, miss, that's it."

"Your order will be $10.55. Please drive around to the first window and pay the cashier."

Slowly, the car pulled to the first window, and Keke paid for the order; then they drove down to the second window to pick up the food.

"Thank you for choosing McDonald's. Enjoy your meal," came the reply as the fast-food worker handed over the food. Larry passed the bag of food to Keke, and she immediately dug in.

"You gotta another call?" Larry asked.

"No, these niggas can wait. I'm eatin'," she replied.

"OK, I'll park then. Ain't no sense burning gas," he commented.

With one hand she devoured the hamburger, while simultaneously texting her girlfriend with the other. Keke stared down at her phone waiting for the return text. How things were going on her friend's end was the only thing on her mind. These two were in a real competition every night to see who could make the most money nightly, selling pussy on backpage.com.

My phone is lit, the text read.

Keke shifted her attention from her food to her phone, dialing her friend's number immediately.

"Bitch, how much you made so far?" she cursed into the phone.

"Almost a stack," her friend lied, trying to impress her. The temptation was too strong for her to resist.

Keke's reaction was as could be expected. She frowned up her face with envy.

"What?" Keke exclaimed. "You gettin' to it? Long you been out here for?"

"Oh, since six o'clock. At first, it was slow. But the last hour or so shit picked up," Tonya smirked.

Larry sat in the driver's seat pretending not to overhear the conversation. He was of such little consequence to Keke that she spoke freely around him. For all intents and purposes, he may as well have been invisible. Keke completely ignored him until she got a new text on her phone.

"Take me to Dyckman," she instructed him.

"Where?" he asked.

"I'll tell you when we get there," she hissed.

Backing out of the parking spot, Larry put the car in drive and headed to the area he was instructed to take her.

"Lemme call you back Tonya. I'ma finish eatin'," she told her. "Talk to you later, bitch!"

"Oh, you goin' out to Queens, to Angel's tonite? It's supposed to be a movie in there. Tekashi 69 gonna be there," Tonya said.

"We there!" Keke exclaimed. "I'll call you when I'm done, or if you finish first, call me."

"Kopy," Tonya replied before hanging up.

Keke finished her meal, and Larry drove to the next destination. Things were looking up; her phone was vibrating like crazy with callers from the Internet looking for sex. Her spirits were lifted when she saw the sheer number of texts.

This might be a good nite, after all, she thought.

Suddenly her phone rang.

"Hey, you doin' out-calls or in-calls?" the caller asked.

"Out-calls. Read the fuckin' post!" she stated before hanging up the phone.

"Ole man," Keke suddenly said, "can I ask you a question?"

"Sure; go 'head," he told her.

"Would you fuck wit' a girl who sold pussy?" she blurted out.

She was suspiciously quiet at the moment as she awaited an answer she may—or may not—want to hear.

Expressionless, Larry continued driving, staring straight at the road. Although her question seemed to catch him off guard, he didn't tip his hand about what he was thinking one way or another. He toyed with the idea of telling her the truth. Perhaps this was the opportunity that he had been waiting for, to get inside Keke's drawers, not steer her in a different direction.

Who am I to judge? he wondered.

Keke had her own life to live, and this was how she chose to live it at the moment. More or less, that summed up how she felt. She expressed that sentiment every day that she called him to take her to work the streets. What she was doing was no one's business but her own. She was at the stage where she didn't know which direction her life was headed.

"You know what they say . . . It ain't what you do; it's how you do it," Larry began. "As long as you're discreet, why should anyone have to know? Think about it like this . . . You don't know what ya mama did to put food on the table or clothes on your back. With that being said, do you think any less of your mother?"

Whether or not she cared to admit it, Larry had a point. So, why should she be ashamed of doing what she was doing? Men do it all the time.

"Exactly," she chimed in.

Immediately, Larry noticed that Keke suddenly looked happy. It was as if he had shed light on a situation that had been bothering her. He didn't know his words were having the desired effect on Keke until he heard her comment.

Keke continued, "The reason I asked that question I asked was, this dude was tryin' to cuff me. We went out a couple of times, and I ain't goin' to lie; I was feelin' him. So I fucked him. Now he wants us to be on some exclusive shit. But I don't know. I was wonderin' if I should tell him what I do or keep my mouth shut. What should I do?"

Personally, Larry thought Keke was crazy. She could deal with one man and get all the material things that she desired. He couldn't understand how easily she could put a price on something so priceless.

"If I were you, I'd just be up front with him. Be honest. That way, he can't ever say you didn't tell him, Keke. He might not like what you have to say, but he can never say he didn't hear it from you first. He's gotta deal with you for who you are, not who he *thinks* you are. And if none of that stuff don't work, fuck 'em. When one man won't, another man will. You just have to find the one that will," he explained.

Larry definitely gave Keke something to think about. Still, she was terrified about what she was doing and the knowledge that she could easily be exposed. Word could get around about her occupation. Say, if she had a fallout with any of her friends, they could take to social media to put her on blast. In this day and age, the thought of that frightened her more than anything else.

Once she ran into an old classmate while answering ads on Backpage. They came to a mutual agreement, *"You don't tell I'm buying pussy, and I won't tell you selling pussy."*

That encounter was the closest she'd come to being exposed. However, it wasn't enough to make her stop.

"So, what you going to do?" Larry questioned her.

Keke answered, "I don't know; I have to think about it."

She refused to make a rush decision, especially about a critical situation like this. Keke would let the thought marinate in her head for a few days before she decided upon anything. She had gotten into the habit of doing what she wanted to do when she wanted to do it. No one could tell her different. Until then, she would just give her suitor information on a need-to-know basis.

"There's nothin' wrong with giving the issue some thought," he replied, accepting her decision.

It was no longer a surprise to him how comfortable Keke felt around him. In many ways, he had come to believe that their working relationship was of greater value to her than having sex with him. Larry knew that Keke wasn't sexually interested in him, to say the least.

"I feel so much better, now that I had a chance to talk about it," she admitted. "Thanks, old man. I don't care what nobody say about you; you all right wit' me."

If nothing else, Larry added a little balance to Keke's life when she needed it the most by giving her a little wisdom and common sense to make a good decision. At times, he was her voice of reason.

"You know, it might require time for you to quit doing what you doing," he said. "Nothing lasts forever."

Keke pretended not to hear him. She wasn't trying to hear that shit. She was going ride this wave for the foreseeable future. The money was too good to give up. Besides, she had an endless supply of product, better than any drug known to man that she could peddle daily. She literally left the house broke and returned with a pocket filled with money.

This old nigga trippin', she thought. *Stop sellin' pussy for what?*

Keke wasn't in the mood to talk anymore. The car arrived at the address, so, it was back to business. Quietly, she savored the silence as much she had the conversation. Now, it was time to get back on her grind. She had some serious partying to do later tonight. If Keke wanted to pop a few bottles, she had to handle her business now.

"I'm here," Keke spoke into the phone. "I'm comin' upstairs now."

Keke exited the car, grabbing a small purse that contained condoms and baby wipes and K-Y Jelly. She had a strong feeling that she was going to have to earn her money the old-fashioned way this time. Larry followed her with his eyes until she disappeared inside the building.

Larry sat in the car vigilant. He glanced at his wristwatch again, although he knew it had been approximately fifteen minutes since the last time he'd looked. As soon he looked up, he saw Keke headed in his direction. Over the past few months, Larry had become a great support system for her. He was one part bodyguard and one part chauffer. He was good company more than anything else since nothing bad ever happened on his watch.

"I gotta anotha call," Keke said, looking at her text messages. "145th Street and Convent Avenue."

Larry proceeded to drive to the next destination. He drove in silence expecting some compensation for the last trip. It never came. Finally, he spoke up.

"Keke, where's my money?"

"Oh, that bump-ass nigga ain't even open the door," she explained. "I stood in the fuckin' lobby ringin' the buzzer the entire time."

Larry had his reservations about her story. Normally, when things like this happened, Keke would complain like hell and blocked the caller's number. False alarms were bad for business. In this instance, she did neither. So, Larry was offended that Keke was trying to insult his intelligence. He didn't know why she didn't want to give the devil his due. Why steal from him, of all people? He was the one who had her back if something happened while she was working the streets.

"Oh, okay," he replied, pretending that her thievery didn't bother him at all.

He was vindictive, however. Larry swore she had another think coming if she thought he wasn't going to get her back for this. He'd just bide his time and pay her back when the opportunity presented itself.

Keke righted her wrong by giving Larry every cent that he deserved from that moment forth. So, besides that "bump" in the road, the rest of their night was relatively smooth. Still, Larry never forgave her.

Suddenly, the rain began to fall, putting a damper on what was turning out to be a profitable night. As the raindrops grew heavier, Larry had to increase the speed of his windshield wipers which caused the windshield to squeak with annoying regularity. Battling the elements and driving were causing him to feel more than a little sleepy.

"I'm ready to call it a night," he stated. "What about you?"

"Nah, I need a few more dollars. I'm goin' out tonite, so I need every dollar I can get."

Larry didn't know if he could endure more calls or trips crisscrossing the Bronx, up to Westchester County, or back to Harlem. He felt he was too sleepy to cover that type of ground, especially in the rain. He knew his driving ability wouldn't be as sharp as it normally would be.

"Okay, just say when. I'm ready when you are," he vowed.

Keke needed a distraction to take her mind off calling it a night while she raced toward the imaginary finish line . . . Her realistic goal of making a thousand dollars tonight. She planned on showing her ass at the strip club, throwing a few dollars and slapping a little ass. Keke was going to do it for the gram. She was going to go live and let these other bitches know just how she was living.

So, she plugged in her iPhone and turned on her iTunes music. At maximum volume, she turned on Young M.A.'s "OOOUUU" song.

"Yeah they hate, but they broke tho . . ." The song blasted through the Honda's factory sound system.

Within a few seconds, Larry reached over and turned the rap song down to a less blasting level.

"Old man, you really blowin' mine," Keke stated, expressing her dislike with his actions.

"What you tryin'a do, blow my speaks or my eardrums listenin' to that crap?" he said. "Turn that shit down."

"Whatever!" she mumbled. "I'll be glad when I get the fuck away from you."

"You ain't the only one," he responded.

Once again, Keke buried her face inside her phone, this time scrolling down her Facebook feeds. She didn't get to look at too many posts when suddenly her phone rang.

"Listen, I need that wedding ring back that you stole outta my house," a voice on the phone said. "Just gimme back my ring, and we'll call it a day."

The stolen ring was irreplaceable; it was given to him by his now-deceased wife, so it had sentimental value. Now, thanks to Keke, it was gone. As soon as she had finished using the bathroom and left the house, his ring had vanished with her.

Over the course of the last few days, the man had tried repeatedly to contact Keke, pleading with her to return the ring. He even offered to buy it back from her. But all he had got for his efforts was a cold indifference. Keke hung up on him, his text messages went unanswered, and she blocked his number.

"Fuckisyoutalkin'about?" Keke responded. "Wrong Backpage bitch! I don't know nuttin' about no ring. Sounds like a personal problem that ain't got nuttin' to do wit' me, my nigga."

However, Keke knew very well what this was all about. She had stolen a wedding ring from a home in White Plains, New York, that had been left on the bathroom sink. The man had periodically called her in an effort to retrieve the ring, but to no avail. Keke couldn't give the ring back even if she wanted to because she had pawned it already.

"Stop textin' my phone. I don't know what ya talkin' about." Keke punched those words into the phone's keys.

"Bitch, you fuckin' wit' the right one," his text message warned. "Hope that ring is worth ya life, you money-hungry ho!"

"Suck my dick! You ain't doin' shit!" she responded before blocking his number.

What the hell was this guy thinking? Keke wondered. She wasn't giving shit back, not even if she could.

Her driver pretended to be oblivious to the entire conversation. But bits and pieces of the exchange had caught his ear. From where he sat, Larry was able to use deductive reasoning to figure out what was going on. Keke had stolen something from the man, and he wanted his property back.

Time and time again, Larry had warned Keke about her bad business practices. *"Stealing is bad for business,"* he once told her. However, Keke didn't listen. She was with the shits, doing anything and everything to get a fast buck. So, she continued to do it, thinking she could always get away with it because she always had. One thing Larry knew about stealing . . . The person who did it continued to do it until they got caught.

Keke had selective hearing. She listened to her driver's advice— if and when the mood hit her. Most of the time, she completely disregarded his opinion. In her book, Larry didn't know shit. He wasn't in the field like she was. Her current frame of mind caused her to be ruthless in her pursuit of the almighty dollar.

Acting as if nothing had happened, Keke jumped right back on Facebook and continued looking at people's pictures and reading their posts. A short time later, her phone rang.

"Hey, ma, you still doin' out-calls?" a woman's voice asked.

Instantly, Keke grew suspicious. She didn't get many calls from females, so she immediately thought this was a cop on her line.

"You not a cop, are you?" she questioned. "You not affiliated with any law enforcement agencies, are you?"

Keke thought her little questionnaire would keep her from being caught up in a vice sting or keep her from getting arrested for prostitution. It was something all the women who sold pussy on backpage.com believed. However, it couldn't be further from the truth.

"Hell, no!" the woman laughed. "I'm not a cop."

There was something about her voice that put Keke at ease. She could tell that the woman was black and that she was from the hood. That was kind of reassuring to her.

"Kopy," Keke stated. "No offense; I gotta ask."

"Heard you," the woman replied. "You can never be too safe out here."

"You got that right. So, anyway, how can I help you?" she said.

"Me and my dude . . ." the woman began, ". . . It's his birthday today. We kinda had this fantasy about havin' another woman watchin' us while we fuck. I know that sounds crazy . . . comin' from a stranger, but it is what it is . . . We wanted to know how much."

"How long will y'all be? Half an hour or an hour?" Keke replied.

"An hour," the woman told her.

"Two hundred dollars," Keke said being greedy, hoping she hadn't priced herself out of a nice situation.

The line went dead for a precious few seconds before Keke heard the woman's voice again.

"Okay, my boyfriend said we Gucci on that price," the woman commented. "He wanted to know if you drink or smoke."

There was no way in the world she was going to drink or smoke with complete strangers. She had heard too many horror stories about people doing so, and someone lacing their weed with Angel Dust or slipping something in their drink—only never to be the same again.

"No, I'm good," Keke claimed. "Text me the address."

"OK. We might be in the shower when you get there, but we'll leave the door unlocked so you can let yourself in."

When the address came to her text messages, Keke was familiar with the location. She had done in-calls in this location on several different occasions.

"Take me to the Holiday Motel," she told Larry. "You know where that's at?"

"Yeah," he replied, too tired for a long conversation.

"After this call, it's a wrap," she announced. "I got some clubbin' to do."

Larry was relieved that this was the last call. He had been ready to go home an hour ago.

They arrived at the hotel fairly quickly, even in all the rain. Keke directed her driver to the room.

"Wait for me. I'll be right back," she assured him.

I won't be right here when you get back, Larry thought.

Now, it was payback time. Larry had purposely waited all night to get Keke back for stiffing him on a payment. He determined that she better find another way home because she wasn't riding with him. Let Keke used the money she stole from him to catch a cab.

Keke exited the car and walked over to the room door, which she noticed was ajar. She listened for a few seconds. She could hear the fake moans from the porno channel that was hooked up to every TV in every room. She also heard the hard sounds of the shower running.

She pushed the flimsy door open and stepped inside, not bothering to close the door. Further inspecting the room, she saw the bed was in disarray. It looked like the couple had begun enjoying themselves before she had arrived. A pair of men's and women's sneakers and shoes and clothes were scattered around the room. Nothing seemed out of the ordinary. Quickly, Keke noticed a stack of twenty-dollar bills . . . money . . . Her money was sitting on top of the table. This was going to be even easier than she thought.

Her greed propelled her farther inside the hotel room. When Keke was halfway to the money, she noticed a quick flash of light from a car's headlight illuminate the room. She looked back to see Larry backing up and leaving the parking lot.

Fuck, she silently cursed to herself. *Where this dumb-ass nigga go?*

Keke continued to tiptoe across the room, careful not to make a sound. When she reached the money, she scooped it up without bothering to count it, reversed direction, and made a hasty retreat toward the door. Suddenly, a shadowy figure slipped inside the room.

"Oh my God," Keke gasped, holding her chest, frightened by his sudden appearance.

Keke's heart almost stopped at the sight of the well-built black man clad in a black hoodie to conceal his identity.

"Suck ya duck, huh?" the guy repeated Keke's previous statement to him.

Suddenly, his voice registered with her. She couldn't believe those words even as he spoke them. She prayed it wasn't who she thought it was. Her luck couldn't be this bad. It was then, and only then that Keke realized that she had been set up. She had been lured to this seedy motel with the promise of making some easy money. Now, she was about to get more than she bargained for.

"Bet you never thought you was goin' to see me again, huh?" he questioned as he slowly approached.

Now, the tables had turned. It was he who was in control of the situation; not she. Keke looked directly into his eyes and saw a deadly serious look in them. She knew she was in bad trouble.

"Listen, mister, I don't know what you're talking about," she said nicely, trying to reason with him. "I don't know who you think I am, but I never ever had no dealings with you. I never even saw you in my life."

As she talked, Keke looked for a way out of the room. Unfortunately, the only way out was through him. She had two options: scream or fight.

"Let me out this room," she said sounding tough. "I ain't got no fuckin' time for this shit. Now, if you would please excuse me."

"Bitch, you not going nowhere!" the man spat, taking a step forward with an intimidating expression on his face.

Quickly, the man removed his hands from his pouch pocket and rushed toward her. A flash of movement from his hand caught her eye. A glimmer of steel made her come to the sudden realization that he held a knife in his hand. The man plunged the weapon into Keke's gut just as she was about to scream. She clawed at his face, to no avail, as he drove the knife into her body repeatedly.

The stranglehold that he placed her in was so strong she felt the life being squeezed out of her as her lungs filled with blood. Her eyes began to bulge as she choked on her own blood. Keke felt herself slipping into the darkness. She was feeling very light-headed as she lost consciousness.

Finally, when the last bit of air escaped her body, he released his stranglehold on her neck. Keke's lifeless body crumpled to the ground. Her eyes were expressionless as they stared up at the ceiling. The man proceeded to rummage through her pockets, taking everything of value from her money to her phone. He even took her identification; he wanted to make it hard for the authorities to identify her body.

When that was done, the man slipped out of the room just as quietly as he had come, leaving a deadly crime scene behind.

****

The next morning, the hotel parking lot swarmed with news reporters and police cars. Yellow tape had sealed off the hotel room to anyone but police officials.

"In the Bronx, the unidentified body of a young African American female believed to be in her late teens to early twenties

was discovered late last night lying dead on the floor by a hotel employee. Police believe that foul play was involved. At the moment, they don't have any witnesses or a motive. It's believed that the woman was killed sometime late last night. Anyone with information pertaining to this crime is urged to call 1-800-CRIME STOPPERS . . ." the Bronx 12 reporter said.

****

Across town, Larry's jaw dropped. He stood staring at the television, frozen like a statue. He couldn't believe what he was hearing. The thing was, he felt a deep sense of guilt, knowing that Keke had lost her life and knowing that he could have possibly prevented it.

As soon as the news flash was over, he grabbed the remote and turned off the television. He found himself experiencing a whirlwind of emotions—anger, sorrow, and regret.

He couldn't help but think, *If only I hadn't left. If only Keke had listened.*

All good things—and bad things—must come to an end, but sadly, hers came to a tragic one.

-END -

WAHIDA CLARK PRESENTS

DIGITAL GANGSTER

A SHORT STORY BY

WAHIDA CLARK

DIGITAL GANGSTER

by Wahida Clark

(2014) BALTIMORE "I hate them nuccas!" James barked with the venom of a viper as the blood dripped from his nose like a leaky faucet.

"Let it go," Tyrone replied, holding his blackening eye as he struggled to his feet.

"I ain't letting shit go! I'ma kill them mutherfuckas one day! Watch!"

James was sick and tired of being picked on, bullied and beaten up. It seemed like his life was just one big bruise of a mistake. His mom was a dope fiend, his stepfather beat him and in school, he was a punching bag. It was enough to make a young sixteen-year-old want to kill himself, someone else, or both.

"It's not worth it, bruh!" Tyrone tried to reason, even though he was just as tired of being bullied.

Unlike James, Tyrone had come to terms with his environment. He knew in the ghetto, you were either a sheep or a wolf, and he had long since accepted being a sheep, because his goal was to get out of the ghetto. Like James, his mother was a dope fiend, too. In fact, they had met because their mothers both went to the same shooting gallery. They had been eleven years old then, but since, they had become inseparable. They had bonded over books.

"What you reading?"

Those were the first words James had ever spoken to Tyrone. At first, Tyrone was a little leery of the chubby, brown-skinned kid thinking he was another bully. But when he had replied, "Donald Goines," James' eyes exploded from his face.

"Aw man, Goines is the truth! That's that old school shit my moms used to like!"

27

They could sit for hours talking about *Whoreson, Kenyatta, Prince* and *Eldorado Red.* They both wished they could be one of those gangsta, debonair characters, because they would have power and respect, which meant no more bullying.

But, James and Tyrone also shared another love, one that would change the drug game forever and make them richer than they would ever imagine.

Computers.

The two of them knew the binary code of programming like they knew their own names. They had taught themselves to write code at the public library, mastering it to the point where they had written programs to do their homework, selling the info to other students and making a tidy profit on the side.

"Tyrone!"

Tyrone and James turned to the sound of the voice, just in time to see Monica and her friend, Tatianna, approaching. Tyrone was mesmerized. Monica was beautiful. She reminded him of a darker version of Rihanna, with her green eyes, sexy and bangin' body with a feline-type presence. Tatianna was the exact opposite, with her high yellow skin and ghetto thick body, and loud gum popping, the typical ghetto hood rat.

"Are you okay? I saw what Pop and Twin did. That shit was messed up," Monica sympathized.

James sucked his teeth.

"They ain't do shit, I'm good." he huffed, wiping away the last of the blood.

"Please. They whooped y'all ass!" Tatianna snickered.

"Tati!" Monica objected, shushing her friend.

"What? They did. Anyway, I don't care about that. All I want is my homework. "You got it?" Tatianna sassed.

James was fuming mad. He glared at Tatianna, who returned his glare with a smirk that said, "Yeah, nerd, you a coward!"

He dug in his book bag and thrust it at her.

"You got my money!" he grumbled.

Tatianna handed him a five-dollar bill, avoiding contact with him like he had the plague.

"Don't let Pop take that too!" she snickered.

Monica shook her head. "Don't pay her any attention, Tyrone. Really, are you okay?"

Tyrone looked away from her dazzling smile. Whenever she was around, he felt a strong connection. But, he was scared to speak up, afraid that she was just being nice.

"I've been worse." He shrugged.

"I wanted to ask you some questions about coding. I'm sure now is a bad time, but you can call me if you like," Monica proposed, handing him her number.

"I'm okay," Tyrone replied.

Monica smiled and walked off.

"I hate that bitch," James grumbled.

"Monica's not a bitch."

"Not her, Tatianna."

Tyrone chuckled. "You hate everybody. Come on."

****

"Man, this computer is slow," Tyrone said, obviously agitated while staring at the screen of his laptop.

"What do you expect? It's four years old," James reminded him.

"We need to sell more homework," Tyrone chuckled

Once the computer blinked to life, Tyrone pressed a few keys to pop open a new window.

"This is what I wanted to show you," Tyrone pointed.

James shrugged. "The dark Web. We've been here a thousand times."

"Yeah, but I've been thinking. This shit is the future of the game. These white boys in Silicon Valley have created a place to go where it's impossible to trace. The key is encryption, Tyrone explained.

"Okay …"

"Bruh, think about it! What do we fuckin' use encryption to create our drug delivery service right here in the hood! No more talking over phones, and we deliver the shit."

James thought about it, then a big, cheese eating grin spread across his face.

"Then we could hack the connect!"

They gave each other a gangster hug and snickered excitedly.

"I'm telling you yo, we are going to change the game!" Tyrone predicted.

"We've only got one problem."

"What?"

"We ain't got no goddamn drugs!" James reminded him.

Tyrone smiled, mischievously. "But I know who does."

"Wait, wait. Let me get this straight. You want to sell drugs online?" Psycho asked, incredulously.

"I know it sounds crazy—" Tyrone began, before Psycho cut him off.

"Crazy? Naw, it sounds stupid! This shit is illegal, yo! We can't just post up and set up drugs.com!"

Psycho hit his blunt and shook his head at the two mad scientists standing in front of him.

Psycho was a lieutenant in the Black Gorilla Family, one of the most powerful gangs in Baltimore.

He looked like the rapper DMX, with the same wiry frame, bald head and intense energy that made him move constantly.

"Look, I like y'all nuccas. Y'all smart as hell, but right now, you too smart for your own damn good," Psycho concluded.

"Naw, yo, you don't understand. We use encryption," James replied.

"You crippin'?" Psycho spat, bristling at the insinuation.

"No, not crippin', encryption." It just means we use secret keys and passwords that make the transaction invisible to whoever we don't want to see it," Tyrone explained.

Psycho nodded.

"Like a scrambler on a cellphone."

"Only better," Tyrone winked.

Psycho thought for a moment. "With something like that, you're gonna need a lot of drugs."

"That's why we came to you," Tyrone answered, trying to subtly stroke his ego.

Psycho laughed. "Man, I'm a corner boy. I ain't movin' no weight. I can see your plan, but you are without a strong connect, so it ain't worth the effort."

Tyrone and James walked away, dejected.

The only thing that lifted Tyrone's spirits was getting a call from Monica.

"Are you busy?" she asked, as if he could ever be too busy to speak to her.

"No, I was just messing around on my computer," he responded.

"Anything other than typing or shopping is confusing. Especially all of that coding stuff," Monica remarked.

"No, it's really cool. I mean, once you get the hang of it."

Tyrone heard a male voice in the background.

"I'm sorry, Tyrone, I was talking to my dad. He's on his way to the station."

"Station?"

"Yeah, he's a detective."

"Your dad is a cop?"

She giggled. "Don't worry, he doesn't know about your homework scam."

He smiled. "I ain't worried, just a little . . . shook!"

"Why? You planning on robbing a bank?" she joked.

"Only if it'll get me a date with you," he blurted out and cursing himself for putting himself out there.

He could hear the smile in her voice when she said, "You don't have to rob a bank to get a date, Tyrone."

Her words set him on cloud nine, but her next words opened the door to hyperspace when she shrieked, "Oh my God!"

"What?"

"It's the TV! Turn it on! It looks like they are rioting!"

Tyrone quickly turned on the TV just in time to hear the news reporter announce: "Yes, Tom, Baltimore has erupted in an orgy of violence tonight as protesters are enraged by another killing of an unarmed black man by police. Trevor Daniels was, according to police, belligerently resisting arrest, but video shot by area residents tell a different story."

The screen was filled with the video footage of two police officers choking Trevor to death while he lay handcuffed on the ground. The camera then cut away to the scene of looters running wild as the local stores became enveloped in angry, scorching flames.

"Monica, let me call you back," Tyrone said, hanging up.

He instantly dialed James' number.

"Yo," James answered.

"You seeing this?"

"What the riot? Yeah shit is crazy!"

"Naw, yo ... it's perfect," Tyrone replied, voice brimming on the edge of enthusiasm.

"Perfect? What you can finally get those new Jordans for free?" James teased.

"I've got something else in mind," Tyrone smiled.

****

"Goddamn yo, that just might work," Psycho cackled with criminal glee after hearing Tyrone's idea.

Tyrone and James were standing in the project parking lot as Psycho leaned on his black Tahoe, his two henchmen, Murda and Biz, flanking him on the right and left.

"Aint no might in it," Tyrone assured him, adding, "while everyone else is looting bullshit, we rob every pharmacy in the city for their Oxys, Roxy and all!"

Psycho nodded, greedily.

"Yeah yo, you little nuccas definitely on to something. I gotta run this by the big Homey, Shaka. But if he say it's a go, get your soldiers ready to rob this city blind!"

Psycho took James and Tyrone straight to see Shaka. He owned a big club in West Baltimore, but because of the riots, he had to shut down for the week. As soon as Tyrone and James walked in they were in awe. There were well over 50 BGF members gambling and partying, while naked bitches walked around dancing, sucking and fucking. Shaka sat in the midst of it all like a Don.

"Shaka, these the little nuccas I told you about. Ty and James," Psycho introduced.

Shaka shook their hands, assessing them with a subtle smirk. Shaka was over six foot three, jet black and looked like Usain Bolt, the Jamaican sprinter. He had a commanding presence and a dangerous aura about him.

"So, Psycho tells me you got a plan that could make us all rich," Shaka stated.

"Indeed," Tyrone confirmed, handing him his phone and added, "Check this out." hHe walked Shaka through the app and showed him how it would work.

"So you saying, all a fiend gotta do is put in an order and we deliver? Nobody will know who or where he sent the request?"

Tyrone nodded. "Exactly."

"Can you make it work all over the country?" James nodded.

"We can make it do whatever we want," he stated confidently, letting Shaka know in a subtle way that they needed them as much as they needed BGF.

Shaka got the message and chuckled. "I think I like y'all lil' nuccas. If this shit work like you say, y'all lil' runts about to be rich!"

Tyrone and James nodded, ready to set shit off.

The next few days were full of protests, looting, burnings and mass arrests. The police even tried to implement a curfew, which no one obeyed. The city was off the chain. It was the perfect time to pull off the plan. The BGF systematically broke in and robbed every pharmacy in the city for all of the Schedule II drugs, including OxyContin, Methadone, Vicodin, Valium and several others. While the rest of the city was looting trivial shit, BGF was carrying out one of the largest robberies in history.

When they were done, they stood around a table that held over 100 million dollars in stolen pills. Shaka, Psycho, James and Tyrone looked at the mountain of multi-colored pills.

"Looks like a fucking rainbow," James remarked.

"Naw, nigga, it's the pot of gold at the end of it." Shaka cackled, giving James dap.

Shaka was taking a real liking to James. He sensed a lot of pent-up anger in him that he felt he could manipulate to his advantage. Tyrone saw it, but he was too excited for it to really register. His plan had him blinded.

****

Detective Tony Roberts stepped into the burned-out shell of Willie's Pharmacy. Each step crunched with the debris and glass of the riot's aftermath. Tony looked around with a hopeless sigh. He hated to see the damage that had been done. Tony grew up in the neighborhood and he used to play video games and buy candy from Willie's.

"As you can see, we outta business."

Tony looked up to see Mr. Willie coming out of the back. He had always looked old, but now he seemed to be broken as well. Tony flashed his badge.

"Detective Roberts, Mr. Willie. I'm here to investigate the break in."

"Ain't nothing to investigate. They took everything," Mr. Willie grumbled, shaking his head and adding, "thirty-five years all down the drain. I got every type of insurance, except riot insurance. They don't offer that. I guess that's the risk of being black. Can't be insured for that." It broke Tony's heart to see Mr. Willie so dejected.

"I sure hate to see this place like this," Tony remarked.

Mr. Willie stopped and squinted at him. "Don't I know you?"

"I hope so. I used to come in here all the time."

Mr. Willie's face broke into a smile. "Mr. Snicker! I remember you. I'm surprised you still got teeth after all that candy you used to buy!"

Tony laughed, happy to be remembered. "I'm still paying my dentist bills."

They both laughed.

"This neighborhood sure has changed," Tony commented.

"For the worse," Mr. Willie added.

"Just know I'm going to do all I can to find who did this," Tony vowed.

"There is one more thing I want to show you," Mr. Willie offered and when Tony saw it, it blew his mind.

****

Tony watched the surveillance tape from Mr. Willie's several times, comparing it to the surveillance tapes from other pharmacies. Once he had confirmed his suspicion, he took his case to the Chief of Detectives, Marilyn Watson.

"Chief, I think we have a problem," Tony stated, as he walked into her office.

"Good morning to you too, Tony," she replied, with a light chuckle.

Tony always liked the Chief. Besides being a good cop, she was easy on the eyes, reminding him of Angela Bassett with a touch of gray hair.

"Sorry, Chief. Good morning."

What you got?"

"This."

Tony dropped a manila folder full of black and white pictures and spread them across her desk.

"These were all taken from pharmacies that were looted around town. They all experienced general looting, but these are pictures of guys who came for one thing. Drugs," he explained.

"You've got my attention."

"They were focused and methodical. They knew what they had come for and that's all they took. Now, I've done a rough tally of what these pharmacies say what was taken and multiplied it by the street value of each pill, you ready for this?"

"No but give it to me anyway."

"Over seventy million dollars' worth of pills are on the street," Tony told her.

Marilyn sat back and shook her head.

"Call the coroner."

****

Tony was exhausted. It had only been a week since the robberies, and the number of overdoses and murders as the cause of death had already skyrocketed, not only in Baltimore, but up and down the Eastern Seaboard and as far to the West as St. Louis. Baltimore was really earning its moniker, Bodymore, because homicides were at record levels. He knew the two were related.

He entered his two-story rowhouse with every intention of going straight to bed, but he found his daughter, Monica, sitting on the couch with a young nerdy dude in glasses. They both had laptops on their laps, so there wasn't anything going on, but still, his only daughter maturing into womanhood.

"Hey, Daddy. This is the guy I was telling you about, Tyrone. Ty, this is my dad."

Tyrone stood up and extended his hand. "How are you, Mr. Roberts? It's a pleasure to meet you," Tyrone smiled.

Tony shook his hand, his detective eye assessing him in one glance. His clothes and sneakers weren't the typical nerds. He had on a pair of brand-new Jordans, a style that he knew cost at least three hundred dollars. Hell, he still had his Jordan throwbacks.

"Nice sneakers, Tyrone."

"Daddy!" Monica whined in an exasperated tone.

What? I just said they were nice," Tony shrugged.

"No, it's cool, my mom bought them for my birthday," Tyrone lied.

In reality, Tyrone had made more money in a week than he'd ever seen, forty thousand dollars. His plan was working better than he had ever imagined. BGF had already reached out to sets across the country, and the money was pouring in.

The only thing he was worried about was James. He had started hanging hard with the

BGF niggas. He had even mentioned joining the gang.

"Are you crazy? This isn't our lifestyle! Let's just get this money and get out," Tyrone had urged.

To which, James replied, "Now it's my turn."

"Tyrone . . . Ty, are you okay?"

Monica's voice brought him back to the present.

"I'm good," he replied, adding with a chuckle, "your dad was grilling me so hard, I thought he was going to arrest me."

Monica laughed. "He's cool. He's just overprotective of me. After all, I am his only daughter."

"He should be. There are a lot of wolves out here," Tyrone stated, then playfully howled like one.

"You're so crazy."

Tyrone pulled out a small jewelry box. "I got something for you."

Monica gasped when he opened it and she saw the floating heart pendant and necklace.

"It's beautiful," she smiled.

"Like you."

That comment got him his first kiss.

Walking home that night, he felt like singing, "To Be Loved" like Eddie Murphy in *Coming to America*. He was walking through one of the most dangerous ghettos in America, but none of that mattered. The gunfire in the background didn't matter, the fiends staggering around him like the walking dead didn't matter. And neither did the Mercedes that skidded up on him, with the driver jumping out and pointing a gun at him.

"Rock a bye, baby!"

Tyrone looked up, startled, but when he saw it was James holding the gun he was flooded with relief.

"Fuck you playing for?" Tyrone yelled.

James cackled as he dropped the gun back on his lap. "Nucca, you was scared to death!"

Once his head cleared, Tyrone noticed the car. "James, I know you didn't."

James nodded.

"Goddamn! I thought we weren't going to buy nothing big!" Tyrone reminded him.

"Shit! This the smallest one they had," James chuckled.

"Man, you know what I mean."

"Just get in. Let's go play Laser tag," James suggested, because he knew Tyrone loved Laser tag.

As they drove, James pumped the sounds of Lil' Wayne loudly. Tyrone shook his head.

"I can't lie, yes. This whip is sick," Tyrone remarked.

"So, cop one. We can push twins."

"I told you, yo, I'm saving my money."

"For what? Ain't shit promised. We could wake up dead. Fuck that, I want mines now," James emphasized with the waving of his arms as if he was casting a magic wand.

Tyrone heard a rumble. "What was that?"

"Nothing," James lied and turned the music up louder.

After a couple of games of Laser tag, things seemed like old times. They were just two young boys enjoying their favorite pastime. Tyrone could see the game changing James, but he felt like he could still reach his friend.

"Man, my whole life I've been picked on, bullied and laughed at. Now I got the money, now I got the power and I'm gonna get my respect!" James barked, as they stood in the parking lot of the Laser Tag Plaza.

"Bruh, it's about the money. Period. Remember we said we'd go to Silicon Valley and launch our own start-up? Stay focused," Tyrone urged.

"No, you stay focused. We in the game now. Anything can happen. Just like I caught you slipping earlier, I could've easily been a jack boy," James huffed.

Tyrone leaned against the trunk of the Mercedes.

"But, what about," Tyrone started to speak, but he heard the rumble again and realized it was coming from the trunk.

"What the fuck!" Tyrone exclaimed.

James laughed. "It's nothing."

"Nothing hell! Someone just knocked!"

James popped the trunk. As soon as Tyrone saw who it was, his eyes got as big as golf balls.

"Fool, you riding around with Tatianna in the trunk?"

Tatianna looked up at him weakly. She wanted to speak, but she was too far gone. She had seen James' Mercedes parked outside of the store, and she couldn't believe her eyes when she saw James come out and get in.

"James!"

When James saw who it was, he started to shine on her, but something deep down inside said, "Let's have some fun."

Tatianna came over, mouth wide open.

"Whose car you done stole?"

James pulled out a wad of hundreds and waved them in her face. "Do this look like I stole something?"

Tatianna couldn't believe this chump-ass nerd had come up so fast. But, money was money, and she was all about that.

I'm just playing, boy," she said, hitting him playfully.

"What you about to get into?" he asked.

"Shit," she shrugged.

He opened the door for her. "Then let's take a ride."

They rode, they drank, and they smoked. He offered her some Oxy. She took them. He slipped some more into her cup, she drank. She nodded, slipping into darkness. When she came to, she was butt naked and bent over the arm of a couch, getting fucked by James.

"Yeah, you dirty-ass bitch! You thought you was the shit, huh? Naw, you ain't shit and that's exactly how I'ma treat you!"

He came all over her back but as soon as he pulled out, an even bigger dick filled her pussy. She looked back to see a big black nucca leering down on her, and behind him were seven more. They fucked Tatianna until every hole in her body was sore.

"Don't worry, baby, I'll take away the pain," James laughed as he stuffed another Oxy down her throat. By the time she found herself in the trunk, she had never felt so good in her life . . . or so low.

"You gonna hook me up?" she slurred, eyes damn near closed.

James spat on the bitch and slammed the trunk.

"What the hell you gonna do with her?" Tyrone questioned.

James shrugged. "Whateva the hell I want. Like I said, it's my turn."

"You fucking crazy!"

"Naw, they fuckin' crazy!"

"Who is they?"

"All my enemies, bruh, all my enemies! All the bullshit I have been putting up with?   Fuck that. No more. You heard what happened to Pop?"

Tyrone looked at him. "No, what?"

"Don't worry," James snickered maliciously, "nucca just don't be weak."

****

"Yo, why your man ain't coming with us?" Psycho questioned, loading his nine-millimeter with hollow points.

"This ain't his thing, yo," James answered from the back seat. His voice sounded strong, but on the inside, he was shitting bricks. He had never committed a murder before, but he had gone too far to turn back. He had mentioned to Psycho about killing Pop. He thought Psycho would put his goons on it. Instead, Psycho had said, "It's about time you put in some work anyway. You said you wanted to get your tag, right?"

"Yeah," James had answered.

"That's what it is then," Psycho had nodded.

Now, he sat in the back seat of a van full of killers. On Psycho's behalf, he knew exactly what he was doing. He didn't like how close James and Shaka were getting. James and Tyrone were their secret weapon, but he felt like Shaka was trying to make them loyal to him. Psycho knew if he had something on James, it would give him leverage. And what type of leverage was better than murder?

They pulled the van up in front of Pop's mother's house. James could see his mother sitting in front of the TV.

"You ready, lil bruh?" Psycho questioned.

James mouth was so dry, he could only nod. Psycho knew what was up and laughed.

"Here, yo, sniff some of this. We all got the shakes catching our first body," he lied as he handed James a small package of tinfoil. He unwrapped it until the small pile of coke stared him in the face.

"You got a matchbox?" James asked.

"Just Scarface that shit, yo, we ain't got time for all that," Psycho spat.

James put the tin foil to his nose and snorted it all. He got more on his nose than in it, but since it was his first time, it was still more than enough to blow his mind. He could hear his own heartbeat banging in his ears like someone was beating an African drum, and his inner warrior was dancing to it, spear and all. His whole body screamed for release as he grabbed the .38 tightly. Psycho could see the transformation right before his eyes.

"You good, lil' bruh?"

When James finally opened his eyes, he was a different person.

"Yeah."

Even his voice sounded different.

James, Psycho and his two goons got out, keeping their eyes peeled for nosy neighbors as they pulled the ski masks over their faces. It didn't really matter in that particular West Baltimore neighborhood, because at least one murder was committed every single night.

Psycho didn't waste time knocking.

Boom!

He kicked the flimsy door in, then rushed in, followed by his murder squad. James was in another world. It was like his body was the video game his mind was playing. He heard his mother scream, his seven-year-old brother cry and Pop's pleas as Psycho's goons dragged him into the living room.

"Come on, man! Wh-what I do?" Pop stammered, until James snatched off his mask and Pop saw his face.

"Remember me, motherfucka?" James screamed out like a madman, kicking Pop in the mouth.

"Man, I'm sorry! I-I-I was just kiddin' with you! I'm sorry!" Pop pleaded.

But his pleas were only making James that more angry.

"Naw, you ain't sorry yet!"

"Pop his ass, lil' bruh! Now!"

Boc! Boc!

Pop howled with pain as the bullets exploded his knee, shattering it to smithereens. Pop's mother cried out in anguish for him and his brother almost collapsed.

"Shut the fuck up!" Psycho gritted, aiming his gun at his mother's head.

Boc!

One shot was all it took. He blew her brains all over her screaming child. He tried to get up and run but Psycho's goon, Murpa, shot him twice in the back of the head and he flopped to the ground, never to move again.

"That's how you kill a motherfucka, yo! Now, kill his ass and let's go!" Psycho ordered.

James looked down on Pop. He was beyond pain. He had stopped crying and was staring at his mother's lifeless body. In that moment, the bullying didn't seem worth it, but James knew he had come too far and his hesitation was only making it worse.

Boc! Boc! Boc!

All three shots blew chunks from Pop's skull, until all that was left looked like chewed up hamburger meat. He slumped, twitched, then laid as silent as a tomb.

Psycho patted James on the shoulder. "You handled your business like a 'G', we out."

James took one last look at the body of his former tormentor, then jogged out behind the rest of the crew.

****

Tony stood over the bodies, covering his nose with an alcohol-soaked rag. The room smelled putrid. For six days, Pop, his mother and little brother's corpses had laid on the floor, rotting. No one had called the police, but the fiends and crack heads had been coming in and out of the apartment, stealing everything the family had. By the time the police found out, everything had been taken except the bodies and the blood-stained carpet.

"Wow. No matter how many times I see it, I never get used to it," Tony remarked to the officer standing next to him.

"And then to rob the victims and just step over their dead bodies is a shame," the officer added.

Tony looked around at the bustling activity of the crime scene. Another officer hurried over to him, carrying a small plastic bag inside of a larger plastic bag. The smaller bag contained pills.

"Detective, we found these in the mother's top dresser."

Tony eyed the bag and grimaced.

"Oxys. I bet they're a part of the stolen pills. Damn, all this over a few pills?" He didn't want to believe it.

His sadness quickly turned to anger.

"All this over some fucking pills!" he repeated, with bass in his voice. He turned to the officer. "We find who is slinging these pills and we find the murderers! Get on it!"

It was ironic that what would eventually lead to James's downfall wasn't the pills, it was the totally unrelated topic of bullying.

For the next few days, Tony was unrelenting in his pursuit of the stolen pills, roughing up and pressuring nickel and dime dealers and fiends alike, but no one seemed to know anything, until. . .

"Okay, Okay, man! I'll tell you!" Peanut screamed as Tony pinned him against the alley brick wall.

Peanut hadn't broken until Tony had shown him the picture of Pop and his family's dead bodies. Peanut had once loved Pop's mother, but he had done her wrong, so he felt like he owed her at least that.

"Listen, the shit is simple. These young boys done went digital," Peanut said.

"Digital?" Tony echoed.

"All you got to do is use this app. You put in what you want, how many you want, and where you want it delivered. It's like Uber for driving deals!" Peanut explained.

"They use some type of encounter, encoder, incognito—"

"Encryption?"

"Yeah, yeah, something like that. All I know is, it makes the transaction untraceable."

Tony thought about it. *What gangsta knows how to design apps?* he wondered. "Who is it that makes the delivery?"

"BGF."

Tony held out a fifty-dollar bill. "Show me."

Peanut eyed the bill.

"Plus, a finder's fee?" he asked, but when he saw Tony's expression, he mumbled, "don't even worry about it."

Tony parked in the cut and scrunched down in the front seat. Ten minutes later, a black SUV pulled up. He instantly recognized one of the men in the car as Tonto, a low-ranking member of the BGF. He watched the transaction go down, the SUV pull off and then Peanut came and got in the passenger seat.

"Bingo," Peanut sang, holding out a small packet of ten pills.

"Ten? They're five dollars apiece?" Tony questioned. His expression showed astonishment.

Peanut cursed under his breath for not pocketing half the pills, then he replied, "They killing, the game, fifty used to only get you two, now it's ten."

"Nobody can compete!" Tony shook his head slowly. "No wonder so many people are overdosing. There is a super abundance on the street. Jesus Christ! It's like somebody turned on a faucet and drugs come gushing out!"

Before Tony could process the implications, his phone rang. It was Monica. He frowned. She was in school; she never called him from school.

He answered the phone.

"What's up, baby girl?" All he heard was the sound of her tears. He sat up.

"Monica, what's wrong?"

"It-it's . . . it's Tatianna, Daddy! They just found her body. She's dead!"

"I'm on my way."

He hung up and dropped the phone in her lap. Tyrone came out of the building and approached. She watched him coming, her mind frazzled, then something happened that blew her mind, despite her sadness. Two guys that were friends with Pop, the same guys that used to bully Tyrone, saw him coming and stepped aside! It was like Tyrone was Moses and they were the Red Sea, the way they opened up to let him pass with obvious difference.

"What was that all about?" she questioned.

"What was what? Why are you crying?"

Monica wiped her eyes. "You haven't heard about Pop?"

Monica frowned. "Pop?"

"Him and his family got murdered last night," Tyrone informed her, thinking, *I know exactly who did it.*

Monica shook her head. "No, I'm talking about Tatianna. They found her body in DRV Hill Park. She had overdosed on pills."

Tyrone's jaw dropped. All he could see in his mom's eye was Tatianna's limp body in the trunk of James' car. He cursed himself for not saying anything, and now she was dead.

"I'm, I'm sorry," was all he could muster.

Monica hugged him. "I can't believe she's gone! It's those pills! Everybody's taking them now! I hate whoever did this! I hate them!" she cried.

She had no clue that every word she spoke was a slap to the face, with the word and hate like a gut blow to his soul.

They both heard a car horn blow. They looked and saw that Tony had just pulled up.

"I-I have to go. I'll call you." Monica walked away. Tyrone watched her while Tony watched him. Not because he had caught them hugging, but because Tyrone had on another pair of three-hundred-dollar Jordan's.

****

Tyrone stormed into the abandoned row house and slammed the door. It was the perfect hide out, because no one would suspect that there was a fully operational, digital command center in the middle of the hood. It was outfitted like a Silicon start-up, with private servers, data storage units and monitors everywhere, all powered by generators to make sure the energy consumption stayed off the grid.

Tyrone was surprised to find Murda and two BGF bitches in their spot, but he was even more surprised to find James sporting BGF colors.

"What up, dawg?" James greeted cheerily, his feet kicked up on the table, where several stacks of money sat, looking delicious.

"We need to talk," Tyrone spat firmly, eyeing James.

James shrugged. "So, talk."

"Alone."

James opened his arms in an expansive gesture. "They my family now, too. Whatever you gotta say, you can say in front of the homies."

Tyrone walked up on James, standing over him.

"You didn't have to kill her, James," Tyrone growled.

"Kill who?" James chuckled.

"Don't play with me!" Tyrone.

James laughed, but his eyes didn't. "You better watch your tone. You see this money? That's our cut for the week. That's what's important. Not some cold, dead bitch that ain't deserve the air she breathe. Focus," James spat smoothly, then leaned over and scarfed a line of coke off the mirror shaped like a Benz.

"Nucca, you ain't shit. You think 'cause you got money, guns and so-called friends, you a gangsta? Fuck outta here, yo, you still that same scared little boy," Tyrone seethed.

As soon as he saw the look on James's face, he knew he had hurt his feelings. He regretted it, but he didn't have time to apologize, because James jumped up and aimed a gun at his face.

"Who the fuck you think you talkin' to? I told you, watch your tone! Shit done changed, and respect is reason one! Nobody is going to disrespect me, ever again, you understand!"

The two old friends squared off. Tyrone wasn't scared of the gun in his face, but he was scared he had lost his best friend forever.

"You gonna shoot, shoot."

James just looked at him, pain and regret in his eyes. He slowly lowered the gun. "Naw, I aint gonna shoot, 'cause I think we understand each other," James spat.

"Yeah, we do. I'm done, yo," Tyrone replied, as he stuffed his money into a duffel bag.

"Done? Naw, brah. It ain't that easy," James spat.

Tyrone snatched up the bag, looked James in the eyes and said, "Watch me."

He walked out, leaving James staring daggers in his back.

Tyrone stepped out on the front porch and took a deep breath. Even the air felt heavy. Stifling. Oppressive. He knew right then he had to get out of Baltimore. He had enough money to go anywhere and start over.

"But where?" he mumbled to himself and his mind instantly answered Silicon Valley.

Tyrone smiled to himself. The decision felt right. It made sense. He stepped off the porch feeling like a burden had been lifted. He didn't notice the nondescript sedan sitting among the other parked cars up the block. He hadn't noticed it on his way in or as it followed him from home.

But, it noticed him, because inside the sedan, sat Tony.

"What have we got here?" Tony asked himself as he watched Tyrone walk up the street with the duffel bag slung over his shoulder.

Tony had decided to follow Tyrone on a whim. He had driven over to his house to have a fatherly talk with him concerning his daughter, but when he had seen him come out, looking around and walking fast, his detective instincts kicked in.

Now he had hit pay dirt. He saw the Mercedes and the shiny black Yukon sitting in front of the abandoned row house, sticking out like a pair of sore thumbs. He waited.

And waited.

And waited.

The sun dropped like a dope fiend on crack and still he waited.

Finally, the front door opened, and two dudes and two females emerged, followed by a haze of smoke. One carried a duffel bag and got in the Mercedes with one of the chicks. Both cars pulled off. The block was quiet, dark and inviting Tony to investigate. He knew it was wrong. He didn't have proper authority. He didn't have probable cause. He didn't have a warrant. But, what he did have was his gut, so he went with that.

Tony jumped out of his car, pulled his B-More baseball cap low and made his way up the block. He looked around as he tried to peep in the windows, but they were blacked out with trash bags from the inside. He went around and found the same thing on every window.

"Well, I guess I don't have a choice."

Tony jimmied the back door. It opened. He stepped inside. He pulled his gun out and entered deeper into the kitchen area. All he heard was the faint sounds of rats scurrying for cover. He entered the living room and his eyes widened.

"Jackpot!" he yelped, looking at all of the computer equipment.

He eyed it all, wondering how it all fit together, then pulled out his cellphone and called the chief.

"Chief, I need a warrant."

He had his warrant in less than an hour. He had the equipment bagged, tagged and transferred to a team of police computer engineers in less than two hours.

But, it only took ten minutes to be definitely disappointed.

"I've got good news and bad news," the head computer engineer stated.

Tony sighed.

"Story of my life. Give me the bad news."

"Everything's wiped clean. As soon as we tried to log in. There was an encrypted secret password we needed to key in immediately upon entry. Whatever happened, it's all gone. Not a zero or one is left. Whoever programmed this system is a fucking genius. Criminal, but genius.

Tony shook his head. "With news that bad, what can possibly be good?"

"This was definitely ground zero for this drug app. We traced the app from your informant's phone, triangulated the coordinates and it definitely came from the block," the engineer informed him.

"Great, well I guess, we go back to basics."

"What's that?"

"Dust all of the computers and equipment for any type of print we can get. I don't care if it's an ass print. I want it!"

****

"Your man has to go," Psycho told James as they drove through the hood in Psycho's new Porsche, like ghetto royalty.

"It wasn't him," James said with attitude.

Psycho looked at James like he had lost his mind.

"Not him! How the fuck the cops know about our spot? The same day? The same fucking day. He walked out and the cops kick in the door! How they know?"

"All they got is some useless hardware. I booby trapped the data," James responded.

"That ain't the point! Your man ratted us out!" Psycho concluded.

James wasn't ready to accept what Psycho was saying, but it was staring him straight in the face. Everything seemed to be pointing in that direction, but James couldn't bring himself to believe it.

"Look, yo, I just need to talk to him. That's all; I can straighten all this shit out," James reasoned.

"Where is he then? The mutherfucka just disappeared off the face of the earth!" Psycho spat.

"He'll turn up," James replied, adding, "The bottom line is, we need to deal with this cop. He fuckin' all over us!"

James shook his head, thinking about what Tony had been up and nonstop. He was harassing BGF in every way he could, kicking in doors, arresting entire blocks full of hustlers, and generally keeping it hot.

"We need to send him a message," Psycho gruffed.

"Two bullets in the brain," James chuckled, evilly.

"We can't kill a cop. This city is hot enough."

"Then what message, James?

Psycho looked at him and winked. "The next best thing."

****

Tyrone looked out over the San Francisco Bay and inhaled the crisp air. He had been in California for only a week, but he already had a beautiful apartment and had even bought a hybrid to blend in with the tree huggers and organic crowd.

"Damn," he said, feeling good and bad at the same time.

Good, because he had made a clean break. He had over two million in cash, and now in a City that didn't know him from Jack. But he felt bad because he wished James was there with him. But he knew that to help a person, they've got to want to help themselves.

Tyrone stepped back inside closing the patio door and sitting down in front of his laptop.

Yo, bruh, where you at?

He stared at the words on his screen. They were from James and they were encrypted. They had a sort of digital bat signal to be able to reach each other. Tyrone thought about replying, but he decided against it. He wasn't going to jeopardize his freedom because of James's foolishness.

Until he saw her face.

It was Monica and her picture was plastered all over CNN News. She had been kidnapped. He logged onto CNN's stream and heard:

. . . "was kidnapped several hours ago, allegedly by a group of drug dealers with a vendetta with her father, Detective Anthony Roberts."

Tyrone couldn't believe his ears. *Monica kidnapped?* There was no way he was going to let something happen to her. One hour later, Tyrone was on a flight to Baltimore.

****

Monica was paralyzed with fear. She was tied to a bedpost in a rundown apartment. She had been walking home from school, when a van skidded up and three masked men jumped out with guns.

"Get in the van!" one ordered, putting the barrel to her temple.

She knew better than resist.

Monica snatched at the ropes binding her, but it was useless. She was stuck.

The door opened and one of the masked guys entered. He shut the door behind him and looked at her. All she could see were his eyes, but the lustful glaze filming them made her squirm and blurt out, "My father's a cop!"

The masked man didn't speak, but he laughed. It was a laugh familiar to her. She eyed the squat chubby figure. The way he stood, his pigeon-toed, slump back stance

"James?" she blurted out, and from the way his body tensed, she knew she was right. "James, I know that's you! Why are you doing this? What did I do to you? Where's Tyrone?"

James snatched off the mask. "You a dumb bitch, yo! You should have kept your mouth shut!"

"But why? Why haven't I heard from Tyrone?"

"He's gone! He left you, bitch! Once shit got hot, he ran like a coward!" James spat.

"Hot? What do you mean?

James stepped closer to the bed. "Oh, you don't know? You mean, he didn't tell you?"

"Tell me what?"

"Your boyfriend was the biggest drug dealer in Baltimore. Who do you think gave Tatianna her free ride up the stairway to heaven?"

"I don't believe you!"

James shrugged. "Believe what you want but believe this, if your Pops don't do the right thing, you gonna be my new slave bitch," he cackled.

The look on his face made her cringe.

****

Tony was getting under his own skin. He had lost five pounds in just one day, worrying so much. The whole force was on it, but he hadn't told them it was BGF because he had been warned.

"Nucca, fall back or you'll never see your daughter again!"

He cursed himself for not moving her out of the city sooner. He had always thought he could protect her, now he saw that he was sadly mistaken.

His mind was a frenzied channel of static energy when his phone rang.

"Roberts," he answered.

"I know where she's at."

His ears perked up. "Who is this?"

A beat.

"Tyrone."

"I see. I know some things about you, too," Tony remarked.

"Well, what's more important?"

"Where is she?"

"Look, I'm telling you, don't bring the whole force. If you do, this shit won't work. We gotta do this my way," Tyrone stated.

"Just tell me where."

"You familiar with Park Heights?"

****

Tyrone gripped the pistol tightly as he slowly and quietly crept up the back stairs of the two-story house. He knew this house like the back of his hand. James's grandmother had left it to him. They had sat in the attic and programmed for hours. He knew every nook and cranny of the house, which was why he knew the basement window on the driveway side wouldn't lock. He flipped the watch with the edge of a discarded Popsicle stick and slipped into the darkness of the basement. He stood still, listening for any sounds. He heard a distant TV and headed toward the steps. He knew which stairs to avoid because they could creak, so his climb was silent. The closer he got, the louder he got. He peered around the corner and saw Monica tied to the bed and James sitting at the table.

"Let her go!" Tyrone demanded as he entered, his gun aimed.

James moved quicker than Tyrone anticipated, grabbing his gun, but he didn't have time to raise it.

"Well, well, back from the dead," James smirked.

"Put the gun down, James."

"Or what? You gonna shoot me? You gonna shoot me, Ty?" James taunted.

"Just let Monica go," Tyrone demanded.

James shrugged. "Come on over and untie her ya goddamn self, you fuckin' rat!"

"Fuck you talkin' about?"

"Don't act stupid, you put the police on our spot!"

"No, I didn't!"

"Then how they know?"

Tyrone was confused. He had no idea the row house had been busted.

"You fuckin' traitor!" James raised the gun.

Boc! Boc! Boc!

The first bullet caught Tyrone in his upper shoulder. The next two split James' chest almost center mass, stopping his heart instantly.

"Freeze!"

Tyrone heard the command, but he was too far gone to care. He had just killed his best friend, the only friend he'd ever known. He rushed over to James, but although his eyes were open, they saw nothing. Tyrone's tears fell on James's face as he knelt beside him and closed his eyes.

"Get up slow without the gun," Tony ordered, his trigger finger a sneeze away from a head shot.

He had arrived just in time to see the exchange of gunfire.

"Daddy!" Monica cried out.

Tyrone looked at Tony as he stood to his feet, hands raised.

"You have the right to remain silent—"

"I saved your daughter's life!"

"Daddy, no!"

Tony gritted, flexed his jaw, then continued. "You have the right to an attorney—"

"Then kill me. Shoot me dead, because I'm not going to jail," Tyrone hollered, meaning every word.

Tyrone looked down at the gun.

"Don't make me do it, son," Tony warned.

"You leave me no choice," Tyrone countered.

As Tyrone bent to grab the gun, everything went in slow motion for Tony. He saw the horror in his daughter's face and the determination in Tyrone's. He took a deep breath and pulled the trigger.

Boc! Boc!

"Daddddyyy!"

Silence.

Tyrone realized he was still alive. He looked up at Tony. He had aimed wide, missing Tyrone on purpose. He eyed Tyrone hard.

"If I ever see you again, I'm putting you under the jail," Tony hissed.

In the background, the sound of approaching sirens filled Tyrone's future with an ominous sense of urgency. Tyrone looked at Monica.

"Ty, don't go," she begged.

The sirens got louder.

"If you're still here when they arrive, all bets are off," Tony said.

Tyrone held Monica's gaze. They exchanged tears like a long kiss goodbye.

"I'm . . . I'm sorry," Tyrone stammered.

"Tyrone, I love you!" She called out as he raced from the room.

Tony picked up Tyrone's gun with a handkerchief and put it in his pocket.

Insurance . . .

THREE MONTHS LATER

Monica had her suitcase packed as she stood in her room, modeling her swimsuit. She saw Tony standing in the doorway, looking at her.

"I know you don't think you're wearing that to Spring Break," Tony remarked.

"Daddy, it's a beach. What would you have me wear, a raincoat?"

"Hold up, let me go get you mine," he half-joked.

"Ha-ha," she responded dryly, putting on her robe and going over to hug her father." I'm going to be okay, Daddy."

Tony held her in his embrace. Since the kidnapping, he had bought a house in Baltimore County. It wasn't ideal, but he needed to get her into a better situation. The pill epidemic was still ravaging the city, with no signs of slowing down. Without James or Tyrone, the BGF lost their digital edge and were being slaughtered and pushed aside by another crew, with an even better app.

Gangstas were going digital.

"I know you are, baby," Tony said, then kissed her on the forehead, adding, "And don't make me follow you to Florida."

They laughed.

"I love you, Daddy."

"I love you too, baby girl!"

He walked out. Monica went over to her dresser and picked up the pendant Tyrone had bought her. She still thought about him a lot.

She wondered if he was safe. She wondered if he thought of her. She wondered if . . .

Her thoughts were broken by a strange buzz coming from her computer. She looked at it as her screen saver was blinking in and out, rapidly and then her whole screen went blank. She hit the on switch and hit several keys, but nothing happened.

"Nooooooooo! I just got this computer," she complained.

The screen came back on, but it was no longer her screen saver. It was a picture of a beautiful beach with the caption, "Fiji Islands."

"Fiji?" she was totally confused until words began to I.M. across the screen:

Wish you were here.

Her heart leaped and a smile spread all over her body. Her phone buzzed with a text. It was an app confirming the transfer of twenty-five hundred dollars into her account. On the screen, an ad for a travel agency popped up.

She smiled mischievously.

"What Daddy don't know . . ."

She promptly booked a flight to Fiji instead of Florida.

-THE END-

WAHIDA CLARK PRESENTS

IN LOVE WITH THE STATES PROPERTY

A SHORT STORY BY
REDS JOHNSON

In Love With The States Property

A short Story By
Reds Johnson

PROLOGUE

Click! Clack!

Click! Clack!

The sound of Li'l Grief's *twin bitches* which were his .357 Desert Eagles being cocked back ready for whatever a fuck boy tried to bring at him. He was sitting in his all-black 2018 Audi R8 with tinted windows and black rims parked on Laurel Street waiting for his target to walk out of the Chinese spot.

The sky was pitch black, and there were very few stars out to cause any brightness. The streetlights flickered, and the wind blew hard, causing grains of dirt and leaves to smack against his car. Not many people were out on Laurel Street that time of night; maybe a few Mexicans, but other than that, it was a ghost town. The Chinese spot was the only thing open because them muthafuckas wasn't going to miss out on any coins.

He glanced at the time on his car radio. It read 11:00 p.m. on the dot. Grief nodded his head as he calmly placed his twin bitches on his lap waiting patiently.

Not long after he set his twins down, he spotted Kevin walking out of the Chinese spot with a bag in each hand and Kia, who was his on-again, off-again girlfriend of eight years.

On my moms, these muhfuckas got me fucked up, he thought as he gripped the Desert Eagle that was sitting on his right thigh.

In one swift motion, he grabbed the car door handle, opened it, and slid out of the car like a thief in the night. Grief had both of his twin bitches crossed behind his back like Queen Latifah did in the movie *Set It Off.*

"Y'all 'bout to have a good muhfuckin' time, huh?" he chuckled as he walked toward them with the twins pointed at them.

"Grief, the fuck is you doin'?" Kia was utterly disgusted already knowing that he was about to be on some complete bullshit.

"Yo, homie, chill the fuck out pointin' that shit at me and my girl," Kevin tried to act tough.

Kevin wasn't even the type of guy to be going toe-to-toe with a dude like Grief. While Kevin pretended to be a killer, Grief, on the other hand, *was* a killer, and everyone knew it.

Grief stood there looking Kevin up and down. He could smell the fear seeping through his pores as he watched sweat quickly appear and glisten on his forehead.

Not once did he say fuck the food and grab the Glock that was on his waist, but instead, he tried to impress Kia thinking his mean mug and approach would handle what he thought was his light work. A typical wannabe-ass dude that didn't live the lifestyle he portrayed and Grief was shocked to see Kia attempt to deal with a nigga of such caliber.

Grief's face was tore up with anger and frustration. He frowned upon the way Kevin spoke to him, and being the type of nigga he was, he didn't think twice about his next move.

Boc! Boc! Boc! Boc!

He let go of his bitches and hit Kevin in each leg twice, causing blood to spatter like an overfilled balloon that'd been popped. The bullets tore straight through his medial and lateral collateral ligaments causing his knees to buckle beneath him.

"*Ahhhhhhhhhh! Fuuccckkkkkk!*" Kevin screamed as he dropped the bags and grabbed at his legs while collapsing to the ground.

Grief smirked at the holes he'd created in Kevin's body.

"What the fuck is wrong wit'chu?" Kia screamed as she attempted to help Kevin. "You buggin' the fuck out, yo, fo'real! Just leave, Grief; just leave!"

After placing one of the burnas in his waistband, he pointed the other at Kia, stopping her dead in her tracks. His eyes dared her to take another step as if to say *I wish the fuck you would help this nigga*. Once he realized she wasn't going to try him, he went in on her.

"Kia, get the fuck in my car!" he snatched her by the arm and slung her toward the car. "I should knock ya fuckin' head off out here actin' like a thot-ass bitch wit' this bum-ass nigga!"

"Don't call me no bitch, Grief, fo'real!" They were having a full-blown disagreement as if Grief hadn't just attempted murder on someone.

"Ain't nobody tryin'a hear that fuck-ass shit! I've been callin' ya muhfuckin' phone all damn day, and you been iggin' me, huh? I wonder why."

Grief yanked the passenger-side door open and pushed Kia in, damn near shutting her leg in the door as she tried to shut it.

"Aaaaaaah!" Kevin was still screaming in pain and drawing unwanted attention.

"Nigga, shut the fuck up. You lucky I don't end ya ass right here, but let this be a lesson; don't fuck wit' mines!" He smiled at the sight of the blood that was seeping underneath Kevin and staining the cold, cement ground. "She throw you pussy, you decline it, understand? She call or text ya phone, you decline that shit, understand?"

Kevin was sweating a whole heap and could barely speak as he clenched his teeth to keep himself from passing out from the pain.

"Oh my gosh! Somebody call the police!" a woman yelled out.

People were now turning on the lights in their homes, looking out their windows, and some even came outside due to all the commotion that was going on.

Muhfuckas can't ever mind they business, he thought.

Grief shook his head and turned around to head to his ride. He gave Kia the look of death as he started up the car and peeled out of that muthafucka, all while making a mental note to make sure Kevin understood him once they crossed paths again. He wasn't beat for any sort of disrespect, and Kia knew that.

She always thinkin' since we on a break that we ain't together. If she ain't wit' me, then she ain't gon' be wit' nobody. Keep fuckin' around wit' the fuck around and fuck around and get her shit pushed back!"

IN LOVE WITH THE STATES PROPERTY

1

Four Months Earlier . . .

"You have a collect call from the state correctional institution Coal Township. This call is subject to recording and monitoring. To accept this free call, press 1."

Kia rolled her eyes as she listened to the automated voice message of the annoying white woman that she'd heard several times a day, every day. She didn't feel like answering her phone, but she also didn't feel like hearing Grief's mouth, either.

"Wassup, baby girl?" he greeted when the call connected.

"What do you want, Grief?" Kia said with attitude.

"Why you answerin' the phone wit' all that hostility? Chill out wit' all that, ya feel me?"

"Like I said, what do you want?" she repeated.

Kia didn't give the slightest fuck about Grief telling her to chill out. She was so sick and tired of the nonstop bullshit he caused and then act as if she had to just sit and deal with it. She couldn't deny the fact that she was in love with Grief, but his insane ways had her completely over their on-again, off-again relationship.

"Don't ask me what the fuck I want like I ain't supposed to be callin' you. I put money on this muhfuckin' phone every month, so I'ma call when I feel like it. Now, what the fuck ya pretty ass doin'?" he asked.

Kia forced herself not to blush by what he'd just said to her. It was just like Grief to say some roughneck and sweet shit in the same sentence having her confused as hell, knowing damn well constantly loving a nigga like Grief was bad for business.

"Grief, I ain't even about to fall into ya trap. I'm not doin' this shit wit'chu. Every time I look, you wanna get on my fuckin' nerves and then act like everything all good—nah, not this time."

Grief blew loud in an aggravated manner. Being locked up was something nobody wanted, and damn sure not him, so the last thing he wanted to do was call Kia and argue about some bullshit when she was supposed to be his peace of mind.

"First off, calm the fuck down and watch who you talkin' to, ya hear?" He paused as if he were waiting for her to respond, but he really wasn't. "I ain't call you to hear all that rah-rah bullshit."

Pssh. Kia smacked her lips and rolled her eyes hard as if he could see her.

"Smack ya lips again, Kia, I promise I'll arrange for me to come to you personally and snatch ya fuckin' lips off ya face." His words weren't a threat but more so a promise.

Kia wanted to smack her lips again, but she knew Grief meant well on his word, and she just ain't have time for the bullshit. He didn't beat on her, but he damn sure didn't mind snatching her ass up, if need be.

"Whatever, Grief. You wastin' this phone call up," she changed the subject.

"That's ya naggin' ass wit' the fufu shit, and I don't give a fuck. I'll just call back. Shit, this ain't gon' go on for too much longer, you know. I'll be home soon." His tone brightened up when the words slipped from his mouth.

There was a quietness that took over the phone. Kia loved Grief something serious, but at times, it seemed as though loving him was the wrong thing to do.

"I know you'll be home soon, Grief," she said in a dry tone.

"Why you respond like that? What, you ain't happy a nigga comin' home? Oh, I guess I'm gon' be cuttin' into ya ho time, huh?" he joked.

"Nigga, shut yo' ass up!" she snapped.

Kia briefly thought back on the day that Grief got cased up over that situation with Kevin and shook her head. She remembered it like it was yesterday, and when it was all said and done, Kevin snitched on Grief, but then quickly recanted his story. They still charged Grief with gun possession, and somehow, his lawyers came up with a gun permit, but he still ended up doing prison time due to being wrapped up in some other bullshit. They purposely prolonged his case so that he could do prison time. The system was truly sick of Grief's bullshit, and he was sick of theirs.

I don't got time for this shit, she thought. He was bound to come home and wreck shit like he normally did, and she just didn't have the time nor the energy to be dealing with his crazy ass. She'd been dealing with Grief since she was twenty-one years old, and if she knew then what she knew now, she probably would have turned the other cheek and run far away from his ass as possible. However, her lust for a bad boy got her caught up in a life that she wasn't prepared for, but she'd grown accustomed to it.

All she could do was waste more time on the phone as she thought about the first time she laid eyes on Grief.

Kia, Ty'Kia, ShaQuanna, and TaQuanna were just leaving a place they referred to as The Spot in Glassboro, New Jersey. It was a little club attached to the back of a liquor store that they went to for good music, good food, and some bomb-ass drinks. Every Friday and Saturday, The Spot was LIT!

"Y'all hold on; lemme holla at my homeboy right quick," ShaQuanna said as she walked over to a muscular, caramel teddy bear.

Kia and the rest of the girls followed her and just stood by the side waiting for her to get finished talking. They weren't about to let her out of their sight because they went by the rule . . . We come together, and we gon' leave together.

"Wassup, Grief?" ShaQuanna greeted her friend with a hug.

"Wassup wit' it, ma? Long time no talk," he smiled and unknowingly had Kia melting on the sideline.

"Yea, long time no talk because ya ass was locked up. I hope you bein' good out here," she laughed but was serious.

"I'm always good," he responded and then took a look at his surroundings. "Them ya homegirls?"

"Yea, they my boos," she gloated.

"A'ight," he nodded. "Take them and go home."

ShaQuanna didn't even need to ask why. Not only because they were already about to head home, but she knew how Grief was, so she knew shit was about to get real, and he was making sure she was out of sight and out of mind.

"Okay." She turned to her girls. "Y'all, we gotta get the fuck up outta here."

Ty'Kia and TaQuanna already knew what was up, but Kia acted oblivious to what was about to go down. It could've been because she'd only been hanging out with them physically for a few months. Although ShaQuanna and TaQuanna were her twin cousins, she really didn't do the going out and partying sort of thing until they practically begged her to come out with them one weekend, and ever since then, she was hooked.

"What's wrong?" she asked.

All three of the girls looked at her with their eyes damn near bulging out of their heads. Ty'Kia took it a step further and frowned her face like "Bitch, what?"

"Bitch, you can't be serious. That's Li'l Grief, and right now, that nigga lurkin' ready to set some shit off. Thank God he knows me because a bullet ain't got no name on it, and he just told us to get the fuck outta Dodge," ShaQuanna explained.

That was the day Kia became intrigued by Grief. Her pussy thumped from her flashback. Her mind said to get the hell away from him, but her heart told her to stay just a little bit longer. It was then that she'd realized that she was in love with the state's property.

2

New Year's Day was just another day for Kia. She didn't give a fuck about it being a new year because it was already fucked up being that she'd lost her mother a year ago on New Year's Day. She was over everything and anyone, and she wasn't for any sort of celebration.

Kia Carter was twenty-eight years old. A pretty, brown-skinned girl that looked like she was living the life of a millionaire on the outside, but on the inside, she was going through it. She was born and raised in Bridgeton, New Jersey . . . one of the poorest parts of Jersey, to be exact. She was an only child and spoiled rotten, at that. She didn't work since her boyfriend was a well-known drug dealer, so, she pretty much had life handed to her.

There she was, staring out the window in her kitchen in a pair of skintight, black Spanx and a white, spaghetti-strap shirt. She had just finished washing the dishes and cooking a bomb-ass brunch when she felt a hard smack on her ass, causing her to snap out of her trance.

Smack!

"Ouch!" She turned around and gave him the look of death. "Why would you do that?"

"What the hell you in here thinkin' about?" Grief asked as he moved behind her and wrapped his arms around her waist.

His dick was hard as a rock, and Kia already knew what he wanted. Grief had only been free from that hellhole of a prison for a good twenty-four hours, and Kia hadn't broke him off with some good-good yet, and his dick was yearning for some warm, phat pussy.

"I'm thinkin' about my mother, if you must know," she said with an eye roll.

Grief paused for a second. He then remembered what day it was and understood her zoned-out attitude. It had been a year since Kia's mother, Tasha, passed away from cancer. It was an emotional roller coaster helping Kia get through that tough time. Things were still hard for her, but it was tolerable now.

"You good?" he broke the silence.

"I don't have a choice but to be," she replied.

Grief loved Kia's strength. That was one of the main things that made a thug like him love her the way he did. She'd been through hell and back with Grief, especially when he was on lock. He thought that she would fold during the times they had to be away from each other due to him being upstate, but she proved to be nothing short of a rider.

Now, here he was, once again standing next to his girl and loving all on her like he dreamed about the many nights he was sleeping on what felt like a cement mattress and a thin-ass pillow with a hospital sheet for a blanket. Those were some of the hardest times of his life, mentally and physically, so being home was a breath of fresh air, and he vowed to never go back behind them bars.

"Damn, I missed you, ma."

Grief held her tightly from behind and kissed her on her neck. The food Kia cooked looked and smelled better than a muthafucka, but the way his dick was feeling, he needed to be in some pussy and release some much-needed stress.

"Gr-ief," she stuttered.

"Grief, what?" he asked while he pulled her into the living room.

Standing in front of the sofa, Grief slid his hand under her tank top and was in heaven as he played with her plump breast. He slid his right hand in her Spanx and began to play with her precious pearl as well, causing Kia's mouth to open in pleasure. Grief could tell that she wanted some dick just as badly as he wanted some pussy because her shit was already soaking wet.

"Grief, stop," she moaned in a sort of a mumble.

She tried to move his hand from her Spanx, but he gripped her tightly with his left hand, and in one swift motion, dug two of his fingers in her pussy.

"Fuck!" she screamed.

It felt good to her, and all she could do was grind her hips, hoping that he went deeper. Grief moved his fingers in and out of her pussy, causing her sticky juices to coat his fingers. It was nothing for him to make Kia come because he owned that pussy, and he knew just what to do to please her the right way.

"Stop playin' wit' me, girl," he whispered, then passionately but painfully bit her on her neck. After that, he nibbled on her ear as her legs began to shake.

He snatched his hand out of her Spanx and stuck his fingers in his mouth.

"Damn, a nigga missed the taste of this."

Kia held onto the arm of the sofa to gain her composure because her legs felt like noodles. Thinking that Grief was done, he completely caught her off guard when he placed his hand behind on the back of her neck and leaned her over on the sofa. He pulled her Spanx down and pulled down his basketball shorts and boxer briefs simultaneously. Grief lifted up her ass cheek and slid his nine-and-a-half-inch dick in her pussy in one swift motion.

"Ssshit," she moaned.

He placed his hands on her waist and went ape shit on her pussy.

Smack! Smack! Smack!

Clap! Clap! Clap!

"Grief, waiiittttt," Kia gasped as she gripped one of the pillows on the couch with one hand and held her stomach with the other because it felt like his dick was about to come through it at any given time.

"Mmm, nah, ain't no waitin'. Take this dick."

He was pounding Kia's pussy like no tomorrow. The house was filled with her moans, his balls smacking against her pussy, and the gushy sounds of her juices. He could feel her pussy lips swelling up as he continued to plow his dick inside of her. Kia was comin' like crazy, but Grief's dick was something serious, and she wanted him to pull out already. So she began to throw her ass back and tighten up her walls.

"*That's* what the fuck I'm talkin' 'bout," he grunted.

"Mm, you missed this pussy, huh?" she talked dirty to him.

Smack!

Grief smacked her ass. "Hell, yea, I missed this shit. You missed this dick, didn't you?"

Kia nodded her head and tightened up her walls once more.

"Hell, yea, I missed this big dick, dad-dy."

By now, Kia was comin' for the third time, and her legs were about to give out on her. Her lower half was tired, and she began to lean over to the side. Grief could tell that he was working her over, so he made sure to hold on to her to help keep her balance, but he didn't stop fucking her brains out.

"Hmm, give me this pussy, ma."

Kia felt Grief's dick in her stomach all while feeling his grip get tighter and his dick pulsating.

"Bust all in this phat pussy, baby," she moaned a wakeful moan.

Grief didn't respond again. His focus was on her ass that kept jiggling each time he slammed up against her and watched his dick disappear like magic. *Damn, I miss this shit,* he thought.

"Mmmm, fuuuck." He squeezed her shoulders tightly as he pressed her body against his and his against hers as he released his warmth inside her.

Kia grinded up against him making sure her pussy sopped up all his nut before he pulled out of her. Her pussy made a fart sound when he pulled out.

"I tore that shit up. Listen to that shit talkin'. I hear you, li'l mama. Daddy's home now." He acted like he was talking to her pussy while he pulled his boxer briefs and basketball shorts up.

Kia looked back at him and smacked her lips before laughing. Sometimes, she couldn't stand him, but other times, she was head over heels.

"You get on my nerves, stupid!"

Smack!

Grief smacked her ass hard once more.

"Make a nigga a plate," he told her before leaving the living room and heading upstairs.

I know this nigga didn't just tear my pussy up to the point where I can barely walk and then got the nerve to ask me to fix him a damn plate. She shook her fuckin' head as she thought to herself.

After Kia was able to walk again, she made her way upstairs to clean herself up. She went into the bathroom and grabbed a few feminine wet wipes to wipe both of their juices from between her legs before sliding her Spanx back on. Then she washed and dried her hands before leaving the bathroom. She peeked in the master bedroom and saw Grief breaking down a vanilla Dutch wrap, and breaking down some weed which she knew was Loud because it diffused throughout the hallway.

She headed back downstairs and grabbed a paper plate out of the cabinet and began to make Grief's plate. French toast, fried chicken, turkey bacon, turkey sausage, grits, and eggs were on the menu. When she was finished fixing his plate, she poured him a nice big cup of orange juice and headed upstairs.

The Loud he was smoking had the whole house smelling like a weed traphouse. She was glad that she lived in a single-family home because her neighbors were damn near down the street, and she lived around a bunch of nosy-ass white folks.

"Grief, that shit stink," she said when she walked in the room and handed him his food and drink.

"Shittin' me. This shit smell good as fuck," he told her.

Grief ain't waste no time going to town on his plate. With a mouthful of food, he looked over at Kia who was now lying at the end of the bed going through her phone.

"Who you was fuckin' while I was locked up?" he wanted to know.

Kia was caught off guard by his question. "Nobody! Why would you ask that?"

"Because I wanted to know who the fuck been hittin' my pussy while I was on lock, so, is you lyin' to me?" he questioned her while eyeing her like a lion stalking its prey.

"Grief, no, I ain't been fuckin' wit' nobody. You shouldn't even question me, knowing damn well we've been dealing for the past eight years," she reminded him.

Grief swallowed the food he had in his mouth and looked at her like she was crazy.

"You act like you forgot that I got cased up because you was runnin' behind another nigga. Stop playin' wit' me, Kia," he warned.

Kia threw her phone down on the bed.

"Ain't *nobody* playin' you, Grief. I said I ain't been wit' nobody while you was locked up, and that's my word. Now, please, chill out and finish ya food." Kia was over the conversation.

"A'ight, if that's ya word, then I'ma take that," he assured her.

"You ain't got no choice but to take it because I would never do you dirty. I've been ridin' wit' you for eight years, so why would I stop now?" Her voice was convincing.

Grief looked her in her eyes and saw sincerity. *I must be trippin',* he thought.

"You right, ma; my bad," he apologized.

Relieved that Grief was done with the conversation, Kia got up off the bed and stripped down ass naked. She grabbed her soft, pink, cotton robe off the back of the closet and put it on.

"So that mean we can make it official again?"

Kia looked back at him. "Duh," she said and then walked into the master bedroom bathroom.

Grief was pleased with her response. He watched her shut the bathroom door, and then he heard the shower cut on. Once he was content that she was in the shower so he could dip out of the room right quick, that's exactly what he did. He made his way downstairs to the basement.

What Kia didn't know was that before Grief got locked up, he stashed away $100,000 and two bricks of raw inside a safe that was in her basement, but to his complete surprise—it was gone.

"What the fuck!" he spat.

Grief thought he was tripping, but the more he looked around, he realized he wasn't. Where his safe had stood, he noticed sneakers and shoes and male clothing . . . that didn't belong to him.

"I know this bitch didn't!" he said through clenched teeth.

Grief could feel his body temp go up. He wiped his hands down his face in an aggravated and stressed manner.

"Fuck, yo! I *knew* this shit was too good to be fuckin' true!"

He turned around and stormed up the stairs two at a time before reaching the top.

"*Kia! Kia!*" he yelled as he ran through the house. "I'ma fuckin' kill you!"

3

Thirty-three-year-old Travis "Li'l Grief" Lewis Jr. was an OG (Original Gangsta). He was the son of the late Travis "Big Grief" Lewis Sr., the OG of the OGs and one of the big homies of the SMM, *Sex, Money, Murder* blood gang which made Li'l Grief automatically affiliated. Born and raised in the nitty-gritty part of South Jersey, Li'l Grief grew to be a straight savage. Standing at six foot two and weighing two hundred and three pounds, he was known for knocking niggas the fuck out. He was the type to tie you the fuck up, cut your tongue out of your mouth, and send it to your mother with a note attached to it.

Not only was he a straight savage, but he was one of the most notorious drug dealers pushing bricks of hardcore raw throughout New Jersey. He and his two right-hand men, Loko and Butta, along with a bunch of young boys, was pushing twenty-five a week and bringing in $750,000 a week. Even when he was locked up, he was still bringing in major dough, and word was, niggas was trying to take his spot, but he held too much weight for them even to compete. Now that he was home, he was ready to make the streets pop again, but the situation he'd just run into put him at a halt.

"Kia! Kia!" Grief burst into the bathroom and snatched the shower curtain back. "Where the fuck is my shit at?"

Kia jumped when he snatched the shower curtain back, and she damn near slipped in the tub.

"What the fuck is wrong wit'chu, and what the fuck are you talkin' 'bout? What shit?" she was confused.

"My muhfuckin' money and work, *that's* what the fuck I'm talkin' 'bout! I left that shit in ya basement before I got knocked, and now the shit not there. Where the fuck is it?"

Kia could see how angry Grief was, and it scared her. She had no clue that Grief left money or work in their house before getting locked up, so this was all new to her. She reached to turn off the shower before turning her attention back to him.

"I don't know shit about no money and work." She was telling the truth.

In the blink of an eye, Grief reached in the shower and grabbed her by her hair and yanked her out of the shower.

"Get the fuck outta here! You think I'm stupid, bitch? Huh? You think I'm stupid?"

"Grief, what the fuck is wrong wit'chu? Let me go! Let my hair go!" she screamed.

"Bitch, shut up! You stealin' from me, and you had some nigga in my shit! I should fuckin' kill you!"

Kia was confused at first . . . until she thought about what Grief said to her when he first barged into the bathroom. *The basement,* she thought. She remembered that a day before Grief was released from prison, she'd taken all of her side nigga's clothes and put them in the basement, not thinking that Grief would go down there.

"Grief, baby, I swear I didn't steal from you. I didn't know anything about no safe, I swear," she pleaded.

Grief was over her lies by now, and every word that came out of her mouth was a lie to him. He pulled her out of the bathroom and dragged her through the bedroom, in the hallway, and down the stairs.

"Ow! Ouch! Grief, stop! Stop dragging meeeee!" she screamed while clawing at his hands. "My skin is comin' off! Please stop!"

From the rug burns and being dragged down two sets of wooden steps, Kia had splinters on various parts of her body. Once they finally made it to the basement, Grief slung her around like a rag doll before letting go of her hair.

"I don't wanna hear that shit. I want my fuckin' money and work, and I wanna know who the fuck you had in my house."

Kia realized there was no way she was getting out of this one, and the only way out was telling the truth about everything. She was forced to admit she had a side nigga while Grief was on lock, but that she didn't know anything about his safe.

"Baby, I swear that's the truth. I didn't know anything about no safe—on my moms I didn't." Kia was in tears as she stared at the clothes that Bandana left at her house, and her attempt to hide them.

Grief looked at her with anger and hate in his eyes that was reflected all over his face. He couldn't believe that Kia would be so grimy to allow another man to come lay where he laid his head at. The same home they'd built together, the same home they'd fucked and made love in numerous times. All he wanted to do was grab his burna and blow her brains smooth the fuck out, but before he did that, he had to get his shit back.

4

The young bul Kia was creeping with, his name is Bandana, was twenty-two years old, and he was an up-and-coming hustla in Bridgeton, New Jersey. He was also with the bullshit the same as Grief, just a younger and wilder version. Bandana was quickly solidifying his spot, and he was doing so the entire time Grief was locked up. He was basically the *new nigga* in town, and he was coming for everything he felt like he deserved.

Chilling on the block on the South Side, hustlin' and doing his thing, Bandana watched as one of his homies, Roll Call, pulled up in his silver 2017 Benz truck.

"Oooweee! That boy clean! Wassup, bruh?" Bandana greeted one of his homies.

"Shit, I can't call it. We creamin' out this muhfucka today, bul, I tell you," Roll Call dapped him up.

Bandana was making hellva noise in Jersey, and Grief had some major competition. He was pulling in $750,000 a week, and Bandana was pulling in $850,000 a week, trying to take Grief completely out.

"Hell, yea. The fuck you thought, nigga? I told you we was takin' this shit over, and that's what the fuck we doin'," he boasted.

Fiends were walking up and down the block, copping from each corner. Bandana and Roll Call stood back and watched like proud fathers on game day. Shit was running so smoothly for them, and pretty soon, Bandana was going to start pushing work in other cities. He wanted his shit to be global and would stop at nothing to make sure it got done.

"You ain't neva lied, bruh. You pulled this shit off in a matter of months, and I still don't know how you did that shit," Roll Call shook his head with a smile.

Bandana had a cocky smile on his face as he walked in the middle of the street and opened his arms wide.

"The city is mines!" He looked back at Roll Call who had just made a quick sell. "Come on, bruh, we got money to pick up."

"Shit, I was about to tell ya Nino Brown ass the same thing," he laughed.

"Yurrrppp!" Bandana called out to a young boy that was standing on one of the corners.

"What up, bruh?" the young boy yelled back.

"Hold the block down, youngin'," Bandana ordered before going toward Roll Call's truck and hopping in the passenger side.

Roll Call stuffed some money in his pocket and headed over to his ride where he hopped in the driver's side and pulled off.

****

"You gon' tell me where that nigga stay so I can get my shit back and then push his shit back?" he said.

Kia was throwing on some clothes as she listened to Grief snap as he paced the room back and forth.

"I don't know where he be at," she lied.

Kia knew exactly where Bandana hustled and chilled at, but she also knew how crazy he was, and she was afraid that if she let Grief know his location, that one of them would end up killing the other, and that was something she couldn't let happen.

"You just gon' keep lyin', huh?" Grief nodded his head up and down.

He lifted the pillow on his side of the bed and removed the nine millimeter he had hidden underneath. He spun around, cocked it back, and pointed it directly at Kia, whose mouth was wide open.

"Bitch! Stop fuckin' playin' wit' me! I want my muhfuckin' money, and you gon' help me get it. You think I'm stupid? You let a nigga come up in my shit, bring clothes and lay the fuck up, but you don't know where he be? Get the fuck outta here, you dirty-ass bitch. I know you know where he at, and if you don't, you better call that muhfucka and find out, or I'ma push ya shit back right the fuck here!"

Tears formed in Kia's eyes. She was scared-ass shit, and she knew the ball was in Grief's court and that she had to play by his rules—or she was as good as dead.

"Fine," she said just above a whisper.

"What the fuck did you say, bitch?" Grief asked with flared nostrils.

"I said fine, Grief. I'll tell you where he is. He's at—"

Grief shook his head *no*. If Kia thought she was just going to drop a location and that would get him off her ass, she had another think coming.

"Nah, ya whore ass gon' take me to him."

5

Grief pulled up on the South Side in his black Audi with Kia in the passenger side. He had his window rolled down, not giving a fuck who saw his face because the moment he saw his target, he was going to start spraying.

"Point that nigga out," he told Kia.

Kia squinted her eyes to see if she saw Bandana, but she didn't. She figured he was probably on another one of the many blocks he owned. There was a bunch of young niggas standing around, but none of them were him, just his crew.

"I don't see him out here," she spoke up.

"You gon' keep lyin'?" Grief gritted his teeth.

He had his nine millimeter gripped in his right hand as it rested on his lap.

"Grief, he's not out here. I'm tellin' you the truth."

Grief didn't know whether to believe her, so he continued to scope the area hoping to see a flashy nigga walking around. Everyone looked like regular nickel-and-dime hustlas, and not one person on the block looked like they were moving any major weight.

Beep. Beep.

Grief beeped his horn to get the attention of one of the young buls that held down the block. A slim-figured dude with a big-ass head and chubby cheeks jogged over to him across the street.

"Wassup, bruh? What you need?" Pudge asked, thinking he was a customer.

"You know a nigga named Bandana?"

Pudge took a step back from the car. He got the vibe that Grief could've possibly been an undercover posed as a street dude. That was something that happened often, and he wasn't about to get caught up, nor was he about to get his homie bagged.

"Nah, I don't know a Bandana. You might wanna take that twenty-one-questions shit somewhere else, bruh. This ain't what you want." Pudge tapped his waistband, letting Grief know he was strapped.

Pudge never saw the gun that was resting in Grief's hand because he would've never come off as cocky as he did had he. Thinking he was helping his homeboy, he had really just put his foot in his own mouth. His answer alone was way too suspect for Grief, which let him know that he knew Bandana, but he wasn't telling him shit about him.

"Cool, well, when you see him, give 'em this for me." Grief pointed his gun in Pudge's direction, causing him to jet away from the car.

Boc! Boc! Boc!

"That bitch nigga gon' feel my muthafuckin' raft!"

Boc! Boc! Boc! Boc! Boc! Boc!

"*Aaaaaaaah!*" screamed the innocent bystanders.

Kia placed her hands over her head and ducked down. Not one dude that was on the block attempted to shoot back at Grief, but they all dove for cover when he let one of his bitches go off.

Scurrrrrrr!

The sounds of Grief's screeching tires peeling off and kicking dust behind him echoed throughout the street. To send Bandana a message, Grief shot up the block. Two of many bullets he let off splattered one of the youngin's melon into pieces of bloody flesh killing him instantly. Just like that, Grief had erased one of the young buls . . . who just so happened to be Bandana's little brother.

6

After what had just taken place, Kia was shaking the entire drive home. It wasn't the first time Grief had shot someone in front of her, but it was the first time that she ever feared for her life in the process of him doing it. The scenarios were much different from then to now. She was praying and hoping that he would just forgive her for what she looked at as an "honest mistake," but the heat coming from his body told her otherwise. She had been crying all day, and she was hoping that Grief would leave to cool off, but that was a *no-no*. He made sure to scold her during the drive home calling her every bitch and ho in the book. His words cut her deeply because he'd never before spoken to her in such a manner. Granted, he got mad, and they argued, but the words that were coming out of his mouth were downright disrespectful and cold now.

I really fucked up this time, she thought.

When they got in the house, Grief headed straight upstairs to the bedroom. Kia followed slowly behind him . . . until she heard a commotion coming from upstairs which caused her to put some pep into her step.

"Grief! What the fuck are you doing?" she screamed at him when she walked in on his tearing up the bedroom.

"Shut the fuck up! I bought this shit, and I'ma do what the fuck I wanna do to it!"

Bang! Bang! Bang!

Grief punched holes in the bedroom walls and swiped stuff off the dresser.

"Bitch, you gon' have another nigga in my shit!"

Bang!

"In the muhfuckin' house I bought!"

Bang!

"I pay the muhfuckin' bills in this bitch!"

Bang!

"I was payin' the muhfuckin' bills in here when I was locked up, and you repay me wit' betrayal?"

Bang!

Grief continued to punch numerous holes in the bedroom walls and even went as far as punching the flat-screen television they had mounted on the wall which he snatched right down and stomped on it afterward.

"Stop!" she screamed.

Whap!

Grief backhanded Kia with his nine millimeter, causing her to fly against the wall and slide down it, whimpering while holding her mouth as blood poured from it.

"I should kill you in here, bitch. You miss ya dumb-ass mom so bad, well, I'm about to send you to that dead bitch."

Tears were pouring from Kia's eyes. The way he talked about her mother broke her heart. The love he'd once had for her was gone in a matter of hours, and for the first time ever, she wished that she would have just accepted Grief's flaws and all because he treated her like a queen, fucked her good, and did right by her. The only thing she hated was his crazy ways and the fact that he was in and out of jail.

Her decision to test the waters backfired tremendously. She wanted to call Bandana and tell him to give back everything he took, but she knew damn well he would probably laugh in her face.

Ring. Ring. Ring.

Kia was still holding her face when her cell phone rang. She was scared to pick it up, but after seeing that it was her cousin ShaQuanna, she attempted to answer it, but Grief stopped her.

"Who the fuck is that?" he asked.

"It's ShaQuanna," she quickly answered with a mouthful of blood.

"Answer that shit and put it on speaker," he demanded.

Kia did as she was told and answered her phone and put it on speaker like Grief told her to. She was going to do any and everything she could to keep him from pulling that trigger.

"Hello?"

"Girrrrl, you ain't hear about that shooting that just happened on the South Side?" ShaQuanna blurted into the phone.

Kia looked at Grief, and he gave her a look like *bitch, you better say the right thing*. Her body was already filled with fear, so she read his expression well and went along with it.

"No, what happened, and who got shot?" She was acting very interested because she genuinely wanted to know who it was that got shot and if anybody heard anything.

"From what I heard was that somebody just pulled up and sprayed the block. Ain't no names right now, but the cops is out deep as shit because somebody got killed," she explained.

Kia looked at Grief who shook his head in aggravation. Not because someone was killed, but because the boys were in the streets deep, and he'd just got out of prison and wasn't trying to go back no time soon. Everything that had gone on was all Kia's fault, and he was going to make sure he never forgave her for the trouble she caused.

"That's crazy," Kia responded as she watched Grief grab a duffle bag from the closet and start throwing his belongings in it.

"Fo' real. But I just wanted to make sure you was good and to let you know to stay yo' ass in the house. The streets is too hot right now, and clearly, people don't give a fuck that it's a new damn year because they still acting the same old way." ShaQuanna was disgusted on the other end of the phone.

She had no clue that Grief was behind the shoot-out and murder that had just taken place moments earlier, and even if she did know, it wouldn't have been surprising for her because that's just who

Grief was. He would come, fuck shit up, and then leave, and there wasn't much that anyone could do about it.

"I'm not goin' anywhere, but I do need to call you back because I got another call comin' in," she lied so that she could get off the phone to see why Grief was packing.

"A'ight, boo. Just hit me up later. I love you."

"Love you more, boo."

Click.

Kia ended the call with her eyes still on Grief. "Where you goin'?"

He glanced over at her and then continued what he was doing. He ain't have shit to say to her, and he wouldn't dare disclose another thing about himself to her grimy ass, so his whereabouts was about to be the least of her worries.

"Grief, did you hear me? Will you please just talk to me? We can get through this. You don't have to leave," she pleaded as she got off the floor.

"Don't come near me. On God, if you come near me, I'm not holdin' back, and I'ma put a muhfuckin' bullet in ya head right here in this room and leave yo' ass here to rot," he promised.

Kia stopped in her tracks because Grief made good on his promises, but that didn't stop her from prying for more information.

"Can you tell me where you're goin' so I can at least know that you gon' be safe?"

This bitch is dumber than I thought, he thought to himself.

"I'm not tellin' you shit, ya hear? I'm safer away from you anyway. You must've hit that wall pretty fuckin' hard if you think I'm tellin' ya snake ass anything." Grief threw the duffle bag over his shoulder and pushed past her.

"Please don't leave me," Kia cried.

Grief never replied, nor did he turn around. He kept on down the hall and down the stairs. Her hopes of him coming back up to talk and fix things were shattered when she heard the door slam shut.

There had been so many times that she wanted to be done with Grief, and now that she realized that they were finally done, she wished they hadn't been.

****

Vrrrrm! Vrrrrm! Vrrrrm!

Bandana and Roll Call were in Millville when his phone kept vibrating on his hip. He reached in his pocket and looked at it to see who the caller was. The name Pudge, who was one of his corner boys, flashed across the screen. The only times they were to ring his phone was to let him know how things were moving and if there was a fuckup.

"Yo, what up?" he answered.

"Somebody just came through and sprayed the block up," Pudge blurted through the phone.

Bandana, who was sitting in the passenger seat of Roll Call's ride as he waited for Roll Call to make a drop, sat up in the seat. He was caught off guard and wondered who in their right mind would want to go to war with him.

"The fuck you talkin' 'bout?" he questioned.

"Man, like I said, somebody came and sprayed the block up, and shit not lookin' too good out here," he explained.

An apprehensive feeling eased its way in Bandana's stomach, and he didn't like the sound of Pudge's voice. If it was the cops, he would've said so, so he knew that something much deeper had taken place while he was out handling business.

"Yo, stop playin' these mind games and talkin' in riddles and shit; tell me what the fuck is goin' on."

Pudge shook his head before breaking the news to Bandana. "Bruh, Kye got hit," he revealed.

His throat got dry, and a knot formed in Bandana's stomach when Pudge mentioned his brother. He didn't want to ask any further questions, but he knew he had to because the weariness in Pudge's voice let him know that there was more that needed to be said.

"Is he okay?"

Pudge was quiet. He looked down the block at the white, red-stained sheet that covered Kye's body and wiped the tears from his eyes before they had a chance to fall.

"Nah, he ain't okay. He gone, B. Kye gone, bruh. His fuckin' brains is all over the sidewalk."

Bandana dropped the phone. It hit the floor and landed by his feet. *Kye? Dead? Nah, this can't be. Not my fuckin' brother, man. Not my baby brother,* he said to himself. All he could think about was his last word to him . . . *Hold the block down.*

7

Grief was on his way to Chesterbrook, Pa. He figured he needed to lie low, and that would be the last place to look for a black man. It was a nice, quiet area, and that was something he needed . . . peace and quiet to figure out his next move being that Kia had fucked his shit up.

He leaned over and grabbed his cell phone that was laying in the passenger seat and quickly scrolled through it until he came across the contact he was looking for. Grief pressed down on the green call button and placed the phone to his ear.

Ring. Ring. Ring.

"What's poppin', blood?" Loko said when he answered his phone.

"That five, you already?" Grief replied.

"That's what I like to hear. Wassup, tho', blood? Welcome home, nigga," Loko said.

Grief wished it was a welcome home, but here his ass was on the run.

"Shit, fuck all that. A nigga outta Dodge right now."

Loko was getting some mean-ass neck from one of the young girls from around the way. He mushed her on the side of her face and slung his legs over the side of the bed.

"The fuck happened?" He was all ears.

"Dumb-ass bitch was fuckin' some nigga in the crib, and he took all my shit, bruh. I mean, *everything*."

Grief knew not to say too much over the phone, and he said just enough knowing Loko would understand him.

"Say whaaa?" Loko was in disbelief.

"I said it already. That bitch grimy as hell. I went straight goofy earlier, and now I gotta lie low. I can't believe that bitch stole from me, yo."

Loko was just as shocked as he was. Never in a million years did either one of them think that Kia would be so low-down and do such thing, but as they got older and continued to play in the streets, they realized they couldn't put shit past anyone.

"This shit crazy, bruh. The whole hunnid grand? Damn, they shiesty wit' it," Loko stated.

It wasn't that Grief was broke because he was far from it, but the money she allowed to be stolen from him was money he was going to use to get back straight instead of going right back to the streets once he was released from prison. He knew the cops were going to be on his ass, and he didn't want to bring any heat his way but leave it to Kia to spoil a wet, fucking dream.

"Straight up shiesty wit' it," he agreed.

"Tell me what you need me to do. You want me to go over there and rape that bitch wit' a hot knife fresh off the stove top?—

Just let me know. I'll burn that whole muhfuckin' house down wit' her ass in it," Loko stated and was as serious as a heart attack.

"I want my shit back first. Give me a few days, and we gon' link, but until then, keep ya eyes and ears open and get back to me if ya hear anything."

"Shit, you already know I gotchu."

Click.

Loko ended the call and stood up. He looked back at the young girl that was lying on her side in his bed ass naked, just waiting to get her back blown out by some hood nigga dick.

"Where you going?" she asked.

Loko leaned down and picked up her clothes before throwing them at her. He positioned his hand like people did when they wanted someone to call them, only he was motioning to his door.

"You gotta get the fuck out. A nigga got shit to do."

The astonished young girl sat up, pouting and looking at him. She couldn't believe he was just going to throw her out like that when she had just got finished sucking his dick just minutes ago.

"Loko, you fo'real?" she asked.

He didn't like to repeat himself and not once did he stutter when he told her she had to get the fuck out. From the looks of it, he didn't make himself clear, so he grabbed her clothes, snatched her young ass up off his bed, and damn near dragged her out of his bedroom and to the front door.

"Are you fucking serious, Loko! Get the fuck off me!" she screamed as she scratched and hit him.

Loko wasn't trying to fight, but she damn sure was going to get up out of his crib. When he had shit to do, pussy was the last thing he was worried about. Indeed, she did have a phat ass, and her pussy was good because he fucked her before, but all that shit had to wait.

"Get the fuck outta here, yo, and stop trippin'. I'ma call ya li'l stupid ass when I get the chance." He pushed her out the door and threw her clothes at her.

"Fuck you, Loko, and lose my fucking number! You think you gonna put ya fucking hands on me and say you're gonna call me? Fuck outta here!"

Loko wasn't trying to hear shit she was saying. He waved her off and slammed his door in her face. He ain't have time to fuss and fight with a bitch, and a random one, at that. There was business that needed to be handled.

8

Later that Tuesday night, after leaving the morgue to identify his little brother, Bandana needed to ease his mind and release some stress, so he went to his brand-new house that he'd just coped not too long ago in Hopewell, New Jersey, which he shared with his baby mama, ShaQuanna.

The moment Bandana stuck the key in the door and unlocked it, ShaQuanna ran over to him and embraced him in a hug. She had just found out that the dude who got killed was his brother, and she knew he was hurting something serious. Regardless of how hard core Bandana was, Kye was his heart, and that was the only person besides his daughter who he had a soft spot for.

"Baby, I'm so sorry."

Bandana allowed her to embrace him, but he didn't say anything in response to what she'd said to him. He was still trying to wrap his brain around the fact that his little brother, his *only* brother at that, was never coming back, and there was nothing he could do that was going to bring him back.

"Talk to me. Baby, please, say something." ShaQuanna had pulled away from him and placed her hands on the sides of his face and examined him like a concerned mother.

"I need some pussy," he finally spoke.

ShaQuanna looked at him with confusion written all over her face. She couldn't understand at a time like this how pussy could be on his mind when he'd just loss his baby brother. She searched his face for some sort of answer, hoping that he was playing, but she could see that he was dead serious.

"I got you," she assured him before pulling him toward the hallway.

She guided him to their bedroom and removed the oversized shirt of his that she'd been wearing. ShaQuanna was ass naked underneath, and that was just what Bandana wanted to see. She tried to be sexy and remove his clothes, but now wasn't the time for all that lovey-dovey shit. He was trying to fuck and knock her walls loose.

Bandana smacked her hands away and gave her a slight shove away from him, then kicked off his sneakers and removed his shirt, jeans, and boxers. ShaQuanna stood there in front of him waiting for him to make the next move. She could feel the tension and knew he had a lot of bottled up stress, and she didn't want it flipped on her.

"Get that ass on the bed," he ordered as he stroked his semihard dick.

She walked over to the bed and tried to lie on it, but he stopped her.

"Nah, turn that ass around."

ShaQuanna turned around and got in doggie-style position. When she bent over, Bandana could see the pink of her pussy peeking through her chocolate-covered lips, and that shit drove him wild. He walked over and positioned himself in back of her, not even fingering her or doing any foreplay to get her wet. Bandana spit on his hand and rubbed it on the tip of his dick and forcefully pushed his dick inside of her pussy, causing her to wince a little in pain.

He placed a hand on each ass cheek and gripped them tightly as he started to bang her out. *Smack! Smack! Smack!* ShaQuanna finally started to get wet down there the more he plunged his dick in and out of her. It wasn't the first time they fucked or had rough sex, but it was the first time she felt like he was going to rip her in the ass.

"Ssss, shit. Take it easy," she managed to get out while jerking every time he went in and out of her.

"Shut up," he grunted and then grabbed a handful of her hair.

He placed his left hand under her chin and held her head back while power driving her from behind.

Clap! Clap! Clap!

ShaQuanna was gritting her teeth together and curling her toes up tightly. Bandana was deep in her guts, hitting the bottom of her stomach while rearranging her organs. She closed her eyes in hopes of him busting soon because her shit was sore by now, and her stomach was cramping up.

Smack! Clap! Smack! Clap!

"Ban-dan-a," she stammered, attempting to get out of his grasp.

He let go of her hair and her face and forcefully pushed her head down on the bed causing her back to make a mean arch.

"Mm, don't run," he told her.

After a few more hard pumps and a couple of ass smacks, he pushed her over, and she landed on her side. He hurried and climbed on the bed as he stroked his dick at a fast pace.

"Mm, fuc-k. Sh-it." He bust all over ShaQuanna's face.

He panted for a couple of seconds before wiping his dick on her face and then collapsing back on the bed. ShaQuanna lay there feeling completely violated. She knew he was going through something, but the sexual treatment he'd just given her was out of line. But she wouldn't dare say anything about it. Instead, she got up and walked wide-legged to the bathroom to clean herself up.

Bandana was still lying there lost in his thoughts when she came back from the bathroom and now snuggled up under him. The last thing he wanted was to be touched, but he didn't want to push her away knowing that all she wanted to do was be a shoulder for him.

Vrrrm! Vrrrm! Vrrrm!

"What up?" he answered in a dry tone.

After fucking ShaQuanna to settle his nerves, Bandana received a phone call from one of his homies who was out there when his little brother was killed. The streets were claiming the nigga in the black Audi who shot up the block was some older nigga named

Grief, and that the chick who was sitting in the car when he did it was Kia. That immediately caused Bandana to push ShaQuanna to the side and sit up on the bed. Once he heard Kia's name, nothing but death crossed his mind.

****

Meanwhile, Grief was already lying low in Chesterbrook, Pa, uncertain whether the cops were looking for him. Either way, he wasn't trying to head back to Jersey until it was definite that he was going to get his shit back; other than that, he was in no rush, especially since he had his right-hand Loko out lurking, doing any of his light work that needed to be done.

Zzzzz. Zzzzz.

Grief was laid up in a town house he rented through Airbnb. His phone was going off like crazy, and he assumed it was Loko with some information, but when he picked it up and saw the name Kia flash across the screen, he quickly declined the call and laid his phone back down.

She dumb as fuck, he thought.

Zzzzz.

Right after that thought left his mind, his phone went off once more, and then a text notification alerted him. He didn't even bother to pick it up because he already figured it was Kia, and he was right. He glanced at the text message which read:

Grief, please answer my call.

Once again, he ignored her. There wasn't anything Kia could do to fix things between them. It was over. They were done. The trust had been broken, and she had betrayed him one too many times in just a matter of months. Eight years down the drain for a piece of temporary dick.

9

It

didn't take long for the word to get back to Bandana, and he didn't hesitate to blame Kia for his brother's murder. If it wasn't for one of his young buls noticing her sitting in the car when Grief shot up the block, he probably would have never known who did it and charged it to the game as being at the wrong place at the wrong time.

"You sure it was that bitch? Don't play wit' me because this shit about to get real ugly out here," he warned.

"Nigga, I'm one thousand percent sure that Kia was in the car. I told you that bitch was grimy from jump," Pudge added.

Ignoring what Pudge said, Bandana was already thinking about his next move. It didn't take him long to come up with the plan to kick Kia's door in and knock the noodles outta her fucking head.

"So, a nigga named Grief and his bitch Kia sprayed the block up and killed my li'l brother? Strap the fuck up because it's on!"

ShaQuaana was lying in bed beside Bandana while he was talking on the phone, so by now, she was aware of what was going on. She wanted to say something to defend her girl, but she was afraid that Bandana could possibly blame her too.

"Bandana, don't go out there doing nothing crazy. You got a family that needs you," she tried to plead with him.

"ShaQuanna, I don't wanna hear that dumb-ass shit right now. This nigga just killed my brother, and I'm killin' everything breathin' around this muhfucka until I'm satisfied." His voice was filled with anger, hurt, and frustration.

"But what about ya family? Me and ya daughter? What about us? We need you, and all you gon' do is go out there and start killing any and everybody? I'm sorry that Kye got killed, but we can't lose you too," she started to cry.

ShaQuanna knew that Bandana was a maniac, but she also knew what Grief was capable of, and it was bound to be a bloodbath. Bandana, on the other hand, didn't give a fuck about what ShaQuanna was talking about, and she knew it because he waved her off while he finished getting dressed, grabbed his gun off the nightstand, and stormed out of the bedroom.

ShaQuanna knew she had to do something, so the second he left to link up with his crew so they could kick down Kia's door, she called Kia to give her a heads-up. Unaware of the fact that Kia and Bandana were creeping on the low behind her back, she still considered Kia not only a cousin but her friend—her best friend.

10

didn't take long for Bandana and his crew to link up the next morning. Pudge, Roll Call, and he snatched a car from Enus mechanic shop and pulled up to Kia's crib which was located on the quiet side between the North and South Side. No conversation took place as they all hopped out of the car, guns in hand, and not a ski mask in sight. They wanted Kia to know exactly who they were because theirs would be the last face she would ever see before Bandana blew her brains out.

Boom!

Roll Call kicked Kia's front door in, and Bandana ran in first with his gun drawn.

"Bitch, where the fuck you at?" he yelled.

They were each running in and out of the living room, dining room, and kitchen before checking all the closets.

"Y'all check upstairs," he ordered.

Bandana opened the door to the basement and crept down each step with patience and focus. It wasn't the first time he'd been down there, so he knew his way around. Finally, he reached the bottom of the stairs. He entered the laundry room that was located on the left side of the basement and looked around. The smell of clean clothes caught his attention, letting him know that Kia was indeed there not too long ago because the dryer had just shut off.

He checked around the corners in the basement and behind anything that one could think to hide in or behind, but still came up with nothing.

"Yo, Bandana! The bitch ain't here," Roll Call yelled down the stairs startling him.

"Don't be fuckin' yellin' like that, dog. I almost shot ya dumb ass," Bandana snapped on him.

"Damn, my bad. I'm just sayin' the bitch ain't here, so what now?" he asked.

Bandana didn't answer him right away. He made his way back upstairs and brushed past Roll Call who was standing in the doorway of the basement. He didn't want to stay in there and debate knowing that someone could've possibly called the cops by now, so he made his way out the front door with Roll Call and Pudge on his heels. They all hopped back in the car, and Roll Call pulled off while Bandana leaned back in the passenger seat deep in thought.

"What we gon' do now?" Pudge wanted to know.

Bandana sighed. "Keep our ears to the streets. That's all we can do right now," he told them.

Their plan to go to Kia's house and kick in the door was successful, but it backfired when they realized the house was empty. However, Bandana was skeptical about the condition the house was left in. Kia could suck a dick and die slow for all he cared, but one thing he knew was that she was clean. So, to see how trashed the house was, and Roll Call and Pudge said upstairs was tore up too, he wondered if the bul Grief got to her first before he did.

****

After receiving the heads-up from ShaQuanna, Kia quickly packed up some clothes and left the house just minutes before Bandana and his crew pulled up. She drove to her grandmother's house in the nearby town of Buena, New Jersey.

She felt like that would be the only safe place since the hood was hot, and she couldn't go to Ty'Kia's or TaQuanna's house because they would've let the cat out of the bag, and she didn't need that shit.

"You all right, baby?" her grandmother Sheryl asked.

"Yea, I'm fine. I just need to be alone right now," Kia said as she massaged her temples.

"All right, now, I'll be in the living room," she told Kia before leaving her to her lonesome in the kitchen.

Kia waved her off and tried calling Grief for the fiftieth time.

Ring. Ring. Ring.

But to no avail did she get any sort of answer. Kia had been calling Grief's phone nonstop to tell him what's going on, but he refused to answer her calls or her text. She knew he was still mad at her for creeping and for getting his safe stolen, but she felt like they needed to stick together if they wanted to come out on top in that situation.

They wanted different things for different reasons, but they were both meaningful. Grief wanted his safe, and Kia wanted her life. The only thing left to do was to call ShaQuanna and thank her for the heads-up, as well as to let her know that she was safe.

11

"Kia, I told ya ass not to get involved with Grief's ass. I mean, he's good peoples, but he's crazy as hell. Now look at you, all caught up and shit." ShaQuanna shook her head as she listened to Kia tell her, her version of the story.

Kia was well aware that Bandana was ShaQuanna's baby daddy, but she'd be a fool to reveal that she had been sleeping around with him, so her version of the story was simply that Grief got jealous of the *new nigga* in town and wanted problems.

"I know, I know, but it was like love at first sight, girl. I couldn't help myself back then. You know, if I knew what I know now back then, I would have never given Grief a chance. I've been tryin' my hardest to get him to leave me alone. Now, he got me caught up in some more mess. I don't know what I'm goin' to do," she cried.

ShaQuanna was hurting for her cousin. She did all she could to keep Kia under her wing and guide her in the right direction away from the bad boys, but there was only so much she could do.

"Baby girl, I'll see if I can talk to Grief, but in the meantime, Kia, please continue to lie low. I don't know what I'd do if something were to happen to you," she said honestly.

She continued to be Kia's comfort for the rest of the conversation.

Meanwhile, Bandana had pulled up to the crib. It had been a long-ass forty-eight hours for him, and he needed to smoke a blunt and take a shot and unwind a little before heading back out to handle business. He walked in the crib and went straight to the kitchen and grabbed the leftover bottle of Henny that was sitting there. He popped it open and took a long swig, allowing the liquor to burn his throat.

"Kia, you overwhelming ya'self, girl, and that's not good."

Bandana pulled the bottle away from his mouth and even stopped breathing for a brief second, so the house was completely silent. *I know she ain't just say Kia,* he thought.

To be sure, he crept down the hall to the bedroom, and sure enough, he caught ShaQuanna talking on the phone to Kia.

"Give me that fuckin' phone!" Bandana caught ShaQuanna off guard as he reached for the phone and snatched it out of her hand. "Bitch, I'ma fuckin' kill you!"

After grabbing the phone and threatening Kia, he hung up immediately. ShaQuanna had moved to the other side of the bed to get away from Bandana, but he was still on her ass.

"Where the fuck is she?" he demanded.

"Bandana, baby, relax. I can't tell you that," she pleaded with her hands in the air in a defense manner. "I know the situation is fucked up, but she's my cousin, and I can't let you hurt her."

When ShaQuaana refused to tell him where Kia was, he decided to let everything out. He'd known all along that ShaQuanna and Kia was cousins, but when it came to getting his dick wet, he didn't give a fuck who shared the same blood or who was best friends.

"You protectin' a bitch that I've been fuckin' for the last year," he blurted.

ShaQuanna's face contorted into a surprised look when Bandana revealed that he'd been fucking Kia behind her back and that his come-up in the game was a result of the safe he stole from Kia's basement.

"Wh-what?" ShaQuanna was in disbelief. She grabbed her chest as if a sharp pain had come about, and she held onto the wall for balance.

"Yea, that shit hurt, don't it? I hope that shit sting so bad the way my heart sting because my brother is dead."

ShaQuanna managed to muster up a few words. "How could you? How could y'all do that to me?"

"How could I do that to you? Bitch, how the fuck could you protect a bitch that got my fuckin' brother killed? My baby brother! Our daughter's uncle and a nigga you done cooked for and broke bread wit'—the fuck!"

ShaQuanna was heartbroken, and she felt like Bandana and Kia had ripped her heart straight out of her chest. This was beyond betrayal, and the fact that Bandana said everything with no remorse in his voice cut her deeply. She knew that a nigga was going to be a nigga, but Kia was her blood, and she knew better. It was one thing to break the girl code by fucking with an ex, but it was a whole other thing to fuck with a dude that one of them was currently fucking with.

"Fuck all that cryin' shit; we'll deal wit' that another time. You need to let me know where this bitch is because she's been fuckin' over everybody—including you. Don't protect a bitch that wouldn't piss on you if you was on fire." Bandana was pulling all kinds of tricks out his bag to make sure he got to Kia.

ShaQuanna dropped to the floor and was balled up crying hard. Even though she was hurt, a part of her still didn't want to reveal where Kia was, but only God knew how much other grimy shit Kia did behind her back, and she couldn't allow her to get away scot-free anymore. Blood made them related, but loyalty made them family, and Kia had been disloyal . . . which no longer made them family.

After sniffling and wiping the snot from her nose like a child with the back of her hand, she looked up at Bandana with puffy red eyes.

"She's at our grandmother's house in Buena. The address is . . ."

12

"Please, no! Don't hurt her! She ain't got shit to do wit' any of this," Kia cried as she watched her grandmother be pulled to the living room floor and kicked in the head.

"Bitch, fuck you and this old bitch! Knock her shit off, Roll Call," Bandana ordered.

Kia's mouth dropped open as she watched Roll Call aim his Beretta .9 mm at her grandmother's forehead.

Boc! Boc! Boc! Boc!

Boc! Boc! Boc! Boc!

The first bullet was lodged in her eye, and Sheryl's face contorted and twitched. Kia wanted to scream, but nothing came out as Roll Call emptied his 16-round clip in her grandmother. The aftermath was a pool of blood and brain matter, along with a pile of shit that Sheryl released when the first bullet entered her body.

"You next, bitch; you next," Bandana mean-mugged her.

****

Loko had made his way to Chesterbrook, Pa, to chop it up with Grief. It wasn't surprising to see that Grief was laid up in some nice shit because that's just how they were. Regardless of any Ls they took, they still lived a comfortable life.

"What up, bruh-bruh?" he dapped him up when Grief let him in.

"Besides the bullshit that happened you see wassup."

"Shit, I heard that," Loko said before taking a seat in one of the leather love seats.

Grief was already smoking a blunt filled with Loud when he opened the door for Loko, so he took a few more pulls and then passed it to him.

"What's the word?" he asked.

Loko took two pulls of the blunt and coughed loud and hard. "Kia's name is all up in the streets." He took another pull on the blunt. "The boys is out lurkin', but it ain't as deep as everybody makin' it out to be. You know they lookin' at it as a job well done because it's another nigga dead."

"What they say about Kia?" he wanted to know.

"Word is, Kia was the bitch in the car when the block got sprayed. So, basically, they callin' her a setup bitch," he explained.

Grief shook his head. If Kia wasn't in the car with him, she would've remained innocent, and he would've been the only target. He wasn't bothered one bit by how the streets were on Kia's head because it made no sense how she played the cards she was dealt in such a grimy manner.

"It is what it is, so fuck that bitch," he said.

Loko shrugged his shoulders.

"Honestly, the shit is surprising to me how shit went down. I would've never thought that Kia would do some snake shit like this because y'all been rockin' for a minute."

"That's what I'm sayin'. At least, be honest wit' a nigga and say you don't wanna be wit' me anymore. Why the fuck would you bring another nigga where I lay my head at and then allow him to steal my shit? Don't make no fuckin' sense, bruh." Grief shook his head in disgust.

Loko chuckled as he shook his head.

"The fuck is so funny?" Grief grilled him.

"I admit shorty was foul as fuck, but come on now, bruh; you wasn't takin' no for an answer. How many times y'all was on and off? Remember Kevin? You ran down on every nigga she was tryin'a have somethin' wit'," Loko told him.

"Man, fuck all the—"

Ring. Ring. Ring.

Before he could respond fully his phone rang. Grief looked down at his phone and saw he had an incoming call from ShaQuanna. He didn't think anything of it because they had always been good peoples. So, he figured she'd heard about what was going on and decided to check up on him.

"Wassup, ShaQuanna?" he answered.

Bingo! Bandana's eyes lit up like Christmas lights. He knew damn well that Grief wasn't going to answer the phone for Kia, and he knew that Grief being a street dude wouldn't answer a number he didn't know, so it was pointless to use either phone. After hearing ShaQuanna mention Grief's name, she gave him the rundown on how she knew him, and once she gave him the address to their grandmother's house, he snatched her phone up knowing that he would need it.

"Grrriieeeffff!" Kia screamed.

The moment ShaQuanna dropped that address, Bandana, Roll Call, and Pudge ran down in her grandmother's shit and held Kia hostage to try to force Grief to come out of hiding.

What the fuck! he thought.

Loko was alert and all ears when Grief put the phone on speaker. He really didn't need to because Kia screamed so loudly that anyone standing near Grief could have heard it. The scream was so loud that even Grief had to pull the phone away from his ear.

"Who the fuck is this?" he asked.

He heard Kia's screams, and he knew that was ShaQuanna's phone, but he had no idea who had it at the moment.

"You know who the fuck this is, nigga. Where the fuck you at, pussy?" Bandana's voice boomed through the speaker of the phone.

These bitches tryin'a set me up, Grief thought.

He was referring to both Kia and ShaQuanna.

"Nah, I don't know who the fuck this is. Stop bein' a bitch and say ya muhfuckin' name!"

"Bandana, nigga!"

Hearing the man on the other end of the phone reveal his name sent flames through Grief's body. He'd been trying to get his hands on Bandana for the last forty-eight hours, and here he was, with the one person he'd least suspect being that he almost knocked her block off for dealing with him in the first place.

"Yous'a dirty bitch. On God, I'ma kill you the next time I see you," Grief said with his nostrils flaring.

Kia cried hard. She could only imagine what Grief was thinking. She wanted to tell him that it wasn't that type of party, but she never had the chance.

"Stop cryin' like a li'l bitch and tell me where the fuck you at! Matter of fact, come over here to where I'm at because either way, I'm splatterin' ya shit when I see you," Bandana warned.

Grief didn't like the tone that Bandana was taking with him, nor did he like the threats he was giving. Bandana was a small fry to Grief, and wherever he went, he got respected because he earned it and people knew what he was capable of.

"Get that nigga address," Loko mouthed to Grief.

Grief placed his hand up as if to say *wait a minute*.

"You got a lot of hostility for somebody who took *my* shit, you bum-ass nigga."

"Nigga, suck my dick pussy! Yea, I took ya shit, bitch nigga, now, wassup?" Bandana bragged.

Grief was heated as he sat on the edge of the couch. He gripped his phone so tightly that he could hear it crack. He knew that Bandana had taken his money and his work but just hearing him confess it sent him through the roof.

"I promise you it's war, my nigga."

"What you tryin'a do, nigga, because it's game time when I see ya dumb ass? You killed my li'l bro, so it's off wit' ya fuckin' head," Bandana kept going.

Grief had no idea that the young bul he killed was Bandana's little brother, but now that he was aware, he played on that shit.

"Yea, I killed ya li'l brother, and what the fuck you gon' do about it? I'ma kill you too, nigga!"

Bandana was waving his gun in the air as he spoke to Grief. Everyone in the room knew that he couldn't wait until he got his hands on Grief so he could do damage, but until then, his anger was being released through a phone call.

"Nigga, you ain't killin' shit, you washed-up-ass nigga. *You* the one that's gon' die as soon as you pull up to get this raggedy bitch." Bandana paused and pointed his gun at Kia's dome. "Yea, we got ya bitch, nigga, and she gon' be dead if you don't come the fuck outta hiding, pussy," he warned.

Aware that Kia and Grief had been dealing for the last eight years, he figured he'd use her as bait. He had got all that he needed out of her and no longer gave a fuck about her, especially after finding out that she was in cahoots with the nigga that killed his flesh and blood.

Grief burst out laughing.

"Man, fuck that bitch. All I want is my muhfuckin' bread and work. Y'all can do what y'all want to her disloyal ass. I was gon' kill her anyway once I killed you, dummy."

Bandana looked at Kia who had a swollen face and swollen eyes. She was looking at him wanting him to feel sorry for her, but he didn't; there wasn't an ounce of care in his heart for her. Her grimy ways got her in the position she was in at that moment.

"Hold on," Bandana put the phone on speaker. "You said *what* now?"

"I said fuck that disloyal bitch. Y'all can do what y'all want wit' her; just make sure y'all give me back my shit," Grief repeated.

Kia gasped for air, as if the wind had been knocked out of her. Bandana was bat-shit crazy, and now that Grief denied her help, she knew she was about to die.

"You hear this shit, bitch? This nigga don't give a fuck about you! Never did and never will! But I don't blame him," Bandana chuckled. "What kind of bitch allow another nigga to come and fuck her in the same bed her nigga sleep in? The whole time this nigga was locked up, I was fuckin' you. I knew you was a snake-ass bitch, but I ain't never think you would go as far as to playin' a role in my brother's death."

More tears rolled down Kia's face.

"I ain't have shit to do wit' that," she cried.

"Yous'a lyin'-ass bitch. How the fuck this nigga know which block I be on if you ain't have shit to do wit' it, huh?" Bandana asked her a question, but he really didn't want an answer because he already knew it. "Exactly. Because you ran ya fuckin' mouth, but that's cool because ya cousin ran her mouth too. ShaQuanna's loyalty lies wit' *me,* bitch. That's *my* girl and the mother of *my* child, so you just as scandalous as they come. Fuckin' on ya nigga and fuckin' ya cousin's nigga."

Grief was still on the phone listening to the words that were coming out of Bandana's mouth. If there was even a drop of love he had for her left in him that was quickly removed by what Bandana revealed. The entire time, Kia was fucking everybody over, and they were just a part of the game she was playing. With nothing more to say, Grief ended the call. For right now, he was going to charge the loss he took to the game, but he made a mental note to finish what he started if he ever crossed paths with Bandana.

"Look at that. Ya li'l boyfriend hung up. I guess the truth hurt," Bandana laughed.

Although nothing was funny, he was laughing to cover up the pain he was feeling. Everything inside of him wanted to find Grief and torture his ass, but the reality was that nigga wasn't coming to him unless he was giving him everything he stole from him—and that was never happening.

Click! Clack!

The sound of Bandana's .22 being cocked back caused Kia to piss on herself. She felt the cold steel touch her temple and just when she thought he was going to put her out of her misery quickly by blowing her brains out, she was caught by surprise when he pulled the gun away.

Kia sighed with relief.

Pow!

Bandana let off one round hitting Kia directly in her chest. She gasped for air as she clawed at her chest trying to rip her T-shirt off to get to the burning sensation that filled her body. The room was getting blurry; everything seemed to be getting dark.

"*Grrrrurghhh,*" she gurgled up blood.

Kia spent eight years of her life being the woman that Grief needed. She did bids with him, put money on his books and commissary, and even sucked and fucked him on conjugal visits along with sending some sexy flicks when she could. Kia made sure his homeboys were well fed and still pushing that raw like Grief wanted, and even did drop-offs for him. She'd witnessed Grief commit several murders and attempted murders, and she grew tired of it all. However, no matter how much she dibbled and dabbled with other men, for some strange reason, she couldn't leave Grief alone. Whenever he wanted her back, she went back and gave him chance after chance.

I guess this is what I get from being in love with the state's property . . .

Those were the last words that cross Kia's mind before she took her last breath.

13

The next morning, Bandana was sound asleep when he heard the sound of a gun being cocked.

Click! Clack!

"What the fuck?" Bandana jumped out of bed, wiping the sleep from his eyes. "ShaQuanna, what the fuck is you doin'?" He stared at his baby mama with a confused expression. She was standing in the doorway with a tearstained face. Her two hands were clutched around the gun she stole from Bandana's closet, and the hate in her pain-filled eyes was shooting daggers at his.

"Nigga, you thought shit was sweet, but it wasn't," ShaQuanna snarled at him. She aimed the barrel at his torso and sucked in a deep breath.

"ShaQuanna, wait! Don't!"

Boca!

"Agggghhhh, shit!" Bandana groaned as he slouched back into the dresser beside the bed and then crumbed down to the floor. The pain in his stomach was nothing compared to the sting of betrayal he felt in his heart. ShaQuanna was his queen, his love, the mother of his child, and his life motivation. But now, she was the one taking his life away from him.

Boca!

Another bullet bit into Bandana's shoulder, and he rolled around in pain.

"ShaQuanna, yo, what the fuck?" He gasped for air and cried out with a trembling voice. "After everything we been through, you're gonna fucking kill me? Bitch, I fuckin' love you!"

"Nigga, you don't love me!" ShaQuanna screamed back. "If you did, you wouldn't have been fucking my cousin!"

"And that's . . . And that's enough for you to kill me?" Bandana questioned with his mouth leaking blood.

"Whoever said I was gonna kill you?" ShaQuanna smirked. "Nigga, I'm not gonna kill you. *He* is."

Bandana looked into the face of the man who stepped into the room behind her and couldn't believe his eyes. ShaQuanna kissed the man on his lips, then stepped aside when he tapped her on the ass.

"Yeah, nigga." Grief smiled at Bandana with his .45 aimed at Bandana's wig. "Remember me?"

Boca!

-The End-

WAHIDA CLARK PRESENTS

The Lick

A DOLLA & DYME SHORT BY

SA'ID SALAAM

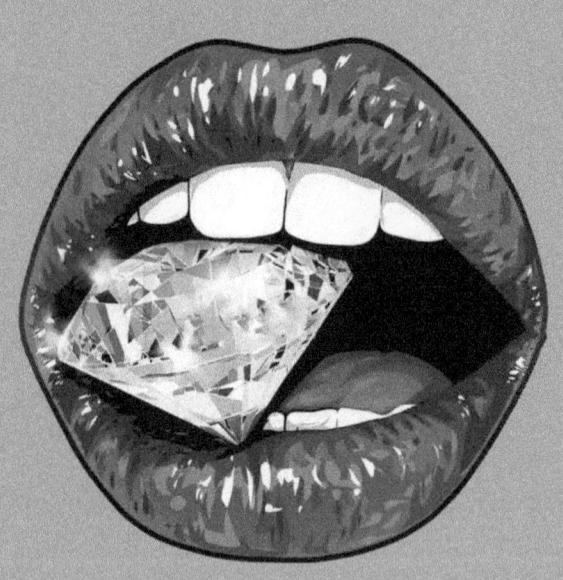

THE LICK

(a Dolla & Dyme short)

Written by
Sa'id Salaam

THE LICK

(a Dolla & Dyme short)

Written by Sa'id Salaam

"Yo! Yo! That's her, B! That's the bitch I was telling you about!" Yayo shouted and pointed when he spotted the same girl from a week ago. Her round, brown ass was jumping and jiggling under a short pair of shorts now just like it did last week. Except last week, he was with one of his baby mamas and couldn't pull up. Now he was with his partner Que, so he pulled up and hopped out.

"Silly nigga," Que said and shook his head. His boss just hopped out of an eighty thousand-dollar car to talk to some hood rat eating a twenty-five cent bag of chips. "Bitch bad, though!"

Dyme was what's known as a fine muthafucka. She stood five foot six inches and had an athletic bod. Athletic as in an ass as round as a basketball and firm breasts the size of regulation softballs. Her pretty brown skin helped showcase her pretty face.

"Ayo, ma! Hold up, shorty!" he said and grabbed her hand. She twirled around and shot him a look that cut like a blade. It didn't draw blood but did get him to let go. "My bad, ma. I'm just tryin'a meet you."

"Well, you have, so . . ." she said and twisted her sexy ass away. Dyme had a naturally nasty walk just from the proportion of hips to ass, but she did turn it up a little since she was certain he was watching. He was—along with every other male on the block. Old to young, all looked at her as she passed by. Even a baby boy spit out his pacifier and gave her a gummy smile.

"Swing and a miss for strike three!" Que teased when he returned empty-handed. It was actually a good thing since they had business. Yayo was one of those clowns who thinks with their dick. He would have blown off their drug deal in a heartbeat if he had bagged the girl.

"Yo, bet a 'huned I bag that bitch!" Yayo dared. Que twisted his face up to show what he thought of betting a hundred thousand dollars on some pussy.

"Or we could go make a 'huned off this deal. How 'bout that?" Que asked.

"Yeah, I guess," he sighed like he'd rather fuck the chick instead of sell a couple of bricks.

"Girl, what Yayo ass talkin' bout?" Dyme's cousin April asked when she made it back to the group of girls she hung out with. They called themselves G.M.G. for "get money girls," but B.A.B. was closer to the truth because these were some "broke-ass broads."

"Same as all the rest of these Brooklyn niggas talking 'bout . . . some ass!" Dyme shot back. She'd been tricked out some pussy a couple of times and wasn't falling for it again.

"Word. I know that's right. Fuck these niggas," they all said, even though Yayo had been inside every one of them, including April on some late-night, last-second, backseat action when he caught her coming home from a party.

"Word," Dyme agreed and opened her bag of chips. She regretted it instantly when every hand extended for a chip. They shared the bag, just like they shared blunts and dick.

****

Yayo didn't give up easily. In fact, he downright stalked the block for weeks on end trying to get the girl. She finally gave him her number, and they began to talk and text and *"like"* and *"share."* But persistence pays off in any pursuit, especially the pursuit of pussy, and Yayo got that pussy.

Weeks of movies, food, weed, cash, and even some much-needed outfits did the trick, and they winded up inside a swank brownstone. Her friends fucked in motels, backseats, and even staircases, but Yayo took her to his main house. He set out the champagne, exotic weed, and even a new phone inside of a new purse. In return, she set out some good, clean, wet, tight pussy. It wasn't tricking since he swore they were in a relationship now.

"Don't play me," Dyme pouted when Yayo settled on top of her. Her body was ready, but her mind needed a little reassuring.

"Never that. You my lady," he assured her with soft kisses as commas. He reached down and rolled on a condom like she insisted. "We is now us."

"OK," Dyme said since that was a fly line. It did the trick, and she gave in and gave it up. She let out a hiss and winced from the pressure when he entered her. Then she got her breathing together and settled in to enjoy her new man.

"Mmm," Yayo grunted and screwed up his face. She did too, wondering what was wrong since he just got inside of her. Two strokes later, he was moaning and groaning like he was about to come. "I'm . . . about to come!"

"Huh?" she asked because that just didn't make any damn sense. He wined and dined her for months and only fucked her for a few seconds? He couldn't even be called a "minute man" since you have to stay in the pussy for a whole minute. April always said that if a dude bust that quick, it's only because a chick got that good-good, wet-wet. It's to be expected, but they will last longer the second go-round. Could be true, but there would be no seconds.

"Mm, shit! That was good. I gotta go," Yayo announced and stood. Dyme was already confused by the microsex, but when he pulled out and got up, he wasn't wearing the rubber!

"The fuck, yo?" Dyme demanded when she reached down and felt the slimy semen he deposited in her vagina.

"My bad," Yayo shrugged and got dressed. It was no big deal to him since he always pulled the trick condom act on young chicks. Meanwhile, Dyme was still in shock, trying to figure out what just happened. His "my bad" echoed in her head the whole way back to the hood. She was in her shower still shaking her head at his "my bad."

Yayo was always throwing her a hundred here or a hundred there, but the hundred he gave her when he dropped her off at her aunt Lynn's house seemed tainted. It felt dirty, and she would have thrown it away if she didn't need it so damn much. The only thing she could do was cry, so she cried. Cried herself a river in the shower while washing his seeds out of her.

****

It took a week of unanswered calls and texts before Dyme accepted that she'd been played. It just didn't make sense since if he was one of them *fuck 'em and duck 'em* dudes. At least, he could beat the pussy up a little bit. He spent all that time, energy, money, and good game to fuck for only a few seconds.

It took a month to figure out that she was pregnant from the brief encounter. She was the only chick she knew who knew who knocked her up without a calendar and phone records to match up dicks. No question Yayo impregnated her, which made her calls and texts even more urgent. She saw the nigga every day when he was stalking her but didn't see a trace of him now.

To add insult to injury to pregnancy, he didn't pay the bill on the phone he gave her so she couldn't even call or text anyone. Now, she never saw him at all . . . until today, that is. The whole crew was posted up at the stoop as the drama unfolded.

"Humph! There go that sexy-ass Dolla!" April said with gusto when she spotted the hood's most elusive pretty thug. Just a sighting of the dude made every coochie on the stoop throb. Even Chattie, and it sent up a puff of funk in the air. His bright smile contrasted brilliantly against his dark skin and turned heads. The pretty thug type that chicks liked.

"He a'ight . . ." Dyme was saying when she saw Yayo pull up and go into the bodega ahead of Dolla. She hopped up and made a beeline over to the corner store, almost getting hit by a gypsy cab when she blindly crossed the street.

"Fuck she got going on?" one of the B.A.B.s asked since she didn't even have a quarter for a quarter water.

"I'on know," April said but kept a keen eye out to find out. Especially since Dolla was heading to the same store. She wanted to run over and ask if he wanted her to roll his blunt, light it for him, and then suck his dick while he smoked it.

Dyme didn't even notice Dolla as she rushed past him and into the store. He noticed her and bit his lip as he watched her phat ass wiggle by. Dyme finally had this nigga Yayo, and he was gonna have to tell her something about something. She caught him in the cooler picking up wine coolers.

"Aw, man!" Yayo groaned when he saw her coming.

"Aw, man, what?" Dyme shouted on the verge of hysteria. All she wanted to do was tell him she was pregnant so he could break bread to pay for the termination. No way would she even entertain the thought of being baby mama number eight.

"I ain't got time for you," he said and stormed off. He saw they had an audience, so he had to put on a little, even if it was a lie. "Plus, yo pussy stunk! That's why I ain't come back for seconds!"

A lifetime of unspoken disappointments flooded Dyme's mind and pushed all reasoning aside—that bullshit her own mother pulled, putting her out over some nigga—living with her shady aunt and ratchet cousin—having to hang out with the brokest broads in the borough—and now her pussy stank! No, that wouldn't do at all. She made sure to keep a nice, clean vagina.

"Ain't got time for me?" she growled and pulled her straight razor as she followed him from the store. She couldn't have stopped herself even if she wanted to. She didn't want to, though, so she savagely took a swipe that opened his face from earlobe to his chin. "Got time for stitches?"

"Oh shit!" the whole block shouted. That included Que sitting in Yayo's car, the G.M.G.s sitting on their stoop, and Dolla who had just arrived.

"Did you cut me?" Yayo asked mainly from everyone else's reaction since the super sharp blade was almost painless for a moment, followed by the burn and gush of blood that seemed to explode on his shirt.

"Mind your business, Dolla," Dolla said to himself. He had a little thing for Dyme but didn't like the company she kept so he kept that thing to himself.

"Bitch, I'll kill yo' ass!" Yayo shouted with his cheek flapping as he spoke. His teeth and tongue could clearly be seen through the cut. He snatched Dyme completely off her feet and into the air by her throat. Que reached for his door handle to go help her because he didn't like seeing women beat up. Neither did Dolla, who was closer.

"Shit!" Dolla fussed at himself when he realized he wasn't going to be able to mind his own business. He pulled a pistol from his back and rushed over. Que fell back to watch the show.

"Choke *me!*" Dolla dared and gave him a backhanded smack with the gun that made the block go, "Ooooh!"

Yayo let Dyme go, and she stumbled away and coughed in search of her breath. Dolla wasn't done yet, so he shoved the gun in Yayo's mouth until he gagged. Que just shook his head at the spectacle and sat tight.

"Do it," Que heard himself say like most sidekicks will do. Every right-hand man wants to be the man instead of the man next to the man.

Dolla felt his finger tightening on the trigger until he was a millisecond away from splatting Yayo's brains on the "rest in peace" mural on the wall behind him. Something shook Dolla's head "no," and he left the pressure off the trigger. He pulled the gun out of Yayo's mouth and dismissed him with a swift kick in the seat of his expensive jeans. Que shook his head again as Yayo ran and got into the car.

"Ain't nobody need your help!" Dyme snapped on Dolla instead of thanking him. Her pride was hurt about getting put on blast and almost getting choked out.

"Whatever. Keep ya legs closed, and shit like this won't happen," he said and continued on his mission.

****

"Roll a blunt?" Que reeled in response to Yayo's request as they rode away from the incident. He took another look at his friend's battered face and confirmed, "Nigga, you need a doctor! Some stitches or sutures or staples or something!"

"Is it that bad?" Yayo asked hopefully not. All that hope was lost when he pulled the visor down and saw his face in the mirror. He had a classic "buck fifty" that would stay with him for life like a case of herpes. "That bitch cut me!"

"Yup," his partner nodded as he steered toward Kings County Hospital. "And that nigga Dolla stuck his tool down your throat."

Both men paused to process those facts. Both recalled the embarrassing sound of him gagging on the barrel of the Glock. They both relived the "ooh!" of the crowd when Dolla slapped a spark out of him. Yayo was content to be alive, but Que knew he had to do something. To do nothing would invite the whole borough to try him. He would be considered soft, and soft niggs are bait. Especially ones with bread like Yayo and Que were getting. He was too young to move to Florida and retire so "get back" was the only option.

"Well?" Que asked since he saw the wheels turning in Yayo's head. If he punked out, Que would pull over and kill him now so he could take his spot. There may not have been any lions and tigers, but the streets of Brooklyn were a jungle.

"I'ma buss that nigga is what," Yayo said unconvincingly. He heard his own whiny tone and tried again. "Nigga gon' slap me with the tool! Yo, I'ma knock son block off! That's on Brooklyn!"

"Humph," Que huffed. It always amazed him when people swore by shit that ain't theirs to swear by. He didn't swear much, but when he did, it was by Allah. In fact, he secretly swore by Allah right then to take Yayo's spot first chance he got. He didn't know who the connect was, so he had to wait. Wait and plot. So while Yayo was plotting, Que was plotting . . . but both were being plotted on at the same time.

****

"Been wanting to rob his soft ass anyway," Dolla growled to himself. He never really liked Yayo, but a bit of jealousy played a part in it. He was a ladies' man himself, so he got just as much ass as Yayo, but Yayo had that check. Money allowed him access to some chicks out of Dolla's pay grade. For now anyway, because he was plotting on a come-up.

His heart broke when word got out he'd sexed pretty Dyme. Her good girl rep made her wifey material since no one wants a ho for a housewife. Not that a ho can't be tamed; it's just a lot of work. Similar to breaking a wild horse, and no one has time for all that.

Then hearing Yayo putting on that her pussy stunk just added insult to injury. Dudes can tell a chick whose pussy stank from two and a half blocks away, and Dyme wasn't one of them.

Dolla peered out his window and saw Dyme and her little crew of girls smoking on the stoop of her brownstone. A half smile turned a corner of his mouth up as he watched her theatrics as she spoke. She waved her hands, flipped her hair, and dipped her hip to help make her points. He could only guess she was telling them what happened with Yayo earlier, and he was right. Some of the girls saw, and others heard about it, but it was still a good story.

"So, I was like 'Sup now, nigga!' He was like 'Chill, yo.' 'I ain't got no chill, yo.' I let that nigga get it!" she said and demonstrated the swipe of the blade that opened his face. "Then son grabbed my neck—"

"Told you not to mess with that 'fuck 'em and duck 'em'-ass nigga anyway!" her cousin reminded. She would know since Yayo fucked her and ducked her too. The other girls nodded since they had experienced the same as well.

"Ooh, then fine-ass Dolla came out of nowhere . . ." Chattie exclaimed and told that part of the story. "Yayo had her in the air and—"

"And what you and Dolla got going on?" April needed to know right away. She'd been throwing pussy at the pretty thug like a white girl tossing a Frisbee in the park.

"I'on even know that nigga!" Dyme shot back. His words from the bodega came back to her. *"Keep your legs closed"* replayed in her mind and threatened to make her smile. She knew he had to care to say that to her.

"Girl, that nigga is a beast!" Chattie said. She shook her head and bit her lip like she had firsthand knowledge.

"Bitch, plu-leeeze!" April said dramatically. "If that nigga turned his nose up at *me*, I *knooooow* he ain't fuck with you!"

"Cuz yo' pussy stink," Monica nodded helpfully. The rest of the crew nodded since it was singing its salty song right now.

"My um . . . pH balance be off . . . and um . . ." she stammered in defense of her funk box.

"Can I finish my story?" Dyme wanted to know. She got no objections and continued. Her girls "oohed" and "aahed" as she played it back for them.

"What you gon' do about Yayo? He may be soft, but you cut his face, yo. He gotta do something about that!" April spelled out as correctly as an Indian kid in a spelling bee. R-E-V-E-N-G-E, revenge.

****

"Word! Fuck that nigga. We out here!" April cheered even though she knew they shouldn't be out anywhere. She knew good and damn well that Yayo had to clap back for getting cut. She was willing, though, because if something happened to Dyme, she would inherit her clothing.

"We out here!" Dyme repeated, even though she knew she shouldn't be. She wouldn't run into Dolla again if she didn't, so yeah, "We out here."

The rest of the G.M.G.s piled into the small apartment and blazed up the few dime bags they scrounged up. It usually took two or three of them to chip in on a ten-dollar bag of weed.

"What you over there smiling about?" April fussed when she saw that faraway gaze and a slight smile on Dyme's face. She didn't like seeing anyone around her too happy. After all, misery loves company, and she wanted everyone to be miserable with her.

"Oh, nothing," she sang and tried to wipe the smirk from her face. It was hard because Dolla's words kept playing in her mind. *"Keep ya legs closed."*

"Yo, let's hit this spot while we can still get in free!" Chattie said since they couldn't afford to pay the cover. Plus, she had temporarily tamed her pussy and wanted to bag a man before it crunk up again.

"Yeah, we need to get up in that piece!" April said and led the charge out the front door.

****

Que was a VIP in Brooklyn, so he bypassed the line and walked straight into the club. He heard the chickens clucking as he walked by, but he was too deep in thought to listen. One, in particular, caught his attention, so he made his way over to shoot his shot.

"Look-it," Lala said to Dyme when she spotted Que approaching. On cue, the whole crew slipped razor blades from their mouths and got ready. The club didn't allow guns inside, so they all carried the blades between their cheeks and gums. They were so good at it, they could eat, speak, and give head without even taking them out. Que would get cut to ribbons if he was on some bullshit.

"Sup, ma?" Que greeted with his hands raised and movement in his hips like he just came for a dance.

"Sup with you, daddy?" she shot back inquisitively.

"Just tryin'a dance, so you can untwist them lips," he said and disarmed her with a smile.

"Ya man still wack!" Dyme insisted and smiled back. "Now, he 'sposed to be coming for me?"

"Eh?" he shrugged. Lord knows she would be on RIP T-shirts had she cut his face, but she was right; his man was wack.

"I'on even know how you work for a nigga like that," she put out since she heard him ask the same thing in his tone. If he protested she would fall back; he didn't, so she pressed on. "I know you loyal and wouldn't move on him, but . . ."

"But what?" he asked so intently, she knew she had him. Dudes were always distracted by her pretty face, phat ass, and slim waist, but Dyme was one smart girl.

"But what if it just happened to happen? Then, the man next to the man could slide over—"

"and be the man!" he finished with stars in his eyes. They exchanged numbers to put their plan in motion. The deal was sealed, but Dyme still needed one more piece to complete the puzzle.

****

"Dolla! A-yo, Dolla!" Dyme shouted up and down the block. She didn't know which apartment building or window belonged to him, so she just shouted his name.

"The fuck?" Dolla fussed when he peeked through the blind and saw the girl. She cupped her hands like a bullhorn and kept on calling. After ten minutes, he accepted she wasn't stopping or leaving, so he grabbed his gat and stepped outside.

"A-yo, Dol—" she said but stopped in her tracks when he barged out of a building taking long, angry strides toward her. She felt her pussy twitch in reaction to the pretty thug in a crispy white wife beater. There was nothing she could do to stop the moisture from gathering in her panties. Dolla didn't even tuck his tool when he came out.

"What the fuck is wrong with you?" Dolla barked outwardly but inwardly thought, *Damn, this is a bad broad.*

"Well, actually, there's a lot of things wrong with me, but I ain't here for all that," she admitted. His fine ass didn't go unnoticed either, but she wasn't here for that either.

"So what are you here for then?" he asked again and scanned the block once more.

"Same nigga looking for you is looking for me. I may just have a way to find him before he finds us," she suggested.

"Do you know what you getting yourself into? Huh?" Dolla shot down at her. "This ain't no little hood rat game you little hood rats be playing!"

"First of all, I ain't no hood rat! If I was, I wouldn't have did what I did. I got honor, and dude dissed me. I'll die about mine!" she said with a fire in her eyes that lit his fuse.

"OK, I'm listening," he said and listened to her plan.

"Can we go inside?" she asked so they wouldn't be on front street.

"No," he said so quickly she had to try to remember what the word meant. They did duck inside the bodega since it wasn't safe to be outside. By the end of her plan, he was all in.

They exchanged numbers and glances up and down before they departed. Neither would admit it at that moment, but it was on from that moment.

****

"That's where he be taking chicks to bone them," Dyme said nodding toward a brownstone. She would know since that's where he took her to bone her. Her face scrunched in disgust as she replayed the incident in her mind.

"And that's where I'ma run up in there on him," Dolla decided. "The best time to catch a nigga with his pants down is when his pants *are* down."

"You say the craziest stuff!" Dyme laughed and lit up his life. He never felt what he was feeling now ever before.

"Yeah, my uncle used to say stuff like that all the time. I ain't always get it, but it seemed to fit," he recalled fondly.

"Only thing, babe . . ." Dyme said with worry in her voice. "Yayo soft, but this nigga Que—"

"Ain't talking about nothing either," Dolla responded sharply. Everyone knew about Que's rep because he was loud and flamboyant. No one knew about Dolla's because real bad boys move in silence and violence. That didn't stop a smile from spreading on his face from her calling him babe.

"He tried to holla at me too," Dyme admitted shyly. She knew it was only because Yayo bragged on her box. Dudes tell other dudes how good the pussy is, so they want some too. Chicks do too and can't understand why their girls fuck behind them.

"Well, holla at him," he said causing her to snap her head in his direction for an explanation. "Go to the movies like Abraham Lincoln."

"Ah, yes!" she nodded when she got it. Yayo was about to get robbed, and Que wasn't going to be able to shit about it. They like to ride together, so they could die together.

****

"Whoa, shorty, save some room for dessert!" Yayo told Kimba from across the table. She was smashing her chicken and waffles while he picked over his.

"Mmm, and what's for dessert?" she dared as if she didn't know. Every chick in the hood knows dick comes with dinner and a movie.

"This dick!" he laughed. She laughed too since he was paying. "Come on; let's bounce."

"Bounce on that dick?" Kimba giggled. He was a known playboy, so her goal was to fuck him, suck him so crazy he'd have to come back for seconds . . . and thirds.

He tossed money on the table for the bill minus the tip and pulled her from the restaurant. She had to open her own door since he opened his own and hopped behind the wheel. She never had a dude open a door or pull out her chair, so she couldn't miss it.

"Go on and warm that motor up," he dared and nodded at her legs.

"Mmm," she hummed and put her feet on the dash and pulled her panties aside. The little circles she made on her clit made her moan and hiss.

"Damn, shorty!" he said and mashed the gas to hurry home and smash that ass. The car came to a screeching halt in front of his brownstone, but it was being taped off by the gas company. "The fuck? Yo, my man. What's going on?"

"Gas leak," the utility worker said from behind the mask covering his mouth and nose. "We have to find the owner to shut it off from the inside."

"This my shit! Come on!" he said and led the way up the stairs.

"You better stay out here," the man told Kimba before handing Yayo a mask of his own.

"A'ight, yo," Kimba said and sucked her teeth. A smile turned her lip up as she watched the utility worker follow Yayo inside with his toolbox. Her work was done, so she raised her hand and hailed a gypsy cab.

"It's in here!" Yayo said pointing to the basement door. He turned around and saw Dolla pull down his mask and pull up his gun. "Son, I thought we was good about shorty."

"Oh, we are," Dolla assured him with a nod. "I'm over that. This is a robbery, homie."

"She told you where I be at," he said shaking his head at his own stupidity. Que warned him on many occasions to stop bringing chicks to the stash spot.

"Yup, now, let's get this bread upstairs," he said. Yayo let out a sigh and led the way up to the second floor. He unlocked a locked door where bundles of cash sat neatly on a table.

"Put them in here," Dolla ordered and opened the empty toolbox. Yayo complied and accepted his loss.

"Man, that's almost eighty bands," he moaned when he put the last of it in the box. He wasn't hurt, though, since he had twice that on the street.

"Now, I heard something about some work?" Dolla asked with raised brows.

"Nope! Que got everything in the street. Ain't nothing here but a few pounds of green!" he said as if he one-upped the jack boy.

"Well, run that!" Dolla growled, ready to slap the smirk off his face.

"Oh yeah," Yayo agreed when he remembered he was getting robbed. He led Dolla into the bedroom to retrieve the weed. The robbery was business, but what came next was personal.

"Argh!" Yayo gagged even louder this time when Dolla shoved the plastic pistol in his mouth. He chipped a tooth, but that was the least of his worries. Dolla grabbed his throat and looked him square in his eyes.

"You dissed my woman!" Dolla yelled.

Yayo tried to shake his head no, but it was too late. A tug on the trigger blew his mind . . . literally, as the wall turned a custom pink from blood and brain matter. Dolla saw the lights in his eyes go out when his soul left his body. There was no turning back now.

****

"So, what made you come hang out with me?" Que asked when he and Dyme got seated for dinner. She agreed to dinner and a movie, knowing what came with it. It didn't matter what was on the plate because dick was for dessert.

"You asked me," she shrugged. "Better question is, why you wanna hang out with me after what I did to your man's face?"

"Cuz Yayo told me you left a puddle in his bed. Not a wet spot, but a whole fucking puddle!" he admitted.

"True, but he also been running around telling errbody my shit stink!" she said, getting mad about it again now. But not for long before a text from Dolla made her smile. Most chicks would have been grossed out by the gory picture of Yayo with his brains decorating the wall. Not Dyme, though. She let out a little giggle.

"Nah, I knew that wasn't true. A nigga can tell if a chick pussy stink from a couple'a blocks away. Son be bugging, yo," he nodded with his own decision to take over his spot. "He on his way out anyway."

"Mmm," she giggled again since she knew he was already headed to the upper room. Que was right behind Yayo and didn't even know it. "Anyway, I did leave a puddle behind. I can't help it. My pussy get so wet I be having to carry extra panties in my purse."

Que felt his dick jump in his jeans when she said that. Then he got an instant erection when she pulled a pair of yellow panties from her purse. Que had heard all he needed to hear when he saw the dainty drawers.

"Fuck this food, yo. Let's get out of here!" he said and rushed her from the spot.

"I got a room," she offered coyly.

"Word?" he asked cautiously. He could give a fuck about saving motel fair. He just wanted to hurry up and take a dip in that puddle. He reached over to feel it, but it was not to be.

"Chill, B!" she said and knocked his hand away. She pledged her pussy to Dolla and vowed never to let another man touch it. "I got a room over in Red Hook. My cousin rented it, but they at the club."

Que nodded and steered the car toward the Red Hook section. He found the motel and parked outside. Que scanned the area for friends or foes before stepping outside, pulling a .40 cal from under his seat.

"What you need that for? I'ma give you the pussy. You ain't gotta steal it!" she laughed.

"Word," he said and squinted his eyes into evil slits. He was a killer himself and killed quite a few dudes just like this. As soon as Dyme unlocked the door, he rushed in with the gun eye high and cleared the room like in a cop show.

"Clear!" she called out and cracked up when his search of the room came up empty. "Really, bruh? You think I was tryin'a set you up?"

"Nah, I even do that when I go to my grandma house," he laughed and set the pistol on the nightstand. That was mistake number two. Number one was taking her call in the first place. "Now get them clothes off!"

"You first. Slow, papi, so I can watch," she said and twirled her tongue around her thick lips.

"Oh, word? You want the Chippendale shit, huh?" he said and grinded his hips.

"Uh-huh," Dyme said and bit her lip so she wouldn't laugh. He made a big show of unbuckling his belt and letting his expensive jeans fall to the floor. He had a decent-size lump of dick in his boxer briefs, but it was about to go to waste.

"You like that?" he asked, and she nodded and bit her lip a little harder. Que reached down and slowly pulled his shirt over his head. When he did, he came face-to-face with his own gun. It looked totally different from this side. The huge barrel looked like the Holland Tunnel, but Jersey wasn't on the other side. "Chill, ma. That shit is loaded!"

"I know," she smiled and pulled her phone. "Come on, babe."

Que knew what was up and wasn't going out without a fight. He was pretty sure that wasn't April she just called, so he had to make his move before whoever it was arrived. She eased over to the door to open it, and he sprang into action.

"Bitch!" he barked and lunged toward her. Lunging requires legs, and a quick shot to his knee nearly took one of his off. The gun barked and sparked, and down he went. "Yeeooow!"

"I bet," Dyme giggled at his howl and turned the knob to let Dolla in.

"You okay? I heard a woman scream," he laughed as he entered the room. He grimaced at the mess the .40 cal made of dude's knee. "Son, you sounded like an opera singer."

"Fuck you, fuck her," he said defiantly. He lived like a man and would not die like a bitch. "Could at least let me fuck her first!"

"*I'll* take care of that," Dolla said and raised his gun to Que's face.

"Wait!" Dyme shouted just before he bust him. Dolla twisted his face up, wondering why she wanted to spare him.

"The fuck?" he asked.

"Let me?" she asked with a wicked grin.

"You sure?" he asked cautiously. He knew once a person opens that door, they can't close it. Murder is habit forming like smoking weed or masturbation. She nodded; he shrugged and stepped aside.

"Not with my own shit, yo!" Que protested when she raised his own gun to his face.

"Beggars can't be choosers," she reminded him and sent a speeding bullet into his face that sent him speeding into the afterlife. She cocked her head and studied the mess she made. Dolla realized he just created a monster. Not that he cared because she was *his* monster.

"Come on, ma. We gotta bounce!" he urged and pulled her out of the room. They tucked their guns and rushed to his car.

"Yo, I'm mad horny!" Dyme said. It was time to take their relationship to the next level.

****

"Well, this is it," Dolla said almost nervously when he pulled to a stop in front of the Park Hill Motor Lodge. He knew there would be heat after both Yayo and Que got their shit twisted. Fingers would certainly point his way since he dissed Yayo. Yayo had a mean team, so he stepped off the scene for a moment. Things would die down once Yayo's old crew finished their power struggle and a new leader emerged. Dolla and Dyme would rob him too on their quest for a million dollars.

"Yup," Dyme said just as nervously. They both knew tonight would be the first night of the rest of their lives.

"You hungry?" he asked despite them just eating an hour ago.

"Nah," she said and followed him into the room that would be their home for a while. She hid the money and weed in her aunt Lynn's house. She found a hole in the closet wall that April would never find.

Small talk was over once they entered the room and sat on the edge of the bed. The first kiss was a memorable peck after locking eyes. The others were lost in a blur of furious sex.

Dyme practically ripped Dolla's clothes as they made out. Then her own without breaking the lip-lock. His sweet tongue only came out of her mouth long enough to pull her shirt over her head. Next, they found themselves face-to-face on the bed.

"I'm going to love you so good. That's my word!" Dyme vowed when they locked eyes once more at the moment of truth.

"And I'm going to love you even better," Dolla declared as he lubed the head of his dick in the slippery froth between her legs. She relaxed and gave herself up to him completely.

Dolla was well hung, but it didn't hurt when he entered her. She was far too turned on and slippery wet to register any pain. She was going to be sore later but only felt pleasure at the moment—a moment that literally lasted for hours as they explored each other in search of what the other liked.

"I'm about to come," Dolla announced like he was confused as to what he was supposed to do about it.

"Come then," Dyme purred and clamped her already snug walls around his dick. He grunted and spasmed in the throes of a good nut. Holding back only intensified the sensation and damn neared killed him. He could have sworn his heart stopped for a second as he filled her with his seeds.

****

Neither recalled going to sleep, but they awoke huddled together in a ball the next morning. His morning erection didn't go to waste because Dyme mounted it and rode off in search of her own orgasm. She found it and rode him to one of his own. They cuddled again and caught their breath.

"Mmm," Dolla moaned as he felt her contractions convulsing on his dick. They milked him dry and made him wonder, "Are you on the pill? Or a shot or implants?"

"No, no, and no," she giggled and wiggled. He didn't go soft, so she kept right on rocking and rolling on the dick. His tone was funny, but the question was valid. Especially with all the kids he just sent speeding up inside of her.

"Okay, daddy. I'll go to the clinic in the morning," she relented. Having him pull out felt like kicking a man out of his home when he needs you the most.

She would love to have his kids one day, just not this day nine months from now. Not in this place, either.

"Okay, baby," he said. He wanted her to have his kids as well but now wasn't the time, and New York wasn't the place. Anywhere was better than here to raise a family.

"We should move. Let's move to Atlanta!" she shouted and rolled out from under him.

"Word?" Dolla asked and thought of his own pros and cons. First, it wasn't Brooklyn, and the score was four to one in favor of the ATL.

"Hell yeah! It don't snow. It's mad money down there. Cost of living is way cheaper," she said, pushing the score to twenty to one.

"We still got sixty bands that Yayo donated to us," he said since they ran through twenty in the week since the robbery. He let her stash the cash since he didn't want to keep it in the room he rented in the rooming house or in the motel room they shacked up in.

"Yeah, I stashed it real good in my auntie's house," Dyme said. She was now happy Dolla put the brakes on their shopping, or she would have spent it all. She spent five grand on a chain and wanted to spend five more on matching earrings and bracelet, but Dolla talked her out of it.

He spent his ten on a used Lexus and new Tims. He'd been broke and homeless before and vowed never to be again. . . no matter who had to get robbed.

"Well, go get it tomorrow, after . . . the clinic, and we out," he said and rubbed her booty. She smiled wickedly and set off round three.

****

"Let's bounce. Let's get up out of here!" Dolla decided seemingly suddenly.

"From the room or . . ." she asked hopefully that she had sold him on her idea of moving down to Atlanta. It was the land of milk and honey compared to the bricks and bullshit of Brooklyn.

"From New York," he said. It wasn't quite as spontaneous as it seemed since he had been weighing it all day. He had no family left, and friends were more trouble than they were worth. Dyme was all he had, and he wanted a fresh start with her.

"Thank you! Thank you! Thank you!" she cheered and planted more kisses all over his face. That led to round two for the day, and it was still morning. Once they wrapped up and showered, Dyme set off to collect her clothes and his money. He had to make a few moves of his own; they agreed to meet up later. When they did meet up, it was more of the same.

****

"We need to hit that clinic now if it's not too late," Dyme moaned after Dolla filled her full of early-morning come.

"For real, though," he agreed since pulling out is much easier said than done. It's unnatural to get to that point, then abandon what got you there. He pulled his deflating dick from her and got up.

Dyme joined him in the shower and ended up with even more come in her. Neither had any self-control when it came to the other. They were soul mates, and only death could separate them . . . unless they died together.

Once they fucked and finally washed, they got out the shower and got dressed.

"Let me help you," Dyme fussed and fixed his collar like he was her son. She hoped to have his son, then sons and a couple of daughters. Ten if it were up to her. She didn't want her children growing up lonely like she did as an only child. Then they could protect each other from scumbags like her mother's boyfriend, James, who got tired of sneaking and eating her out. Now he wanted to fuck her. She confided in KC, but he got mad and cut her off.

She ran away to her aunt Lynn and cousin, April. Life was crowded and chaotic with them, but no grown man was sneaking in her room trying to fuck her, either, so it balanced out. Her biggest problem was ratchet-ass April wearing her clothes and going through her belongings.

"Thanks, babe," he said once she fixed his collar. They looked around the motel room to make sure they didn't leave anything since they would not be coming back. Then they rode over to the clinic to put her on something before he knocked her up.

"Um, excuse me?" Dyme fussed at some young chick staring at Dolla like he was a rap star. He did have that look and that aura about him. He was larger than life, and she would just have to learn to live with the attention it brought. "Ain't you here to get rid of them crabs?"

"Chill, Dyme," he said, holding her arm as the girl rolled her eyes and stole another quick glance. He was used to the attention but humble enough to still not understand it. Chicks dug him everywhere he went.

"Let me catch you looking at him when I come out!" Dyme dared when her name was called. She went to the back and got a six-month prescription for Dolla to come in her. Once that was done, it was off to Aunt Lynn's house.

"You just missed your cousin," Lynn said when Dyme walked into the house.

"Missed her where?" Dyme wondered since April never worked, and it was too early for the club. It was too late in the afternoon for a booty call since dudes would drop her off first thing in the morning.

"Girl, she done picked up and moved to Atlanta! I believe she done met some nigga on Facebook," Lynn said, since she had met one herself. In fact, she had just put some pussy pics in his inbox before Dyme arrived.

"Say, word! I . . ." Dyme began until a sinking feeling came over her. Her heart sank, and she knew what she knew before she got upstairs to check.

"Oh no!"

****

"Yo, I can't believe this—" Dyme began but stopped short of lying to herself. Why wouldn't she believe that April would steal from her when she'd been stealing from her since she arrived? First, the change out of her pockets, to socks and panties. Now, she just snaked her for everything she had and what she didn't have— including Dolla's dough from robbing Yayo. A man died for that, and she just walks off with it for free.

"What's wrong, chile?" Dyme's aunt Lynn asked in response to the scream Dyme let out when she found her closet and stash spot empty. Even she knew something was up when her daughter suddenly bounced with more stuff than she owned.

"April jacked me. She took everything I own, yo. She ain't leave me nothing. Not even my dirty clothes!" she whined. "And my man's money. Tens of thousands of dollars!"

"That girl ain't shit!" Lynn slipped. She usually stuck up for her sorry-ass child no matter what. She was now as mad as Dyme hearing how much money she ran off with and didn't leave her any money. "I heard her telling someone she was moving to Atlanta."

"Wow. She even stole my plans. Now, how I'm supposed to tell Dolla?" Dyme moaned. She failed him, and all their money was gone.

"Suck his dick first. Then give it to him straight," she suggested. It was actually a good idea but deceptive, so she decided to give it to him straight. Still, she had to make up for it, so she searched her mind for a quick lick. She saw a name and number on a piece of paper April had left behind. She saw why she left it behind once she read the name.

"Shit!" she fussed when she read Goose's name and number. He had plenty of money but was known to be a sexual sadist. Chicks threw the pussy at him because he was rich, but he still took it anyway because he was a rapist.

Knowing she had to make up the loss, she picked up the paper and made the call.

"Who?" Goose asked and frowned up when he answered the unknown number.

"Dyme, April cousin," she repeated. "From Marcy. You don't remember me? Wow!"

"Oh yeah! Young, pretty bitch with that phat ass!" he recalled. He had checked her out as much as he checked out April when he rolled up on her. She looked young and didn't have a reputation, so he didn't pursue her.

April went out with him once and wasn't the same when she returned the next morning. She had a few hundred dollars in her knockoff purse but was in shock for a couple of days.

"That's not exactly how I would describe myself, but, yeah. So what's up? You tryin'a hang out or nah?" she cut through to the chase.

"If you fucking. You fucking?" he wanted to know. And if nothing else, he should be given credit for transparency. He wasn't with the movies, or dinner, and didn't even have a subscription to Netflix. He was trying to put his dick in some pussy—end of story.

I mean, we can go. I'm saying, I-I," she stammered.

"Nah, yo. If we fucking, say we fucking. If not, get off my phone. There's plenty of pussy in Brooklyn, so don't waste my time."

"Okay, we fucking. Dang!" Dyme fussed. It was crass even for a chick from the projects. They made plans, and he got off his phone. She stayed on hers and called her man.

"Sup, ma? I'm headed your way now," Dolla said when he took her call.

"'K," she said and decided to wait until they were face-to-face to tell him. In the end, she took her aunt's advice and gave him some head before breaking the bad news to him.

"I'm about to—" Dolla warned when he reached the point of no return. It was enough warning for Dyme to get him out of her mouth and finish him off by hand.

She smiled in amazement when the baby batter exploded from his dick and landed everywhere. She stroked his thick shaft until he was spent, then went to get a soapy washcloth from the motel bathroom to wash him off.

"Okay, now, what's up wit' you?" Dolla asked knowingly. The upside to having a soul mate is them knowing you like a book. The downside is them knowing you like a book. He knew something was eating her before she ate the dick.

"Man, April done hit the stash. You trusted me to keep your money, and she found it. Stole err cent—even my dirty clothes. I ain't got shit except what I got on!" she whined.

"Damn, yo!" Dolla shouted and shook his head. He felt as bad for Dyme as he did about the money. He knew the streets were talking about Yayo getting hit up and people knew they had beef. "How we supposed to move to the A now?"

"I got us another lick. Dude named Goose from Bed-Stuy."

"Goose, the Killer? The nigga who be raping chicks for money? You bugging, yo," Dolla insisted.

"I'll do it myself. Just give me the banger," Dyme offered.

"Oh, you a killer now, huh?" he laughed and was actually a little turned on. "Got one little body under yo' belt and now you ready to go murk something, huh?"

"Yup!" she insisted and stuck her chin up.

"Okay. We gon' see what you talking 'bout, but, uh . . ." he said and reached between her legs. She gladly gave him what Goose was never getting and would die trying.

****

"Yoooo! This some HGTV-type shit right here!" Dyme sang as Goose led her into his waterfront loft in downtown Brooklyn.

"Thanks. Nothing like that small-time cat Dolla, huh?" he asked and laughed at her shock. "Oh, a nigga did his homework. I'on just stick my shit in anybody."

But you'll fuck a nobody, Dyme thought to herself. Dolla told her sometimes it's best not to say nothing and just listen, so that's what she did.

Goose lit a blunt of some fruity-flavored weed and introduced her to the good life.

"Dom P, while you was drinking wine coolers," he said as he retrieved a bottle from the ten thousand-dollar fridge.

"Mmm," she said with her lips pressed tightly so nothing else would come out. Especially that good weed he had. She hoped there was a stash of it somewhere so she could take it too. If not, she would clip the blunt so she could save some for her man. The conversation started off weird, then got worse.

"Most people like to do things the easy way. Me, I like things the hard way. Feel me?" Goose asked and handed Dyme a glass of champagne.

"Not really," she said and took a sip. "What exactly does that mean?"

"It means I'm gonna take that pussy. I want you to try to stop me. I mean, like really fight me. I'ma hit you off real good, but I like what I like," he explained.

"Yo, that's the craziest shit I ever heard in my life. Straight up, and I'm not with it," she said and took a final pull on the blunt.

"That's what the fuck I'm talking about!" Goose cheered. He assumed she was getting into character, and it turned him on. He had her on tape saying we fucking, so it was whatever with him at this point.

"I'm out, yo," she said and went for the front door. She really did want to get away from the sicko but knew Dolla was on the other side of the door. A switch hit inside of Goose's twisted mind, and he snapped.

"Drink my bubbly and smoke my weed, and you talking 'bout you out?" he shouted and attacked. He ran up and tried to get her down so he could rape her right there on the spot.

"Get off me, nigga!" she shouted and fought for her life. Dyme had been fighting her whole life, but fighting not to be raped gave her energy and strength she didn't know she had.

"*That's* what the fuck I'm talking about!" Goose cheered when she split his lip and scratched his face. He was rock hard and ready to fuck. Dyme put up a better fight than most and actually made it to the door. She managed to unlock it before Goose snatched her away and threw her down. He had her right where he wanted her and went for his pants. He was so focused on getting his dick out that he didn't hear death rush through his front door.

"Sick-ass nigga!" Dolla growled as he wrapped his muscular arm around Goose's neck. Goose was so used to fighting chicks he was no match for a man. He could only pull at the meaty arm cutting his wind off. A body needs oxygen to fight, and he quickly ran out of both.

Dolla felt him go limp but kept on squeezing. He squeezed until he passed out, then kept on until he passed away. He dropped him next to Dyme and went to check on her.

"You a'ight, yo?" he asked even though she was clearly shaken up.

"That nigga is crazy!" she shouted and scooted away from his corpse.

"Go wait in the car!" he demanded and pushed her to the door. Once she was out, he pulled his gun and pumped a couple of rounds into Goose's head for Dyme, then got to searching for valuables.

"Jackpot!" Dolla cheered and pumped his fist. He was glad Dyme was in the car, so she didn't see the little happy dance he did. The safe was closed but not locked, so a simple turn of the latch gave up its goods as quickly as Chattie on a first date.

"Man," he said and twisted his lips at the content inside. There was a few hundred thousand dollars' worth of bonds which were worthless to him. They came with tracking numbers and signatures that could connect him to the dead guy. A pair of plastic pistols with extended clips and silencers attached made him smile. He grabbed the twenty grand in loose cash, the jewelry, and turned to leave. He remembered his manners as he stepped over the corpse and nodded.

"Thanks for donating to the Dolla and Dyme get-rich-or-die-trying fund," he said and stepped from the house. Dyme was bundled up in the blanket with a blank look on her face. "You good?"

"Huh?" she asked and came back to the present. "You straight? We straight?"

"A little. Son keeps his bread in the bank. We got some traveling money, though."

"Well, let's travel then!" she laughed and off they went. Next stop was the ATL.

****

Dolla walked out and took a deep breath to inhale the sweet Brooklyn aroma for the last time. It's a mix of curry, good weed, arroz con pollo, pretty women, and new sneakers. His face scrunched when another scent invaded his melancholy. He scanned the streets and saw the cause. Chattie was two and a half blocks away and closing in. He turned to escape but heard his name.

"Yo, Dolla! Dolla, you hear me!" she said and rushed in his direction.

"Sup, ma?" he asked and turned into the wind so it would carry the funk two blocks up.

"I heard about April. She foul," she said as if she wasn't foul herself.

"Yeah," was all Dolla had since he didn't do gossip. He turned to finish his mission of getting breakfast for the road while Dyme went to the weed spot. Neither had left New York before, so they figured they would load up on green before they got ghost.

"Where Dyme?" Chattie asked after a scan up and down the block didn't produce her.

"At the whatchamacallit," he said which means none of your business.

"Shit, so come up for a second," she said and batted her eyes. She was pretty, but pretty funky too, so his head shook before his mouth opened.

"I'm good, ma. I'll tell Dyme you asked about her," he said and turned into the bodega. He ordered beef pastrami, egg, and cheese sandwiches on Kaiser rolls and grabbed her favorite orange-pineapple juice.

Dolla couldn't believe the people around Dyme who claimed to love her yet harmed her. Her mother put herself over her daughter and allowed a man to touch her. Her cousin steals all her money and clothes, while her funk-box friend just tried to fuck him.

His chin lifted in pride knowing he was the one who would love her and protect her. Verses from the Qur'an always seemed to pop in his mind when he needed them.

"Men are the protectors and maintainers of women."

Dyme was his woman, and that's what he planned to do. She was all he had and vice versa until death did them.

****

"Welcome to Atlanta!" Dyme cheered and cheesed as she read the sign welcoming them to their new city. They made the 13-hour drive in two days and five hours because they had to stop and fuck several times on the side of 95 South, motels, and once in a while, he drove. Each was a new toy to the other, and neither could get enough.

"Now what?" Dolla heard himself say. She knew he wasn't asking her since she picked up on his habit of vocalizing his thoughts. She also knew he would have an answer. He would lead, and she would follow. She could only hope he didn't lead them over a cliff, because, again, she would follow. Dyme turned the radio on while the wheels turned in his head.

"Join us at Chaos, the ATL's hottest new club! Special invited guests include . . ."

"That's where she gonna be!" Dolla said it at the exact second it popped in her head. She nodded in agreement.

"Word. She gonna find the hottest club in the city. I just hope we ain't too late!" she said as she checked her cousin's Instagram feed. She could have at least blocked her if she was going to stunt with their stolen money. April was balling out of control on their dime.

"Too late for what?" Dolla asked since he never expected to see a dime of that money back. Thieves never return what they steal, no matter what.

"Before she . . ." Dyme began until she caught on too. She shrugged her shoulders at what she knew was to come. A violation like that only has one recompense. "Oh well."

"I'll do it since she your family," he offered since they were now on the same page.

"And that's exactly why I'ma do it. I can't believe she would do me like this! She always be wanting whatever I get!" she pouted as a lifetime of indiscretions flooded her mind. "This is on me. I got her."

Dolla wasn't surprised by Dyme's sudden change of mind. The one thing he taught her was never to allow anyone to snake you—family or not. Dyme was learning well, which made Dolla proud. He had a pretty chick that was a go-getta and wouldn't hesitate to leave a bitch stinkin'. That, to Dolla, was definitely worth bragging about.

"That's prolly why she offered to blow me last week," he guessed. He didn't have to share that since April was already as good as dead. He just wanted it to be brutal. The low growl emanating from the passenger seat said it would be brutal indeed.

They drove through the city of Atlanta and settled in the northern suburb of Marietta. It was twenty minutes away from the action, yet busy enough to blend in. Dyme went to the restaurant next door while he registered and got their room.

"Need some help?" she offered when he began to unload the car.

"I got it, ma. Set that food out. I'm starving!" he said and passed her the key card.

"I got something you can eat," she purred seductively. He twisted his lips into a frown just like the last time she suggested it. Just like he did whenever she suggested going down on him, especially since she was practicing on him every day. She always heard April and Chattie telling their blow-job tales about driving dudes wild and couldn't wait to have a man of her own to try it out on. Her cousin and friends may suck stray dicks like stray cats, but she waited for a man of her own, and now she had one.

She heard some dudes would wait awhile before going down on a chick to put some distance between them and the last dick. Also to ensure that it's their pussy before they eat it. None of those things applied to them, and it was definitely his pussy. They had the rest of their lives, so she would wait before asking again. Like maybe give him another week.

"I need some clothes," Dyme pouted when he set the bags down. He still had all of his clothes while she had none. She would only bring an overnight bag each night when she spent nights with Dolla.

April even stole her dirty clothes from the hamper. Her fault for showing off matching bra and panty sets to a chick whose bras and panties never matched. A lone tear slipped, and her lips began to quiver as she got emotional.

"We'll go tomorrow," Dolla said to comfort her. He wanted her angry, not sad, so he scooped her up and planted some kisses on her face.

"The food gonna get cold," she warned since she was getting hot. Dolla nodded his head toward the microwave and walked her over to the bed. The young couple made love like a couple of young people in love. The food would have to wait.

****

"Let's go out, check out the city," Dolla suggested after they awoke from a nap. Three rounds of sex, followed by dinner put them to sleep like a baby in a car seat on the highway.

"Uh-uh, I'm good," she moaned and flipped over in the bed. A smirk spread on his face knowing he dicked her down so well, she couldn't get back up.

"Well, I'm going for a ride," he said and rolled out of bed. He slipped under the shower to wash away the residue left behind from her juice box.

Dolla was a goon at heart but allowed his woman to buy some fancy clothes she wanted to see him in. He pulled on a pair of the designer jeans and loafers and matched them with a tasteful button-down shirt.

"Eh," he chuckled at his well dressed reflection in the mirror. He looked like one of those fancy dudes he liked to rob, but he liked the look on him.

He snuck a kiss on Dyme's cheek, then moved up and placed another on the cheeks on her face. His mission was to learn his surroundings, so he turned the GPS off and felt his way around. They arrived here on 75 North, so he reversed course and pulled onto 75 South.

Once he reached downtown Atlanta, he navigated the surface streets. The scenery went from swank to dank when he reached MLK Boulevard. He shook his head when he realized that if a tourist to any city in any state wanted to buy weed, crack, or pussy, all they had to do was find MLK. He was pretty sure this wasn't the dream the reverend had.

"Humph?" Dolla wondered when he drove past a well-lit building with a parking lot packed with luxury cars. He had to pull a U-turn to come around for a closer look. The sign above read "Dimes," so he pulled in to check out the scenery.

"Twenty dollars!" a pretty, yet ratchet hostess demanded and stuck her palm out the window. Dolla was slow moving, so she left her news feed long enough to look up at him. Her face changed when she saw the new face. One look told her the pretty thug wasn't from around here. "Heyyy"

"Um, hey?" he repeated. He would soon get used to the down south version of "sup, yo?" He reached into his pocket and pulled out a large roll of cash. "Twenty?"

"Uh-huh, go on in!" she smiled, blushed, and batted her eyes. He nodded his thanks and stepped inside.

Dolla stopped dead in his tracks when he reached the bowels of the establishment. He squinted his eyes to decipher the smells rushing toward him. This was a strip club, so he quickly recognized pussy and baby oil. Then perfume, cologne, alcohol, weed, and tobacco, but through it all, he smelled cash. Lots and lots of cash.

Cash rained from several sources throughout the club. One dude actually had a gun that spit cash out the end. It was a virtual gold mine or mint. He knew right then he was going to rob the place. He followed his nose and ended up at a velvet rope that separated regular people from very important people.

"A hunnid for VIP section, my nigga," a large bouncer boomed down at him. Dolla almost laughed at him as he went back into his pocket.

"All I got is a hundred," he said deliberately to correct him as well as show him he wasn't intimidated. He stepped aside, and Dolla entered. All the booths were loaded with dudes who were loaded.

One dude wore so many diamonds that his whole booth twinkled, twinkled like little stars. He flicked dollars in the air toward two dancers he barely even looked at. A scan of the dimly lit club showed several more dudes flossing and spending.

Nah, I ain't robbing the club. I'm robbing all y'all niggas, he thought and nodded.

"You tryin'a get a dance, handsome?" a voice asked, disturbing his thoughts.

"Huh?" Dolla asked as he looked at the woman standing over him. She leaned her crotch toward him like a good salesman does when trying to sell something. He couldn't tell if she was good looking or not, because she had quite a few aftermarket parts. God is perfect and would not have put her together like that. Her breasts, lips, and ass were all spare parts and extras.

"Dance? Strip club? I'm a stripper," she smiled and showed a diamond-laced front tooth. He scanned her from head to camel toe to toes and back to the camel toe.

"Sure. Why not?" he shrugged.

"Twenty dollars a song," she said and unhooked her bra. The custom-made titties didn't budge when she did.

"Hope the DJ ain't playing the mixed tape," he laughed and scanned the room once more. The dancer looked back and saw he wasn't paying her much attention. Either way, he was paying her, so she kept shaking what the doctor gave her.

"Instead of paying by the song, why not just give me a grand after we close and I'll show you how the South was won," she offered with everything that came along with it.

"Some other time, maybe," he said after the song. He paid for the next song and stood to leave. He left but planned to return. Soon. And he was bringing Dyme back next time.

****

"Guess we can go shopping now," Dolla gave in after Dyme put it on him real, real good. He had been a little stubborn after her cousin made off with their money. After all, April stole from them, not just him.

"I know that's right," she giggled since she knew she just put it on him. She thought she knew the power of the pussy, but she had no clue just how powerful it was. Many men had been corrupted or ruined from the pursuit of pussy.

They dressed and set out to the nearest mall in search of much-needed clothing. Dolla was straight since his stuff hadn't been in Dyme's closet. If so, April would have run off with it too. The grimy broad even scooped up the loose change she found so she wouldn't leave her cousin anything. It was payback for being prettier, smarter, and cleaner than her.

They ended up in the huge mall and took in all the strange sounds and sights. Mainly the people.

"We ain't in New York no more," Dolla remarked as they took in the dress and talk of the natives.

"Why they won't finish they words? Why they ta' li' thi'?" Dyme frowned as if it irritated her, then cracked up as she imitated them.

Luckily for Dolla, she wasn't one of those perpetually angry women and was still able to laugh, despite the rough hand that others dealt her. She could be blamed for the way she played some of those hands too, though. Dolla reminded her that there was much more to life than what was directly in front of her.

"I'on know. They just talk funny down here, yo. Naw'mean?" he replied like New Yorkers don't speak funny themselves.

"Word up, yo," she said and dipped into a store. She racked up on jeans and designer tees, while Dolla browsed through the women's negligees.

"Can I help you?" a salesclerk asked so seductively, Dyme snapped her head from across the room. Dolla stifled a laugh when she came rushing over.

"Naw, he 'ont need no help, or herpes, or whatever else you got!" she said as she rushed over. "I can smell the yeast coming out your shit now!"

"Dyme, get help, ma," Dolla cracked up. He laughed so hard and so loud, Dyme had to repeat her question.

"I said, what you doing over here anyway? Dang freak!" she laughed. He was an old-fashioned T-shirt-and-panties type of dude, so she didn't understand his sudden interest in the fancy stuff. She was about to find out, though.

"Oh, nothing. Just grab a few things just in case. You never know. You know?"

"Mmm," she said and side-eyed him skeptically. She grabbed a few boy shorts and bra sets and put them with the rest.

"Don't forget something for the club. We going out tonight!" he reminded.

"That's right. Chaos!" she smiled wickedly. She planned to bring some chaos to April's life when they caught up with her.

****

"Yeah, y'all broke bishes. This is how rich bishes stunt!" April said as she went live on her IG.

"This chick wearing my shit, and it don't even fit her!" Dyme moaned as she watched the feed. April didn't even bother to block

151

her so she could stunt on her. She wanted to cry seeing her fancy clothes stretched beyond capacity.

"Man, she done spent all our little bread!" Dolla said when he saw the big bag of fluffy buds on the glass table. The weed was a hundred dollars for a quarter ounce, and the apartment ran a grand a month. April paid her rent up and furnished the joint with the stolen money. She wasn't worried about a job for monthly bills since she had a vagina for that.

She would just sling that salty pussy far and wide like a boomerang and let it bring in some money. That was her plans for the night at the club. Meet some big ballers and shot callers to help pay the bills. She went live to show off for the rest of the G.M.G.s back at home, but one M.D.C. was watching right there in Georgia. Dyme was one Mad, Dangerous Chick.

"A bitch went from the block in Brooklyn to the good life!" April said on the video as she scanned her surroundings.

"Dummy!" Dyme announced when the sign of her apartment complex came into view. She snatched Dolla's phone to check it so that she didn't have to cut the live feed.

"Yo!" Dolla protested at the rude interruption, especially since his gallery was open to his favorite pics.

"Bruh, you looking at pictures of pussy? Wait, that's mine!" she laughed, then pulled up the complex. "Concept 21, Norcross."

"Got her?" he asked hopefully. He knew the money was lost the second she ran off with it. All that was left was revenge, and he wanted all of it.

"I got her!" she said as the Google earth popped on the screen. She had the whole layout to the whole complex except her apartment number.

"Guess we still going to the club, huh?" he asked.

"Yeah, but we can't go in. She gon' take flight if she see us," she sighed.

"We'll just lay on her in the parking lot then. We can check out the club some other time. I got another spot we can go . . ." he said, putting her on their next move.

****

April arrived by Uber but knew how she was getting home when she saw the parking lot to the club. It was loaded with fully loaded luxury cars. She was hoping for the owner of one of the several Bentleys out front but would settle for a Benz if push came to shove. She was still balling off Dolla and Dyme's dimes, so she bypassed the line and used the VIP entrance. She knew good and well the only time she came close to being a VIP is when she got burned and had a very, infected pussy.

These ATL dudes didn't know any better, and she was new pussy. New pussy has a new car smell the first time you get it. Now, April had a new city of dudes to get run through.

"Dang, shorty," a gold-toothed player said and reached for her arm as she neared to the bar. "Let me buy you a drank."

"Naw, cuz, you gonna want me to sit here while I drink it," she declined. There was too much money in the club to get sidetracked by a drink.

"Fuck you, then, ole lame-ass, fuck-ass, bitch-ass . . ." the man spat as she walked away. Atlanta people sure know how to curse you out. April wasn't shit, but you couldn't tell from the naked eye. She turned heads as she strolled through the club. She spotted her target for the night and headed his way. He was dressed to impress in silk, diamonds, and platinum and was about to get some pussy for it.

"Whoa, li'l mama!" he said when she sashayed by. He too reached for her wrist but didn't get dissed.

"Excuse you?" April said minus the venom as she turned like she was seeing him for the first time. Little did he know, she calculated his net worth just by what he was wearing. He had two lumps in his pants, so she hoped one was cash and the other one dick because she wanted some of both.

"My bad, shorty! I'on mean no harm. My name is Nino, but you can call me Nino," he greeted.

"Yes!" she cheered because a name like Nino explained one of the lumps. He removed a large roll of cash from the other and paid for the bottle of bubbles that just arrived.

"My name is Dyme," April said. Why not use her name too since she had Dyme's clothes on her body and Dyme's money in her purse. Only thing she didn't have was Dyme's pussy in Dyme's panties she was wearing.

"Well, Dyme, what you say we get out of here?" Nino said since he knew a freak when he saw one when he saw how she eyed the money. The couple of grand she salivated over was just play dough, so he didn't mind using it to play in some pussy.

"I say hell yeah," she said and stood. He grabbed the bottle of champagne for the road and led her outside.

"She just came out," Dolla announced and regretted it instantly. Dyme abandoned the blow job she was giving so she could get a look too.

"Grrrr," Dyme growled when she saw her cousin wearing her outfit that didn't fit. It was supposed to be tight, just not *that* tight. April was a whole size bigger and packed in the clothing like a sausage.

"You picked the wrong trick, homie," Dolla said to Nino who couldn't hear him. Dude was about to be a casualty of war and didn't even know it.

"Who you stay with?" Nino asked since he couldn't bring her to his house.

"I stay by myself!" April said with the pride that should be reserved for chicks who stayed by themselves because they worked hard or smart and paid their own bills. Not for them who stole from their family and left them high and dry. She gave the address which he entered into the GPS.

Nino tried her up and whipped out his dick for the ride. He got some expert head as he followed the turn-by-turn directions to her complex. Sucking dick in the whip can actually work for or against a chick. It can be an appetizer to show what's to come when they reach their destination . . . or sometimes not.

"Shit!" Nino grunted and filled her mouth with baby Ninos just as they reached her complex. The night was young, and he was a freak, so he decided to see what else he could get into.

"Here we are," she said with come on her breath and went right back to chewing her gum.

"I'ma have to take a rain check. Here," he said and handed her half the cash and the half bottle of champagne.

"*That's* what's up," April agreed because she was up almost a grand already. Plus, the night was young, and she too was a freak, so she planned to head back out as well.

April rushed upstairs to put her cash up and call for another car. She left her door ajar since she was coming right back but heard it close from her room.

"Came back for some of this pussy, huh?" she smiled as she came back out. The smile disappeared in an instant when she saw a nine-millimeter instead of Nino.

"I wouldn't touch that funk box if it was the last pussy on the planet," Dolla growled.

"Yes, you would, my nigga. Stop fronting," April laughed. She knew this could go either way, so either way, she wasn't scared.

"Where my money at, April?" Dyme asked rather calmly. Her cousin knew then which way it would go. Only killers are that calm. She never knew her little cousin to be a killer, but the demeanor was unmistakable.

"Gon', yo. I spent that shit," she said, waving her hands around to show her purchases. "Now, it's plenty bread down this bitch. I know how y'all get down. We can—"

No one knew what was coming next because Dolla swung the gun so hard, it broke her jaw. Dyme rushed over, grabbed the designer scarf around her neck, and pulled it tight. She pulled so hard that the silk burned her hands. She pulled so hard, April forgot about the pain of her broken jaw. She let out a gasp that would have to go down as her last words. She and Dolla locked eyes while Dyme squeezed. He saw the flicker of life just before the lights went out.

"She ain't in there no more," Dolla told Dyme, but she kept on squeezing. He had to come over and pry the scarf from her hands. "She gone, yo."

"Bitch!" Dyme said and stopped just short of spitting in her lifeless face. That would have left DNA that would tie her to a murder scene.

"Find whatever cash we can find and get your clothes!" Dolla said as he collected the bag of weed off the table.

"She can keep them clothes," Dyme frowned. She found the money April just sucked out of Nino's dick, and they fled the apartment complex.

"Let's make a stop before we go back to the room," Dolla said. It wasn't a question, so Dyme sat back for the ride. She felt nothing after just killing her kin since she deserved it.

****

"What is this place?" Dyme frowned when Dolla pulled into the parking lot.

"What's the sign say?" he said and braced himself for the pop that always came when he answered a question with a question.

"Boy!" came the pop. "I can read, but what this got to do with us?"

Dolla didn't reply; instead, he sat back and let her figure it out on her own. She looked at the packed parking lot and nodded. Her pretty head kept nodding when a Lamborghini pulled up to the valet. A man got out dripping gold and diamonds and tipped the attendant from a large roll of cash before he stepped inside. She watched the valet pull the four hundred thousand-dollar car into a separate area full of other exotic cars.

"Yo, this place is a fucking gold mine, yo!" she gushed. "Only what's our way in here? Just run in, guns blazing and . . . nah. So how do we get to the money?"

"Well, it is a strip club. I mean, if it was a male joint I would dance, but it's a gentlemen's club, so . . ." he said and let her finish that part too.

"Oh boy!" Dyme sighed when she filled in the blanks. She blew her breath again and followed him inside.

****

"Hey there, handsome," Diamond greeted Dolla when he returned with Dyme.

"Sup, ma?" he replied and scanned the area. Meanwhile, Diamond was busy scanning Dyme from head to toe. If she had a dick, it would have been hard.

"Who dis?" she asked curiously.

"My girl, Dy—" he started, but she jumped in to finish.

"Meoshi!" Dyme cut in before he gave her real name. Besides, she always wanted to be a Meoshi, and now she was.

"Well, hey, Meoshi. Can you dance?" she asked into the cleavage poking out the top of her shirt.

"Can I! Y'all do the Bruck up down here?" she asked, but her brain caught up, and she realized that's not what she meant. "Dance, dance? No. I don't have the body for all that."

"Say what? Girl, stand up!" Diamond demanded. Dyme did, and she checked her out, then spun her around to look at her ass. Dolla was almost jealous at the way she was eyeing his woman. He realized he would have to get used to it for Dyme to dance in the club. She would have to dance for them to get the inside track on all the ballers who frequented the place. "Chile, you fine as hell!"

"You think so?" Dyme giggled and cooed, almost making Dolla bust out laughing at her act.

"Girl, you gon' make a band a night easy just working the pole and table dances. Even more if you get up in VIP. Even more if . . ." Diamond was saying but caught herself before telling her about all the money to be made turning tricks with customers since she was with her man.

"Okay," Dyme giggled again and batted her eyes. Dolla was impressed by her acting skills.

"Come on. I'm finna take you up to meet Ant. He the owner," she said and looked to Dolla. He gave his permission with a nod and off they went.

"Who?" Ant yelled from behind his desk. Diamond didn't respond since she didn't have much respect for the man. Instead, she opened the door and walked in.

"Ant, this Meoshi. She finna dance here," she practically demanded.

"You know she gotta audition!" he said, blinking in Dyme's stunning beauty

She was nothing like nothing he'd ever seen before. He got rock hard in an instance at the prospect of auditioning her. That meant free pussy for him since he couldn't care if a girl could dance or not. He was more concerned with what that mouth do.

"Naw, she ain't here for all that! Plus, her man downstairs right now. You know ain't nothing like her in here, so quit playing!" she demanded like it was her club. She was a star, so he let her have her way. For now, because he was gonna get to Miss Meoshi one way or another.

With that, they were in.

****

Dolla and Dyme knew this club was the ticket to their mil ticket. Their million-dollar goal, so they could go wherever and do whatever they liked. Neither had an invention or patent, so they planned to steal it.

They knew these dope boys were sitting on plenty of cash to donate to their cause. They started from zero and didn't plan to stop until they reached a million.

The "Dolla and Dyme get rich or die trying fund," but who was first?

"Is that him?" Dolla asked, squinting through the dimly lit club. The ice on the target's neck illuminated him, putting him on Dolla's radar from all the way across the room. The dancer in front of him looked in the direction he was looking while still popping her caramel ass cheeks in his face.

"He shole look like the one," his equally ambitious partner Dyme said, licking her lips at the tasty lick in front of them. A good lick has a taste, and it's sweet. After wearing a three-thousand-dollar designer outfit and another ten around his neck, they were going to need a shot of insulin after this one. "It sure looks like him."

The mark must have wanted to get robbed when he pulled out a wad of cash and made it rain on the two dancers dancing in front of him. It was mainly ones and fives, but he still wouldn't have been doing it if he weren't caked the fuck up. He could be charged as an accessory to his own robbery for flossing so hard. His Instagram post could be used against him in a court of law or holding court in the street.

"Yeah, that's him, daddy," she purred like she does when her kitty is stroked. He wasn't supposed to be touching it since the club had a no-touching policy, but it was his pussy, so he would touch it when and where he wanted. "See, if I bust a nut on your hand, you gon' swear I did you wrong."

"You do, and I'm gonna bend you over this table and give you the business. *All* of it!" he warned and lolled his head back in laughter. His bright smile contrasted brilliantly against his dark skin and turned heads. The same heads quickly turned back away since Dyme was quick to beat a bitch up over her man. He felt the same way and stopped fondling her when some locals watched him play in her pussy from a few tables over. He used the liquid she leaked to smooth the thick waves on his head since it worked better than Murray's.

"I'm down," she dared and would have done it if he wanted. Dolla was the first man to treat her right, so she was down for whatever he wanted. What he wanted now was to relieve all the city's clowns of their money.

What set Dyme apart from most of the highly made up strippers was she was naturally pretty. She was pretty but as rough as a dirt road.

Her round face needed little embellishments to turn heads. A little lip gloss on the thick lips beat all the beat faces in the club. She further drove the value of her vagina up by not tricking with the ballers. Now, they chunked bands at her to get her home and fuck. She accepted a few times, but they were the ones who got fucked. Fucked out of their money, drugs, and jewels, that is. Not one lived to tell about it.

"Nah, can't lose sight of buddy. Sic him," he laughed and sent her on her way with a slap on her ass. The low-budget ballers laughed at the display and earned an angry scowl from Dolla.

He knew they were a problem when they kept staring at them. In his native Brooklyn, New York, eye contact which was considered a challenge. Staring could get you killed in the blink of an eye. An Atlanta, Georgia, stare was slightly slower, so it took two blinks. They proved his point when one of them reached for Dyme as she walked by. He could hear the music from The Omen playing in his head when dude grabbed her wrist.

"Let us get a dance!" the spokesman insisted and tried to pull her close. She used a martial arts move and twisted herself out of his grip. Dolla knew his girl could handle it but stood just in case. He didn't bring a gun in but knew how to use a beer bottle as a club and knife, if need be.

"Unhand me, nigga!" she fussed as she came free. She saw Dolla rise and knew she had seconds to defuse the situation before he lost his mind and blew the lick. "First of all, if all y'all malt liquor-drinking niggas need one bitch for a table dance, you can't afford me!"

"Ooh!" his partners jeered, trying to get him to turn up. These were the type of broke goons who got into some shit everywhere they went. They got into more fights than into a woman, so the strip club was as close as they came to some pussy. Dyme beat her feet and put some distance between them before security or Dolla intervened. Security would have evicted their asses from the club. Dolla would have evicted their souls from their bodies.

"Fuck you looking at?" the spokesman dared when he saw Dolla looking their way.

"My bad, shorty," he said like a local and raised his hands in surrender. This wasn't the time or place for confrontation, so he put it in reverse. He summoned a waitress with his hand and sent them a round of drinks on him. It was the least he could do for the condemned men. They didn't know it yet, but their last meal was their last meal.

"Damn! Who the fuck is that bitch?" Po-boy asked the stripper working in front of him when Dyme sashayed through the VIP section. Her round ass did its little dance as she walked without even trying. She had a naturally nasty walk that she couldn't turn off if she wanted to. It could turn up, down a little, but never off.

Po-boy got his name as a skinny child but never changed it even he got his weight. His financial weight, that is, because the six-footer was still rail thin with large eyes that made him look like a cartoon character. He really was poor coming up and couldn't afford to keep a chick. He made up for it now by tricking almost every night.

"Her name is Meoshi, but she ain't gon' fuck," Diamond replied and shook her ass a little harder. She couldn't stand Dyme's pretty ass since she had to fuck and suck these salty dicks to compete with what the pretty girl could make just from dancing. She had to wear so much makeup and wigs to fake being pretty that she resembled a transvestite. A few guys actually thought she was a dude when they took her home, only to be disappointed she was really a girl in boy shorts and not a boy. This was Atlanta, after all.

"All bitches fuck if the price right! Call her over here," he said and shoved some cash at Diamond to send her on her way.

"Bitch-ass nigga," she fussed as she went to carry out her mission. She stepped back into her boy shorts and rushed to catch up. "Yo, Dyme. That nigga with the ice want you. We can take this nigga to the motel and work a band outta his ass!"

"We?" Dyme laughed at the attempt to be down. The veteran stripper made it known she wanted a taste when Dyme first started working here. Either she or the owner Ant got to sample all the products. All except Dyme, that is.

"I'm saying, though. You know these trick niggas be wantin' to see some freaky shit! They spend more money to see two gals," she explained. She and Ant had a standing bet to see who fucked her first, so she wouldn't take no for an answer.

"Hell naw," she said since the regular no didn't get it. She looked over at Po-boy and scrunched her face up like he was ugly, then turned away. The snub drove her stock even higher.

"Told you she be on that bullshit. Shit, I'll grab any other one of these hoes to come with us. We'll freak yo' skinny ass out!" Diamond dared and lolled out her tongue to show off her well-used tongue ring. It touched as much pussy as dicks since she went both ways and sideways. She was a true trisexual who would try almost anything sexual.

"Her!" Po-boy cheered, pointing at Desire. She was his first choice until Dyme sauntered by. He may not have gotten her tonight but vowed he had to have her.

Dyme threw up one finger toward her man as she entered the dressing room. He understood it to mean "one minute" as she dressed in her street clothes. He hoped it didn't take much longer since the club was closing, and he had one last thing to do before they retired for the night.

"You ready?" Dyme asked as if it were she who had been waiting on him. She looked just as sexy in the short skirt as she did in stripper clothes.

"Yeah, come on!" he urged and rushed her toward the exit. He spotted who he was looking for just as they pulled from the parking lot. Dyme saw them too and smiled. People always talk about the murder but not the fuck shit that prompted it. These dudes were disrespectful and were about to get disrespected in the worst way.

"You drive!" Dolla said and went to retrieve the long bag from the trunk. He came around to the passenger seat, but Dyme had beat him to it. He could only shake his head and handed her the bag. "Here."

Dolla came back around and jumped behind the wheel. She pointed left in the direction of their prey, and he pulled out after them. Meanwhile, she got the grill ready for the cookout.

He smiled at the sexy sound of her racking a round into the AR-15 submachine gun. It had a modified stock that let it rip almost fully automatic. It could empty the 100-round clip in seconds. She removed the safety and waited on her shot to take shots.

"We'll catch 'em on Griffin Street," he said as they bent a corner. She rolled down her window as he closed the distance between them. They made it easy when the driver pulled to a sudden stop when he saw a crack addict called Rabbit waving at cars. Her head game was the stuff of legend. She could make quick work of the four dicks in four minutes and get another blast.

"Suck a nigga dick or something," the driver proposed. It was his car which meant he had first on her tongue. Rabbit opened her mouth to name her price until she saw Dyme rolled out the passenger window and up the rifle. The men all turned to see whatever made her eyes go wide as a hit of the city's finest dope. None of them liked what they saw.

"Oh—" would be the last words the driver got to utter in this life before she blasted him into the next. The shit that was to follow would have to wait until he got to hell.

The gun looked more like a flamethrower as it threw round after round into the car. The men in the back tried to duck behind the door, but the heavy 5.56 rounds didn't give a fuck about a car door. They ripped through it, and them, and out the other side. The front passenger made a break for it but didn't get far. He only made it a few feet before a shot to his back knocked a lung out of his chest. She gunned Rabbit down as an afterthought so she could never testify.

"Yo, that shit was dope!" Dolla said as he pulled from the curb. He mashed the gas and put some distance between them and the murder scene. "That shit made my dick hard!"

"Nuh-uh!" Dyme dared and reached for his crotch. Sure enough, it was as hard as a scorned woman's heart. She knew just what to do with a hard dick and leaned in to do it.

"Shit," Dolla said as her hot mouth welcomed him inside. Her slow stroke, kiss, lick, suck, had him fucked up, and he knew they wouldn't make it good.

He reached under her skirt and played and played in her puddle, and they both knew they wouldn't make it to their suburban hideaway. Dyme giggled when he snatched the car to a dark street. He pulled her on top of him and slid her thong aside. She shoved her whole tongue into his mouth as he wriggled himself inside of her.

"Shit!" she cussed from the pain his pleasure always brought. She decided to make him feel it, then took, and bit his bottom lip.

"Grrr," he growled from the taste of blood in his mouth. He palmed the basketball-sized cheeks and bounced them up and down on his dick. The smell of fresh gunpowder mixed with the sounds of her splashing juice box drove them both wild.

"Mm, that's it. Get it," she urged even though he was hurting her. His guttural grunts signaled the end was near. She gripped the headrest and threw her hips into overdrive.

Dolla's whole body seized and shivered when he began sending a torrent of semen into her. He leaned up and matched her kisses until the spasms of orgasms subsided.

"Whew!" he exclaimed when his breathing returned to normal. He patted her ass signaling her to get up. She did and fell over into the passenger seat. His dick was still too hard to put up, so he drove off with it still out.

"You know I ain't done, right?" she said wickedly.

"I'll pull over again if you want," he dared, but she declined.

"Nah, I need some space," she said and leaned back for the ride. She rode him backward once they got back to the room.

They made love until the crack of dawn and then finally got some rest. They were going to need their strength for their next lick.

Catching licks is a lot like eating pussy. You do it once, and you'll do it again.

ALL HAIL THE

STREET KINGS

A SHORT STORY BY

HOOD CHRONICLES

All Hail the Street Kings

Written by
Hood Chronicles

All Hail the Street Kings

by

Hood Chronicles

All Hail the Street Kings is my submission for your Street Tales anthology. It's centered on the vicious Blake family in Macon, Georgia. Dealing in drugs, prostitution, and every facet of the criminal underworld, the Blakes have a no-tolerance policy for disrespect. When Jamar aka Hotspitta attempts to leave the family behind for hip-hop stardom, he pays the ultimate price. The leading character, Trevonte, then migrates from Atlanta to avenge his cousin's horrific death. In doing so, his plans lead him to infiltrate the Blake organization and destroy them from within. I hope this story is acceptable and to your liking.

Sincerely,

Hood Chronicles

The Blake
Brothers

1

"You already know what it is! Drink 'til you throw up in this bitch," Jamar exclaimed, causing a stampede at the bar.

Geronimo and his brother sat in the back of the jam-packed venue shaking their heads in disgust. Jamar had taken notice of his one-time business associates, yet attempted to pay them no mind. He was well aware of what they were in the building for and was determined not to let them ruin his wonderful event. After all, everyone in the club was there to party hard and commemorate a dream come true. Not just anybody's dream, but Jamar's dream of finally hitting the majors!

Nothing more than a repeat offender, convicted felon, and drug pusher, Jamar was known to the streets of Macon, Georgia, as a menace without a cause. That is . . . until Geronimo brought him into the family and gave him purpose. Now, everybody in MacTown was well aware of the Blake family tree. There was not one branch on that tree that you wanted to cross.

The Blake family had their hands in every illegal activity taking place in every single hood in Macon. Eerie stories of workers committing suicide rather than come up short with the family's money began to circulate through the projects like old Negro fables.

Geronimo and his only brother, Julian, were of a special kind of crazy. The brothers never did *anything* without adding a new meaning to the word OVERKILL. Severing heads, burning bodies, and the like was normal for the two. To make matters worse, they never did anything behind closed doors. All of their brutal and horrific murders were done in broad daylight for public display.

Jamar wasn't a fool. He knew what they were there for, but he turned up his bottle of Cristal and prepared to take the stage. Inking a major deal and signing to one of the hottest record labels in the hip-hop world, Jamar aka Hotspitta was enjoying his local support and throwing a bash to celebrate.

"Without further ado, ladies and gentlemen of the MacTown, I bring to you the man of the hour to perform his smash hit 'Let 'Em Know' . . . our very own . . . Hotspitta!" the club owner Money announced.

With his microphone in hand, Jamar took the stage. The patrons went wild as the music began to play. With his dreadlocks tied back into a bulky ponytail, the six-foot chocolate rapper let the vibe take over as he bounced from left to right.

"Look at this ho-ass nigga," Julian said.

"Don't worry about it. If he thinking a little fame can save him from us, then he got life fucked up," Geronimo added while downing his Hennessey.

"Somebody better let 'em know who they fuckin' wit'. I'm a nigga comin' straight up out that gutta bitch. Glock cocked with them hollows in the chamber. Cross me wrong, then you know I'm gon' pain ya!" Hotspitta chanted to the hypnotic beat of the 808 drums.

Pushing each other from side to side, the partygoers were in a frenzy. Amused by the sight of women twerking and guys throwing up gang signs, Hotspitta knew he had everyone in their own zones. Sweat poured from his head as he went set by set until he had completed all the songs in his catalog.

Once the music stopped, reality returned. Jamar enjoyed the love that everyone showed him but knew that the time had come for him to address a bigger issue in order to let the world know where he stood.

"Check this out . . . Y'all calm down 'cause I got some real shit to say," he began. The crowd began to simmer as Jamar awaited pure silence. "Okay, peep this . . . Every muthafucka in here know my background. In and out of prison since a teen, flooded the streets with the work, fucked half y'all niggas up for being mad that I was fucking half of y'all broads," he teased.

The entire audience burst into laughter. Geronimo and Julian weren't the least bit amused as they moved toward the front of the stage.

"On some real shit, I ain't up here glorifying what I done in these streets, but damn it, I did it! Any lyric you hear me spit, you gon' be able to vouch for a nigga and say, yea, he did that!"

Again, the crowd erupted in a thunderous roar and applause.

At that moment, Jamar saw his two former business partners surface. An evil smirk spread across his lips as he continued. "Yea, it's a lot of muthafuckas out here that don't wanna see a nigga doing good . . . but I say . . . fuck 'em!"

Holding the mic out to the crowd, he smiled at the Blake brothers as the audience exclaimed in unison, "Fuck 'em!"

"No matter what, I got the Mac on my back, and my success is our success. Real niggas never forget where they came from. Y'all enjoy the rest of the night and know that you got a real nigga riding for the city!" he finished while making his way off of the stage.

Ladies swarmed him as he moved through the crowd with two huge bodyguards keeping them at bay.

"Say, bruh, I think you need to holla at us," Geronimo said, stepping in front of Jamar.

His two bodyguards jumped in front of him, immediately shielding their boss from any imminent danger.

"It's all good," Jamar acknowledged as he headed to the VIP section with the brothers and his bodyguards.

Seated in the glass room lounge, Jamar could still view the party people as they continued to dance their night away.

"What's on you boys' minds?" he asked the Blakes.

Julian chuckled before responding. "My brother took you in when you didn't have a pot to piss in or a window to throw that shit out of. Now, you rapping and shit, and the same muthafuckas that put you on, you just want to up and abandon?"

"Last time I checked, the Blake family didn't need nobody. I hustled plenty of work for your family, and now I'm going legit! That's that," Jamar spat defiantly.

Geronimo turned his head to two partygoers positioned directly outside the glass room. With a head nod, the signal had been given. Rising, Geronimo moved toward the corner with his brother.

"Muthafucka," Geronimo spat vehemently, "the Blakes don't *need* anybody, you ungrateful piece of shit!"

At that moment, Jamar and his bodyguards hopped to their feet. Out of the corner of his eye, Jamar saw the two partygoers draw weapons on the VIP section and squeeze.

"Shit!" Jamar yelled.

The bullets came at a rapid speed—only to be halted by bulletproof glass. After unloading their clips, the shooters were dumbfounded as everyone raced to the exits. A stampede of frightened patrons rushed out, trampling over one another.

Drawing his weapon, one bodyguard went for the door while the other covered Jamar. Pulling his firearm, Geronimo sent a hollow tip into the back of the bodyguard's head. He instantly collapsed at the door. Unleashing his twin Glocks, the other bodyguard rolled over and fired on Geronimo who quickly took cover.

Attempting to retrieve his weapon, Julian was a tad bit too slow. Jamar charged toward his enemy and tackled him through the frigid bullet-riddled glass. As they tussled on the dance floor, Jamar knew his best option was to get lost in the crowd. He leapt to his feet while Julian fired at any and everybody. Narrowly escaping outside, Jamar followed a female to her vehicle and jumped inside.

"Thank you," he said, looking out at Geronimo and Julian as they angrily scanned all of the faces in the parking lot.

Jamar ducked his head down as he rode right past the furious brothers. Realizing that it was a lost cause, the Blakes raced to their vehicle where their two shooters were waiting. The quartet spun out of the parking lot, making their way to a junkyard. Confused, the two shooters were instructed to exit the automobile. Doing as they were told, the pair stood eye to eye with the seething brothers.

"You two fucked up in a major-league way tonight. You do know that, right?" Julian questioned, unleashing his .357 Magnum.

"We didn't know the glass was bulletproof," one of the boys uttered.

Geronimo instantly kneed the guy in his crotch and wrapped both of his hands around his neck, attempting to choke the life out of him. The other turned to view the scuffle in tears. Taking the butt of his weapon, Julian began to pistol-whip him as well. Finding themselves bound and gagged, the two boys knew that they would never see their families again.

Geronimo and Julian placed tires around the boys' necks and doused the tires with lighter fluid. The two sobbed uncontrollably as they were forced to await death in one of the most horrific fashions. Striking two matches, the Blakes each set a tire on fire. The dual pain of melting tar scorching their flesh while burning flames engulfed their skulls produced an agony beyond belief.

As they headed back to their car, the brothers realized that they had worked up an appetite.

"I'm feeling like a chili cheese pup. What about you?" Julian asked.

"Krystal's it is," Geronimo agreed while pulling away from the burning bodies.

Fuck the Blakes!

2

"Good morning, ladies and gentlemen! I wanna thank you for waking up with us and tuning in to 97.5 radio! Today, we have a special guest. The MacTown's very own Hotspitta!" the radio host announced while he sat comfortably over his switchboard.

Directly across from him, Jamar sat with a scowl on his face and a visible expression of anger in his red pupils.

"What's good, world?" he greeted the listeners.

"Okay, let's hop right into this interview because I been watching your come-up for a long time and got nothing but respect for the real hustlers."

"Right . . . right," Jamar agreed.

"Let the people know your current situation, Hotspitta, and what's the word with this new deal?"

Stroking his chin, Jamar leaned over into his microphone, and for the first time, a smile spread across his face. *"God is good, man. A few reps from Universal sat in on a couple of my stage performances and saw how I moved the crowd. One of them gave me their card, and when I read the imprint, I was like, yea, right, but I called, and they sent me a first-class ticket to their New York office. You know I'm outta the hood, so all that Grey Poupon on a jet and limos wasn't something I was used to,"* Jamar admitted.

Laughter rang throughout the studio.

"I know that's right," the cohost Lady Shyne said, smiling flirtatiously at the guest.

Jamar caught her seductive gesture and smirked before continuing. *"Anyway, I got up in there, and I couldn't clear the metal detectors 'cause I had my .40 on me. They was like, 'Yo, you don't need that up in here,' and I'm like, 'Hell, you can get killed anywhere, so I need my pistol everywhere!'"*

"Noooo, you took your artillery to the meet with label execs?" The host shook his head in disbelief. *"Now, that is a comical story to share later on after you've made history. I see it coming."*

Jamar nodded his head in agreement. *"I appreciate that because I most certainly am trying to deliver."*

"Okay, Mr. Hotspitta, on behalf of the ladies, inquiring minds wanna know if you are on the market," Lady Shyne questioned.

After a quick smile and flushed cheeks, he answered, *"Actually, I'm seeing somebody and think this chick might be the winner. I mean, she good people, with curves for days, and a heart as big as her backside,"* he teased.

An inviting smile spread across Lady Shyne's lips as she shook her head in disbelief.

"On that note, let's go to a quick break, play a few of Hotspitta's classics, then take a few calls on 97.5!" the host said as the On Air sign went dark. "Excuse me, you two. I have to make a quick call. Hotspitta, you're doing great. It's a pleasure to have you, brother."

"No doubt! It's a pleasure being here," Jamar said, accepting the host's gracious handshake.

Once the pair were alone, Lady Shyne spoke. "Oh, I got a heart as big as my backside, huh, nigga?"

Jamar burst into laughter. Balling up a napkin and throwing it at him, she chuckled.

"You know I gots nothing but love for you, baby." He smiled.

"You better! We linking up later still?"

"You making that mac and cheese a nigga be fiending for, right?"

She blushed. "I got you, boo."

The couple had secretly been unofficially an item for the last three months. Being celebrity figures, they both thought it best to keep their relationship status hush until they were fully aware that what they shared was real. Love filled their hearts when it came to each other. Unfamiliar with such intense emotion, Jamar was internally confused, which kept him silent. Scarred from too many in her past, Lady Shyne remained quiet until she was assured that he was nothing like the rest.

As the host returned with a Brisk ice tea in hand, Jamar, as well as Lady Shyne, switched back into business mode. The On Air light came on, and so did everyone's microphones.

"All right, all right, all right! We are back in the house with our crazy, cool guest, Mr. Hotspitta, and it's time to allow some callers to holla at the man as promised. Caller, you're on the air. What's your name, and where are you calling from?"

"What up, cuz? This Travonte up in Atlanta."

Hearing his younger cousin's voice made Jamar instantly light up like a Christmas tree. Jamar recalled the last time he got out. Travonte put three stacks in his hands to help him get back on his feet. Ever since the two were kids, they had much love for each other. After Travonte's mother came into a better job situation, she took herself and little Travonte to Georgia's capitol. Both being only children without siblings, they viewed each other as brothers and always maintained a close kinship.

Travonte was making a name for himself in the streets of Atlanta. He caught his first murder case at twelve on his mother's boyfriend. Finding the man choking his mom on the kitchen floor, little Travonte reached for a skillet and caved the man's head in.

While spending a year in a detention center, he made alliances with his best friend, Spud. Spud was from Bankhead, and his uncle had a sweet connect when it came to narcotics. Once the detention center was behind the boys, they both went to work for Spuds's uncle, Mr. Lewis. The boys learned quickly how to survive against all the odds . . . MURDER!

"Man, what you got going on? We gotta link up!" Jamar replied enthusiastically.

"Hey, I'm all for it! All you gotta do is say when, and I'm on it," Travonte assured between puffs of Kush.

"Sound like you over there on one, bruh," the host teased.

"Yea, I stay on one, but check it; I gotta bounce 'cause these folks pulling road blocks. Holla at me, cuz. I'm proud of you!"

"Most definitely, cuzzo!" Jamar exclaimed.

"That's love," Lady Shyne said. *"Next caller, you're on!"*

"Hotspitta?" the feminine voice said.

"Yea, you on. How you doing this morning, baby?"

"Oh my God! I can't believe I'm speaking with you!"

The whole morning crew had to cover their ears as the woman screamed.

Jamar laughed. *"Hey, I appreciate the love, little mama, but I need my eardrums."*

"Oh, I'm sorry! I just love your music. When are you coming to Savannah?"

"I actually have a show lined up there in about three weeks, so be ready, baby girl."

"I will be!"

"Thanks for calling in," the host said. *"Now, let's take another caller. Hello, you're on . . ."*

As soon as the caller spoke, the entire mood went somber. *"Yea, this G from the Mac. Yea, I'm right here, homie, and I wanna know how you made it outta that club the other night."*

Jamar recognized Geronimo's voice clearly, and he grew angry. He was preparing to answer his question when the host started speaking.

"Hey, man, that's a topic we choose not to touch on, so thanks for calling in, but we gotta move along."

"Nigga, you better not go to no more callers before he answer this Blake's question!" Geronimo spat.

Lady Shyne, as well as the host, realized that they were speaking with Geronimo. Everybody knew that the Blakes felt some type of way about Jamar distancing himself from their murderous family ties.

"No, I will answer G, 'cause it do need to be addressed. I made it out 'cause the Blake family so weak they hiring little boys to do a man's job," Jamar retorted.

Letting out a hearty laugh, Geronimo spoke. *"Are you implying that my family had a hand in that? Little brother, we've always had nothing but love for you."*

"Listen, you may have a few killers on the payroll, but I'm hands-on, and I can get it done myself. Fuck the Blake family!" he snapped.

Geronimo's reply was calm and low as he continued. *"That must've been the hardest statement to ever come out of a coward's mouth, but I salute you for being courageous enough to make it. Sweet dreams, rap star."*

The studio was completely silent as Geronimo's line went dead.

"All right, we gotta pay the bills and take a commercial break," the host stated, *"but stay tuned for more of your hottest hip-hop music!"*

As soon as the On Air sign went dark, the host and cohost swarmed Jamar with concern.

"I really don't think that was a wise move. Don't get me wrong, I know you are a grown man and all, but you're a public figure now. These guys can pretty much track your every move," the host said.

Jamar pushed away from the desk, stood tall, and repeated himself. "Like I just said, fuck the Blakes! Don't no nigga think he gonna run my life. I could give less than two fucks how them bitch-ass niggas feel about me. I'm self-made. So again, fuck them clowns!"

Lady Shyne followed her secret lover out into the hallway as he stormed out. "Baby . . . Baby!" she exclaimed, grabbing hold of his wrist.

Pausing, Jamar turned to face his woman. Fear of the entire situation could be read in his eyes. Sweat beads began to form on his forehead. He could barely look her in her eyes. He began pacing back and forth as he quickly realized the gravity of the matter.

"If you don't listen to anybody, take a deep breath and listen to me," she said. Jamar looked deep into her dark brown eyes as she spoke. "Everybody knows that you are not weak. Your street credibility speaks for itself. Right now, you're on the path to greatness, so the devil is working overtime to knock you off track."

Jamar listened attentively in total silence as she continued. "These Blakes are ruthless and feel betrayed simply because you want better for your life. Do not give them the satisfaction of watching you unravel."

For the first time since hearing Geronimo's voice, Jamar formed a smile. He wanted to plant a loving kiss on his woman's lips but opted simply to poke her in the side instead.

"Stop it, silly!" she giggled, batting his hand away. "You know I'm ticklish."

Suddenly, the sounds of automatic gunfire erupting caused everyone to hit the floor. Jamar recognized the sound of heavy artillery. There wasn't a handgun in the crowd. What he heard was the sound of assault rifles.

Within the blink of an eye, it ceased. They raced toward the lobby. The tragic scene they saw was brutal—broken glass, bullet-riddled walls, and blood from several wounded. Standing in the midst of the madness, Lady Shyne broke down into tears. Jamar caught her before she collapsed to her knees.

"It'll be all right, baby; just stay strong," he said, not really even believing his own words.

Tears poured from her eyes as she clung to him as tightly as she could. Security raced downstairs to the scene and sirens were heard approaching in the distance. All of a sudden, a yellow Lamborghini sped up with its doors lifted wide.

"This was just a warning, pussy-ass nigga! It's fuck you, now, homeboy," the driver said before speeding away.

"Oh my God," Lady Shyne said, bursting out into more tears.

"No no no! Baby, you got to pull it together! Right now! It's time to think, not breakdown," Jamar acknowledged, giving her a gentle shake.

Pulling herself together as best she could, she wiped her eyes as police and paramedics flooded the scene.

"It's obvious that I'm not safe here, and neither is anybody that I'm around," he admitted.

"So, what are you saying?"

"I'm saying that I gotta go somewhere and lie low until this shit blows over."

"You used to run with these dudes. There isn't anywhere you can go around here that they can't find you," she reasoned.

"Who said anything about around here?" he replied, retrieving his cell phone. "Obviously, I have to leave the city."

"Who are you calling?"

"My cousin in Atlanta."

"The one who just called in to the show?"

"Yea, that nigga won't hesitate to come help me out. He's one of the few people that have held me down whether times were good, bad, or ugly!" he admitted, as they waited patiently for Travonte to answer.

"Who this?" Travonte's voice came through the line.

"It's me, Jamar."

"What's good, cuz?"

"Man, everything all bad, and I need your help now more than ever," Jamar confessed.

"Lay it on me, homie. You know I got you," Travonte assured him.

"You know I was making plays for the Blakes, right?"

"Yea, I heard you was making moves but weren't too familiar with no Blakes."

"Well, shit went sour when my deal came, and I wanted out of the game. Them niggas tried to kill me at the club the other night and just shot up the fucking lobby of the radio station. I need out of this city ASAP!"

"Fuck! I'm 'bout forty-five minutes away. Pack your shit. As a matter of fact, fuck that shit! Just say your good-byes and bring ya ass, nigga, 'cause I'll get you a whole new wardrobe," Travonte joked.

Lady Shyne could see the relief in her lover's eyes and felt better herself.

"Thanks, cuz. I knew if I could count on anybody, it would be you," Jamar said gratefully.

"You already know it."

"One more thing . . ."

"What's up?"

"If you don't make it in time, I want you to know that Lady Shyne at 97.5 is wifey. Nobody else knows that, and in case this shit don't fly right, I want you to help her grieve me by being that ear to listen. Also," he whispered, turning his back on Lady Shyne, "take care of my daughter."

"Nigga, you gonna be all right! Quit tripping," Travonte replied.

"Bruh, promise me, on some real shit," Jamar insisted.

"You got my word."

Jamar let out a deep breath as a sense of relief washed over him. "Thanks, cuz. I love you like the brother I never had."

Both men's lines went dead. Jamar turned to give Lady Shyne a huge hug.

She was eager to know. "So, baby, what's the word?"

"He's on his way to come get me now. I'm gonna be in Atlanta. When I get situated, I'll send for you. Right now, I gotta go and let my daughter know that Daddy won't be coming around for a while."

Hurt filled his eyes. She knew that his four-year-old, Boopie, as he affectionately referred to her, was his heart and soul. Even though his baby mama didn't always see eye to eye with him, she could never refute that he did his best to take care of his only child.

Checking his watch, Jamar knew he was running short on time. "I'll holla later," he said, racing off to his vehicle.

Mixed emotions filled her heart as Lady Shyne watched him run away. She longed to feel his lips against hers but knew that publicly, it was a no-go. Especially since things had gotten so hectic for anybody close to Jamar. She contemplated when she was going to see him again as she went back inside the studio to help the host shut down for the day.

****

Pulling up to his baby mama's house, Jamar parked and jumped out. He looked both ways before crossing the narrow street. When all was clear, he raced over to ring her doorbell. As soon as she opened the door to let him in, Brenda gave Jamar a tight hug.

Surprise laced his words. "You all right?"

"I didn't know if you were dead or alive. All I knew is that you went off on a Blake, and the radio station got shot up. It's all over the news."

Jamar shook his head. "Calm down. I'm gonna be leaving Macon for a minute. I don't know for how long, but my cousin is on his way to pick me up right this sec. I came to tell you and Boopie before I go."

Tears welled in her eyes as she grabbed hold of his hand. "Jamar, I know that we have bumped heads on several occasions, but I want you to know that you have become a better man, and you deserve to have this success. Whatever you have to do to protect yourself— then do it."

Jamar smiled and kissed his ex on her forehead. "Thank you. Where's Boopie?"

No sooner than he said her nickname, Boopie came crashing into his legs on her Big Wheel. "Daddy!" she exclaimed, hopping up.

Scooping the precious child up into his arms, he squeezed his baby girl tightly. "There you are, you little rug rat," he teased, swinging her around in the air. The child giggled at her silly papa. "I need to talk with you, and it's a serious one." He placed her back down on her feet. Nodding her head, the child urged him to continue. "Well, Daddy is going to have to go away for a while."

"For how long, Daddy?"

"I don't know yet, baby," he admitted. Jamar's heart instantly tore apart, as well as Boopie's mother's, to see sadness spread across the child's little face. "Chin up, Boopie! I'm going to call you every single day until I can get situated and have you be with me. I promise it won't be too long."

The young child threw her hands up, signaling that she wanted a hug. Jamar swiftly picked his daughter up. Her arms locked around his neck.

"Okay, Daddy, but hurry back."

It took everything in him to fight back his tears. A piece of him feared never getting to see her tiny face again, but he knew to have any options, he had to escape MacTown.

He looked at his baby mama and said, "Brenda, I'm about to run out to the car. I forgot some money in the glove compartment that I wanna give you. It's a few stacks that should help you out with Boopie 'til I'm situated."

Brenda nodded her head in agreement.

Jamar carried his daughter, as he walked out the door, heading to his car for the money. "You really gonna miss me, Boopie, or are you just fronting for Pops?" he teased, standing her on her feet so that he could unlock the door.

"Ummmm, fronting!" she joked, giggling.

Jamar burst into a hearty laugh as he unlocked his car door. Retrieving the envelope of money, he shut the door and picked Boopie back up. Brenda took a look out of her blinds and saw a strange vehicle block Jamar from making his way back across the street. Jamar took a deep swallow as he spotted Geronimo and Julian seated in the back of the car. An unknown man pointed a Desert Eagle out of the window at him.

"That's the *real* hot spitta right there," Julian joked in reference to the gun.

"This nigga said fuck the Blake family?" Geronimo added, a sinister look spread across his face. "Well, now, who's fucked?"

Boopie began to cry as she witnessed the gun aimed at her father.

"Listen, just let me put my daughter down," Jamar pleaded.

"Nigga, fuck you! Pull that trigger, Teague," Geronimo ordered.

Without hesitation, he squeezed the trigger of his triangular-nosed .50 caliber weapon. The hollow-tip bullet that he sent took out a chunk of the left side of Jamar's skull as it ripped through his flesh. Blood splattered all over Boopie's terrified face as she was dropped on the cold, hard, concrete pavement. The gunshot instantly killed Jamar as his corpse collapsed beside his daughter.

Julian exited the vehicle and unleashed his semiautomatic to make an even clearer statement. He unloaded fourteen more shots, all in Jamar's face and neck. Paralyzed in fear, Boopie lay beside her father screaming. Tears flowed from her eyes like a waterfall.

Brenda raced out into the street as the Blakes nonchalantly pulled away without worry. Grabbing her baby in her arms, she shielded her from the sight of Jamar's mutilated body. Spectators came out of their homes to witness the horrific sight of the dead man. Many began to vomit from viewing the atrocity. Neighbors helped Brenda and Boopie back into their home, while others called the police. Although everyone saw exactly what happened, nobody said a word. It was obvious that the Blakes were not a family that you crossed.

Chasing Ghosts 3

Three weeks had passed by since Jamar's funeral. The cries of Boopie's little voice could still be heard echoing within Trevonte's head. So many people and so many celebrities were in attendance. Some of Trevonte's most favorite artists were there, but he paid them all no mind. All he could do was stand by Brenda's side as she tried to calm Boopie's weeping eyes.

It was to no avail, however. The fact that the service had to be a closed-casket ceremony only added to the rage burning inside Travonte's heart. A whole city was in fear of people that bled just like them. Trevonte couldn't understand it. He was raised to fear no one besides God because people could kill you, but only God could destroy you over and over again.

As he looked around the room, he saw so many tears and long faces. All the while, little Boopie never stopped her screams. Looking into his baby cousin's soul, Trevonte knew that he could not, and would not, allow his cousin's death to be in vain. Right then, he made up his mind that he was going to kill every single Blake breathing in Macon, Georgia . . . or die trying.

Hearing a knock at his front door, Travonte grabbed his .45 and tucked it in his waistband. Spud exhaled a cloud of weed smoke as he waited for his partner to answer the door. He began to cough on the exotic smoke as he saw Travonte appear as it disintegrated into the atmosphere.

"My nigga, you have got to try this shit right here," Spud said, handing over the blunt.

Travonte took a puff as the two headed back inside. "This shit is good as fuck," he agreed.

"Yea, I don't know where Unc got it from, but it's potent bud," Spud replied.

Travonte plopped down on the sofa and cut on the television screen. As if he had seen a ghost, one of his cousin's last videos made was blasting from the flat screen.

He sighed. "Ain't this 'bout a bitch."

Spud knew how hurt his partner was from the loss of his cousin. "Shit still fucking with you, playboy?"

"It ain't gonna stop until I kill them muthafuckas, bruh."

Spud smiled. "I thought you might say that, so I did a little digging for you."

Travonte watched as Spud tossed a couple of photos on the coffee table. Reaching forward, he saw the first one was of Spud's uncle, Mr. Lewis, and three unfamiliar men. A red marker had circled the three men's heads.

Travonte was curious. "Who are these niggas?"

"The general, captain, and lieutenant of the Blake army," Spud answered before taking another tote off the blunt.

Travonte sprang to his feet. It was obvious that the old man was the father, but he didn't know who was who out of the sons, and neither did Spud.

"How does your uncle know these muthafuckas?"

"Man, Unc know every muthafucka in Georgia that got they hands in dirty money. When you went to Macon for your cousin's funeral, he was looking for you, so I told him what happened. That's when he told me he knew the Blakes and sent his condolences. He pulled out some old pics that he had of their family. I swiped a few to give you a glimpse at the muthafuckas we gotta murder." A wide grin lit up his face.

Travonte had to smile, too.

One of the things he admired most about his friend was that he was down for whatever and always had his back. If Travonte went to war with the world, then he would bet his last penny that Spud would be by his side with his guns blazing.

"Unc said them Blakes dangerous like on some Genghis Khan-type shit, though. A nigga gotta come correct 'cause they got mayors, police, judges, and all in they pockets," Spud informed him.

Travonte fell back down on his couch and had to rethink some things after hearing that statement. He was used to banging it out with street thugs and hoodlums, but never a real organized syndicate that was so well connected.

That's when it hit him!

"Spud, what's that old saying, man . . . If you can't beat them, then what you do?"

"You join them."

"And that's *exactly* what the fuck I'm gonna do 'til they asses are all six feet deep," Travonte pledged.

Spud was a bit confused. "How you gonna do that?" he wondered.

At that moment, everything seemed to stop as Travonte picked up the other photo of two women. One was an older woman who appeared to be in her late fifties. She was still a glamorous sight to behold, although the younger woman is who captivated him.

"Who are they?" he inquired.

"That's the momma and daughter Blake. Unc didn't remember they names, though, either. He just called them Buddy and Li'l Buddy."

Spud laughed.

A devilish smirk spread across Travonte's lips.

"Nigga, what you thinking?"

Travonte marveled the young woman's beauty and knew that he had to have her. The young lady was golden brown, with hazel-green eyes, a small waist, and thick thighs. Her wide hips made her lower half resemble a wishbone. From the top of her honey-blond braided head to the sole of her pigeon-toed feet screamed sexiness and sophisticated elegance.

"Li'l Buddy is my key into the Blake family, and I guarantee she open up doors unforeseen," Travonte said, retrieving his keys.

"Where we heading to, nigga?" Spud inquired.

Travonte dashed to the front door. "I don't know where *you* going, but *I* got some folks to holla at in Macon. When I need you, I'll hit you up."

"That's a bet! Be safe."

"Always," Travonte replied, patting the .45 in his waistband.

****

Julian pushed both doors open as he strolled into the strip club with three of his goons in step.

"Damn, that bitch got a phat ass!" one of the men exclaimed.

Julian had to admit she did.

"A new face with a big ass and small waist," Julian spoke as he approached the stage where she was dancing.

She climbed up the pole, wrapped her strong legs around it, and dropped her head upside down toward the floor. It was amazing to the crew how her large breasts failed to knock her unconscious.

Noticing Julian, the young dancer quickly became nervous. This was only her third night working in the club, but she heard nothing but terrible things about Julian's behavior when it came to the dancers. All of the bouncers, as well as the owner, were far too bitch made to try and check a Blake, so she knew that if any problems popped off, then she would be on her own.

Julian was already putting a down payment on the prize in his eyes as he began tossing hundred-dollar bills on stage. She slid to the floor, gyrating and rolling her hips to the beat. Julian took notice that whenever the two made eye contact, she quickly broke it. Wanting to know if his mind was playing tricks on him, he decided to keep his bills and probe the young sexpot later.

He moved down the stage to another dancer and began to make it rain for the stripper. Relieved that he had found a new interest, the young girl finished off her set and retrieved all of her bills.

"Give it up for Lucky Charms, fellas," a lovely worker said, preparing to announce the next dancer to hit the stage.

Watching Lucky Charms disappear downstairs, Julian recognized his cue. When he made his way into the dressing room, he spotted the girl tallying up the proceeds donated to her worthy cause.

"Hello, ladies," he greeted.

"Hey, Julian," the girls chanted in unison.

The fear he had instilled in them was obvious.

He posted up beside Lucky Charms. "I don't believe we've had the pleasure of meeting."

She ignored him as she continued to count her money.

Thoroughly entertained, he allowed himself to play her game. "Well, let me be a gentleman and introduce myself. I'm Julian Blake, and each of those Ben Franks you're counting came from the flick of my wrist."

She looked up at him. "Thanks."

The expression that he gave her told the others that Lucky Charms was cruising for a bruising.

"Let me try this again," he started. "My name is Julian Blake, and I'm finding it hard to believe that none of these ladies have informed you that I own this city. Since this club is in *my* city, then *I* own it! Since you shake that big, fluffy ass that you're sittin' on in *my* club, in *my* city, then, bitch, that must make you *mines* too!" he snapped, grabbing her by the throat and kicking the chair from underneath her.

Her eyes began to bulge out of her head as he choked her. Both of her arms were wrapped around his wrist in an attempt to free herself.

"You bitches get the fuck out of here and leave me to find out how lucky this here ho charms really is," he demanded, tossing her into the middle of the floor.

The rest of the exotic dancers scattered and hurried out of the room.

"Please don't hurt me," Lucky Charms begged, climbing to her feet.

Julian smiled as he began stuffing her hard-earned money into his pockets.

"What are you doing?"

"Taking what it costs for me not to hurt you," he teased, forcing the last bill into his pants. "Oops . . . Looks like you're still a little short, though."

Rushing over to him, she made the mistake of reaching for his pockets. In one swift motion, the backside of his hand connected with her face. She crashed against the table. Stunned, her hand flew to her face.

Julian stalked up to her. "Are you mentally fucking retarded or something?! Do you *not* grasp the concept of just shutting the fuck up and letting shit be?"

With her arms on the table behind her, she looked Julian in his eyes. "Please don't take my money. I really need every cent. My three-year-old is autistic, and his medical bills are sky high. My baby daddy is locked up, so I'm a single mother just trying to make due with all of this temporarily," she pleaded.

Julian studied the young woman. In a simple pink bra and panty set, she was gorgeous. High-yellow complexion with dark brown eyes, Lucky Charms was built like a black stallion. Her hips were extremely wide, and her rear was a whopping forty-six inches. He took notice of her long Brazilian weave shimmering down her back and flat stomach. Resembling actress LisaRaye by face, Lucky Charms was a beauty queen.

"Very touching story and all," he extended his hand to caress her trembling cheek, "but everybody has issues."

Instinctively, she cringed from his touch.

Anger shot through his veins. He was real tired of her charades. "You know what? You are a real disrespectful bitch, and I'm gonna teach you how to act around men of power," he snapped, punching her to the floor.

Blood trickled from her nose as her face began to swell. She lay on her back in a daze from the impact of the powerful blow. This allowed Julian to mount her body with his slender frame. He quickly undid his pants and whipped his penis out.

"You little nasty bitch. I got something for you," he hissed, ripping her panties off.

Regaining her composure, she began to scream and throw fists in rapid succession. Julian quickly overpowered her and stuffed her panties down her throat. He repeatedly punched her in the face until her nose was broken, both eyes were swollen shut, and her jawline was fractured. Lucky Charms's entire face was purple from the bruises. She realized fighting back was to no avail, so she finally decided to cease resisting.

She shrilled in pain when she felt the penetrating stroke of his penis forced inside of her. Tears streamed down her face as he thrust forward over and over again.

Julian was enjoying himself. He pulled the woman's voluptuous breasts from her bra and began to fondle them. Whimpering cries escaped Lucky Charms's lips, but he didn't care.

She wished for death as Julian pumped in and out of her. To be violated in such a fashion seemed to rip her heart and soul from within and cast it away to the swine.

Next thing she knew, he was harshly biting her nipples. Then, he began slapping her breast as hard as he could.

"Yea, you little freak ho. Take this dick!" he spat as he pushed himself deeper and faster.

Praying for it to hurry up and be all over with, Lucky Charms lay stiff like a corpse not wanting to provide her attacker with any extra pleasure.

Angered by her lack of performance, Julian grew frustrated. "Okay, you little come-catching bitch, you wanna act like you ain't feeling this dick? I got a trick for that too."

Withdrawing his bloody penis from her womb, he flipped Lucky Charms over onto her stomach and admired her huge backside. Pulling both cheeks apart, he found her virgin anus and stuck his middle finger as deeply as he could inside. The feel of his finger forcing its way up her rectum caused her body to jerk as she tried to crawl away.

Tired of her antics, Julian balled his fist up and jumped up on her back. "You . . . stupid . . . fuckin' . . . bitch!" With each word, he punched her as hard as he could on the side of her head.

Blood began to leak from her ear as the ringing noise in her head blocked out all sound. Focusing back on her rear, Julian took a glob of saliva and spit it between her cheeks. He took the head of his dick, massaged the sticky fluid back and forth between her ass, then leaned over onto her back. Unable to see or hear, her body quaked from the fear of what was to come next.

"You 'bout to love this," he whispered, sliding his forearm around her throat.

Locking and squeezing his arm, Julian held the poor woman in a submission hold as he utilized his other hand to hold his throbbing manhood.

"Aaahhhh!" she howled as he forced himself inside her tiny hole.

The size of his dick instantly ripped her apart the deeper he went. Tightening his muscles around her neck, Julian began to choke the woman. Banging himself harder and harder, he realized that she had fallen unconscious from a lack of oxygen. He released his grip and allowed his hand to take hold of her long hair. Yanking her limp head back, he fucked her as hard as he could manage. Watching the waves of her jiggling rear flow up her back had him on the verge of a climax.

Two strippers accidentally came downstairs and spotted the horrific scene. Blood was all over the floor from her bloody nose and leaking vagina. Realizing that it was Julian and seeing Lucky Charms's swollen face, neither girl wanted any part of what was taking place. Spinning around on their heels, both women fled in haste.

It wasn't long before Julian reached his orgasm. Feeling its thrilling approach, he released her hair from his palm. Her face fell flat on the concrete. Instantly, both of her lips burst open while all of her front teeth were knocked loose. Jumping up, he threw Lucky Charms over onto her back. He stood over her chest, squeezed his dick tight, and pumped it back and forth.

"Oh shit," he gasped as his seed began to spray.

Making sure every drop fell on Lucky Charms's bloody and battered face, he aimed to add insult to injury. As the blood and come slid down her bruised face, the battered girl simply lay in tears as she came to. Julian fixed himself up, brushed off his clothes, and wiped the sweat from his face.

Heading back over to his victim, he stood over her and spit into her face. "That'll teach you some respect, you nothing-ass bitch!"

Stepping over her body, he headed back upstairs as if nothing had happened.

****

Pulling up to a small house, Travonte put his car in park. He swiftly exited the vehicle to make his way onto the porch. He rang the doorbell. After a brief pause, the door swung open. Lady Shyne smiled and gave Travonte a friendly embrace before inviting him inside.

Keeping true to his word, Travonte made sure to offer Lady Shyne his shoulder to lean on while he was in Macon for Jamar's funeral. After speaking with her, he realized how hard it would have been to have to go through such a loss with no one to truly understand that she and Jamar were in love with each other. To possess a secret love and lose it as a secret gives one no real form of closure. To confess her feelings for him now would make her look like a groupie, at best. All Lady Shyne could do is reminisce and share stories with Travonte about what once was.

Although he had no problem listening to her pour out her affection for Jamar, at the moment, Travonte came for answers. As they sat on her couch, he jumped right into it.

"I need to know who is who."

Lady Shyne watched as he laid the photos in front of her. She didn't have to give any thought as to who the people were in the pictures. Pointing to the largest of the sons, she said, "This is Geronimo Blake. I mean, his real name is George, but the streets call him Geronimo."

Travonte looked at the man and paid close attention to whom he heard so many feared.

"And this dude here is Julian Blake. The nigga love pussy!" Lady Shyne informed him.

Travonte looked as if he wanted her to elaborate.

Lady Shyne caught the hint, and so she did. "He terrorizes the strip clubs. Any new chicks that don't get with his program, he beats their asses and rapes them." Travonte was already disgusted as he took mental notes. "Not only that, but he's been known to go to college campuses and leave with some of the students—willingly and unwillingly. The nigga used to frequent Wesleyan University like it was the Boom Boom Room," she caustically joked.

Travonte had heard enough. "Back to this Geronimo nigga. What's his character flaws?"

"He's greedy. His problem is power. He has it, but is so obsessed with making sure people know he has it that he overdoes everything! For example, the nigga came to our radio station 'cause a rapper was in the studio that he didn't like. Reason being, the rapper had a line in one of his songs that could have been a disrespectful shot at the city.

"In order to clear it up, we gave the artist our platform to speak his peace. Geronimo was not satisfied with that and barged in there with his goons. They ended up beating our security team down, and

Geronimo choked the rapper out in the name of MacTown," she said, shaking her head at the whole ignorant episode.

Travonte shook his head too, realizing just how stupid the large man was.

"Oh, but the icing on the cake is when the video of him choking the rapper out surfaced on WordStar and YouTube. The rap artists' career was over, and Geronimo became a local hero for holding down the Mac. That is . . . until he killed some poor sap in front of the liquor store for looking at his longtime girlfriend inappropriately."

"Oh, he do got a soft spot! What's her name?"

"Evelyn Monroe. She owns a clothing boutique for women on the South Side. You can always find her there. She is very hands-on with her business, and I heard she's the same with handsome young men," she admitted.

Curiosity piqued his interest. "Well, how old is she?"

"Geronimo is thirty-four, and I know she has him by at least seven years. She's a real cougar, or as us black folks are called, a Thunda Kat," she chuckled.

Travonte smirked before holding up the other photo. "What can you tell me about her?" he inquired, lust filling his eyes.

Lady Shyne observed the photo closely. Travonte looked puzzled. He expected her to go rambling off hidden secrets about the Blake daughter as well but drew a blank.

"I've never seen her before, but this older woman is the first lady of the Blake family. Her name is Misti Blake. Maybe this is the daughter," she reasoned, growing excited.

"It is. I do know that much," Travonte replied.

"Oh, wow. Where did you get this photo of her?"

"A friend of a friend. How come you can tell me any and everything about the rest of the family and nothing about her?" he probed.

"Because she's low-key. Everyone has heard of a daughter in the Blake family, but it's more like a myth. It's said that Misti cheated on Harold Blake, her husband, and became pregnant with a baby girl. Harold was so furious that he told her he would only forgive her if she put the child up for adoption. And she did."

"Damn, so she doesn't carry the Blake family name?"

"No, but rumor has it that on her eighteenth birthday, Misti pleaded with Harold to allow her to meet her child whom she had been secretly keeping up with all those years. Growing soft in his old age, he granted her permission, and she finally met her siblings and was introduced to the Blake lifestyle, but was nowhere near as insane as the rest of her family. I heard her name was Bethany, but don't know how true it is."

Travonte was in awe of the mysterious beauty and story, but more so than anything, he needed facts. "I'm gonna be relocating to Macon, so best believe, we're going to find out if there is any truth to this myth. I guarantee that the Blakes will pay for what they did to my cousin," he vowed.

Lady Shyne nodded her head in agreement. She knew that Travonte meant every single word. Leaning over to embrace her new companion, she made a silent prayer to protect Travonte as he embarked on his quest for vengeance.

Operation Infiltration

4

Travonte took three weeks to come up with a plan to infiltrate the Blake family ranks. It took nerve to do what he was planning to do, but every time he looked at Jamar's photo and thought about Boopie, he knew he had no other alternative.

Checking his watch, Travonte exited his vehicle and prepared to put his plan in motion. As he entered the boutique, he spotted a young woman at the cashier desk and figured she couldn't be Evelyn.

"Excuse me, I came in here last week and bought this lingerie for my girlfriend, and I need to return it," he insisted, placing the bag on the counter.

"I'm sorry, sir, but we have a no-return policy."

Faking an attitude, Travonte demanded to speak with the owner of the establishment. Not wanting to make a scene, the young woman quickly headed to the back. Travonte hid his delight when he watched her return with none other than Evelyn Monroe. He studied the woman from head to toe. The pencil skirt that she had draped around her thick thighs instantly caught his attention. He indiscreetly admired her as his glance traveled up to her peeping full bustline.

Evelyn blushed as she spoke. "Is there a problem that I can help you with?"

Travonte licked his lips. "I thought we had one, but I just came up with a solution," he flirted.

"And what might that problem and resolution be?" the pint-sized mulatto beauty wondered.

"Follow me, and I'll tell you," he assured her, drawing her away from her young employee.

Evelyn took notice that he had walked her over to the lingerie section of her boutique. She too had been secretly admiring him. Travonte was a chocolate man with a naturally athletic build. He was a few centimeters above six-two and carried his height well. His low-cut fade made his baby face stand out even more to the sexy Thunda Kat.

Catching a quick glimpse of his crotch area, she knew that the young man had to be packing. Attempting to remain professional, she was prepared to take this conversation wherever he intended to go. The closer he got, the more intoxicating was his enchanting cologne. Her vaginal muscles began to loosen and moisten as he started to speak in his delicate, yet masculine tone.

"I purchased this very same ensemble for my girlfriend for our anniversary last week, which I have here in this bag," he began. Evelyn remained silent and nodded her head, encouraging him to continue. "Well, she caught me in bed with another woman—her mother, to be exact. Therefore, I no longer have a girlfriend and wanted to return this to your store."

"I'm sorry, sir. Really . . . her mother?" Evelyn questioned in awe. A chuckle escaped her lips.

A smirk spread on Travonte's face as he spoke. "I know, right, but she has always known that I have a fetish for mature women, and one day, her mother and I were at the house waiting for her to return. Mom was drinking, and I had a few shots with her. That led to my face being buried between her thick thighs."

He licked his full lips for effect.

Picturing his pink tongue and juicy lips between her thick thighs caused Evelyn to squirm.

"You okay?" Travonte asked.

"Yes, and I do apologize, but we have a no-return policy, so you have to find someone else to give that to," she admitted while trying to regain her composure.

"Which brings me to my resolution. How about I buy ten more just like it?"

"And why would you do that?"

"Because I wanna see you in all ten of them sprawled across my sheets."

Evelyn's cheeks turned a crimson shade of red.

"Listen, I saw you in here last week and found out that you run this place. There was no episode with a chick and her mother. I just thought I'd let you know what I like. If you're interested, then my number is on the tag of this lingerie. You can use it anytime, day or night."

His dark brown eyes galvanized Evelyn, and she was aroused by his boldly stated words. "How do you even know that I am available?" she asked, folding her arms across her chest.

"I don't know anything except that when a person really wants something, then they make themselves available to attain it. Hopefully, you want to feel me inside of you as much as I want to feel you coming all over me."

He handed her the bag.

Evelyn was speechless as he strolled out of the clothing store. Heading back into her office, she quickly pulled out the lingerie and searched the tag. To her amazement, numbers were there, but not to a phone.

"Meet me here at nine," she read as she browsed over the hotel address. Shaking her head with a chuckle, Evelyn Monroe was now figuring how she could ditch Geronimo to test out her new tenderoni.

****

Spud had been tailing Julian Blake from strip club to strip club for over a week. Not wanting to blow his cover, he only ventured inside twice to see how foolish Julian really was over women. Just as Lady Shyne had informed Travonte, Spud saw firsthand how reckless the younger Blake was when it came to pussy.

Reaching in his pants pocket, Spud pulled out a thousand dollars. "I want you to fuck this nigga's brains out for this stack," he instructed before handing the money over to the prostitute in his passenger seat.

"No problem," she smiled, popping her bubblegum. She exited the vehicle and hit the corner, waiting for her mark.

Spud had come up with a plan to round up a few Atlanta whores and introduce them to the Mac. He, like all hustlas, knew that new pussy was the best pussy to a trick. The strategy was easy. Spud would be introduced as an out-of-town pimp who was considering relocating his stable to the Mac. His ploy would be his interest in finding a local to help him set up shop.

Travonte hand-selected ten girls to help them pull off their plan, and even Uncle Lewis pointed the boys in the best possible prospects' direction. Uncle Lewis didn't know what the boys wanted them for besides one hell of a night and didn't bother to ask. Now was the time to show and prove.

Rolling up a blunt, Spud watched in the distance and waited for his entertainment. It took nearly an hour for Julian to exit the strip club, and Charlotte was right there waiting. Spud had shown her a photo of Julian, so she knew he was the right target. Tipsy from the alcohol he consumed inside the club, he spotted Charlotte in the near distance and pepped up quickly.

"Damn, I ain't never seen you around here before," Julian stated, approaching her.

Charlotte shot him a charming smile before replying. "I'm definitely not from around here. My daddy figured that Macon would be a little more profitable for our talents, so he planning on moving us out here."

"Us?"

"Yes, me and all of my gorgeous sisters," Charlotte purred.

Julian licked his lips as he looked her up and down. "Well, baby, if your daddy plans on making any money out here, then he needs my approval."

Charlotte smirked. "Well, he isn't too far away for you to talk to. I would rather you do because we are anxious to get started down here and bring a lot of delight to the Mac."

Julian nodded his head with a devilish grin. "Where this nigga at?"

Charlotte didn't hesitate to escort Julian over to meet Spud.

Exhaling a cloud of smoke, Spud stepped out of his car to greet his enemy of a friend.

"Is there a problem?" Spud asked with his pistol in hand.

"No, daddy!" Charlotte said, hugging him. "This gentleman says that he can help us do our thang out here."

A smile replaced his frown as Spud put away his firearm. "My apologies then. You can call me Spud," he said, extending his hand as a generous gesture.

Julian apprehensively accepted his handshake. "So, I hear you been doing big things and wanna bring your business out here?" Julian questioned.

"Exactly, but I'm not the type to step on anybody's toes. I have heard about a family out here that has everything on smash, and I definitely ain't trying to cross them. Shit, I think with their assistance, this ho money can go even further," Spud confessed.

Julian didn't have time for small talk and got straight to the point. "Listen, this is *my* city, and that family you're talking about is *my* family. I am Julian Blake, and if you have more dime pieces like this one in your stable, then I am all for helping you grow."

A huge smile spread across Spud's face. "Consider me down, Mr. Blake, and since we are going to be doing business together, enjoy a free sample of our fine products."

Julian was taken aback as Charlotte pushed him up against the back alley wall. Dropping to her knees, she swiftly unzipped his fly and retrieved his manhood. He grabbed a handful of her hair and began to pump himself into her hungry mouth.

Spud got back in his vehicle and chuckled. "This is going to be as easy as taking candy from a baby."

****

Lady Shyne could not believe her eyes as she spotted Evelyn Monroe pulling into the hotel parking lot. Her clock read three minutes 'til nine, and she was on time. Lady Shyne quickly gave Travonte a call.

He picked up on the first ring. "Hello."

"She is on her way up," Lady Shyne beamed.

"Good. She's alone, right?"

"Yep, all by herself."

"All right, I'll be ready and waiting for her. You can go home now and get you some rest," Travonte said.

"Cool. And you better put it down," Shyne teased with a giggle.

"Oh, you can bank on that," he replied while clicking off.

A knock came at the door, and Travonte casually strolled over to answer it. Once she saw him appear before her eyes, Evelyn could not wait to devour the young man. He opened the door shirtless with a glow of baby oil sparkling from his ripped abdomen. The linen shorts he had on displayed his length as he moved to the side for her to enter.

"Nice to see you again," he said while placing a hand on her waist to help usher her inside.

She smiled. "Likewise."

Travonte took notice of the zipper at the top of her pencil skirt and quickly unzipped it. The back of her satin panties came into view, causing Evelyn to spin around and catch her skirt before it fell to the floor.

"If I didn't know any better, I'd take it we've known each other for years," she hissed.

Travonte ignored her words and backed her up against the hotel dresser. Bowing his head, he parted her lips with his tongue and forced it deep inside her wet mouth. Her breathing deepened as he manhandled her round breasts with his strong hands. Her nipples began to protrude through the fabric of her bra and blouse. Wrapping both arms around his neck, Evelyn sat back on the dresser and hungrily suckled his stiffening tongue.

Travonte pulled back and shot Evelyn a devilish smile. "Let me really show your sexy ass what this tongue was made for," he smirked.

Evelyn sat back while he peeled her skirt down from around her luscious hips and tossed it to the floor. Pulling her panties to the side, he took his index and middle fingers and placed them gently on her bloated clit. Evelyn's lips began to tremble as he rubbed his fingers up and down, back and forth, across her clit. Viewing the wetness of her womb, Travonte lowered his head and flicked his wide tongue up the middle of her moist centerpiece. She then took one of her legs and threw it over his broad shoulder. The farther she spread herself, the farther he thrust his tongue.

Caressing the back of his scalp, Evelyn began to pump her pussy on his tongue while he moved his fingers in rapid succession. She began to squirm and smear her love oils all over his thick lips as she wiggled in bliss.

"Feed me that pussy!" he cried out as he continuously lapped away at her sugary tunnel of delight.

Switching up, he plunged his fingers deep within her tight confines until he felt the flimsy nub of her G-spot. Puckering his lips around her throbbing clit, Travonte began to tug at her G-spot with vicious strokes. Evelyn's head was spinning as she rode his fingers like a champion thoroughbred.

Slurping away at her nether region, Travonte could tell by her sudden quakes that she was on the verge of a powerful climax. Suddenly, Evelyn let out a loud shrill as come sprayed forth from her juice box. He made sure to savor every drop as he did his thing. In his mind, he had a mission to complete for his cousin, and this tramp was simply a perk that would eventually become a casualty of war.

Evelyn attempted to catch her breath as she trembled upon the dresser. Without hesitation, Travonte dropped his sweats revealing his rock-hard penis. Right then, she knew that she was in for one hell of a night!

Appearances

5

Awakening to the sound of his buzzing cell phone, Travonte noticed that Evelyn had vanished. He couldn't recall at what point she had left but managed to remember all of the freaky details of their intimate encounter. Groggy, he retrieved his cell and answered the caller.

"So, how did things go last night, Macaroni Tony?" Lady Shyne teased.

Wiping his weary eyes, he replied, "Things went just as expected. Well, looky here . . ." Travonte spotted a letter written and lying on the table beside the bed. He began to read its contents into the phone. *"I thoroughly enjoyed our time spent together and would love to do this again very soon. Here is my cell number . . . I am hoping to hear from you very soon as well. Kisses and hugs,"* he finished with a delighted smile.

"Ah, Negro, don't go to feeling yourself just yet. We still got work to do so get yo' ass out here because I'll be pulling around to the front entrance in about ten minutes," she said.

"Oh, damn! I almost forgot," he replied, hopping out of bed.

"See you in ten," Lady Shyne said signing off.

Travonte reached for his pants and began to get dressed. It slipped his mind that they had intended to meet Misti Blake at her highly publicized charity event for at-risk youth. Travonte questioned whether the event was actually a charade to front for the family's illegal money, but figured the kids were benefitting, either way, so reasoned that it balanced itself out. Heading into the bathroom, he washed his face, brushed his teeth, and prepared to head downstairs.

Lady Shyne sat patiently outside scrolling through her phone. She fought back the tears as pictures of Jamar caused memories to flood her mind. She missed him so much and wanted an end to come to the Blake family and their reckless disregard for anybody else's life. Hearing the door open, she put her phone away and leaned over to hug Travonte.

"Let's ride," he said, smiling.

Without hesitation, Lady Shyne turned the key in the ignition and hit the gas.

****

"Teague, come and meet Mr. Lombardi," Misti called out.

Following instructions, the young man headed over and extended his hand to the man in a friendly gesture.

"I will leave you two gentlemen alone now to do what you do."

She smiled as she spotted Terrence. Terrence Beeman was a prominent lawyer for the family. He had a number of judges in his pocket because he was the governor's favorite nephew. Besides his unyielding loyalty to the Blake family, he seemed to be an average Joe around the city, but he was anything but average to Misti Blake. The two had begun sleeping together after Mr. Blake drunkenly busted Misti's lip in a fit of rage. In all of their years together, he had never put his hands on her, but within the last year, he had become colder and had less tolerance for her. It appeared to Misti that with old age came paranoia, and Harold Blake was a dangerous man when paranoid. Unbeknownst to their children, they rarely shared the same bed at night, and only remained together due to Misti's fear of leaving. Harold was more concerned with image.

"Talk to me," Teague said as Mr. Lombardi and he casually walked through the crowd.

"I confirmed that a fleet of Maybachs, Porsches, and BMWs would arrive around ten thirty tonight for the family. Four of each," Mr. Lombardi informed him.

Teague stroked his chin and paused in his step. "That's only twelve whips. Why three short?" he questioned, his voice rising in anger.

"Yes, and I do apologize, but Mr. Rose opted to go with another buyer this time, and he requested more vehicles for a fairer price," Mr. Lombardi said.

Teague shot the man a look of death. Mr. Lombardi felt a twinge of fear grip his heart when, all of a sudden, a smile replaced Teague's frown. "I understand. Money talks while bullshit runs a marathon," Teague joked.

A sense of relief could be heard in his voice as he accepted Teague's handshake. "Thank you for being understanding, although I'm not. I told Mr. Rose that we have been doing great business with your family for a decade and now for a few extra grand he wants to risk losing such a well-established associate?"

"And his response was?"

"That his wife wants to vacate in Australia this year, and the Drummonds are going to see to it that she does," Mr. Lombardi admitted.

Teague stroked his chin. "A man has got to satisfy his wife's desires. See you and Mr. Rose at ten thirty."

"Later," Mr. Lombardi agreed.

The fact that Mr. Rose had made a side deal with the Blakes' rivals left a bad taste in Teague's mouth. He hated the Drummond family and their rising power in the city. Mr. Rose had sealed his fate, and Teague was gonna make sure that he personally sealed his casket.

Terrence watched as Misti helplessly put a seductive sway in her hips as she approached him, smiling.

"Pleasure seeing you here today."

"I know that I said I might have to miss it, but you know I love to see the delight on your face when you're surprised," he smirked.

"Good job, sir," she giggled.

Travonte and Lady Shyne stood directly across the room watching the two as they conversed like schoolkids engrossed in a teenage love affair.

"You see this shit?" Lady Shyne asked.

"Yea, there is definitely more to this story than meets the eye," Travonte assured her.

"That's Terrence Beeman, the governor's nephew."

Travonte chuckled. "So she got a thing for politics."

The two continued secretly to spy on Misti and her budding romance in silence.

"Maybe we can sneak off when all of the children arrive for a moment, and I can give you a surprise," Misti teased.

Terrence turned up his cup of cranberry juice and prepared to walk off. "Simmer down. We are in public, and I actually do enjoy living at the moment," he said, drawing distant.

A frown quickly replaced her smile. It truly irritated her that Terrence was so spineless, but then again, she knew that he had good reason to be. If Harold ever found out about her promiscuous ways, then she knew that both her secret lover, as well as she, would have hell to pay. She allowed him to stray as she mingled with the crowd until the kids appeared.

Travonte and Lady Shyne were bored out of their minds as the hours slowly passed by. The only thing that kept them alert was laughing at the sleeping children. All investors in Misti's event felt the need to give overly long speeches on where they could have been if they weren't so smart! The whole scene was patronizing, to say the least.

Travonte began to ask if Lady Shyne was ready to leave when suddenly, his heart skipped a beat at the sight he beheld.

"It's her," Lady Shyne acknowledged.

Travonte focused on Bethany's every move as she drew near her mother for a loving embrace.

"Damn, she is beautiful," he said in awe.

Lady Shyne shook her head. "Focus, Negro!"

"Oh, I'm focused," he mused.

Travonte and his accomplice mixed with the crowd as he patiently waited to catch Bethany by her lonesome. He decided to head outside into the park area for some fresh air—only to realize his moment had arrived.

"Excuse me. I'm new in town, so I'm sure that I don't know you, but I would really like to change that." He extended his hand. "You can call me Tre."

She blushed as she accepted his hand. "My name is Bethany."

"Nice to meet you, Bethany. I don't want to come off strange, but I noticed you hugging the lady of the evening. Do you know her personally?"

"As a matter of fact, I do."

"Well, I would be honored if you could tell her that she is really doing something wonderful for these kids."

Bethany smiled before replying. "How about *you* tell her?"

"Don't mind if I do," he beamed.

Lady Shyne couldn't believe her eyes when she spotted the trio conversing. Travonte had Misti and Bethany laughing at his witty conversation and appeared as if he had known them for ages. Suddenly, all laughter came to a halt as Harold approached with his sons.

"Harold, this is Bethany's friend, Tre. Tre, this is my husband and our two sons, Julian and George," Misti introduced.

"Pleasure to meet you, gentlemen," Tre greeted, extending his hand to Harold.

The elder of the Blakes accepted his hand while the brothers sized him up.

"Where y'all find this character?" Julian asked, purposely trying to intimidate him.

Trevonte remained cool and spoke up for himself. "This character's name is Tre. You would want to remember that."

"And why would he want to remember that?" Geronimo said, stepping to place his large chest in Tre's face.

Bethany tried to intervene, but Misti held her back by the wrist.

Stepping closer, Tre replied, "Well, George, I heard that no business gets handled in this city without the Blakes cosigning. Since I'm new to this area—and very much a businessman—I'm sure we'll cross paths again."

Julian and Geronimo looked at him like he was crazy. Harold smiled.

"Let's go outside for some air," the old man began. "We have things to discuss."

As the Blake trio went on their way, Misti whispered to her daughter, "I like this fella."

Bethany blushed and pulled Trevonte away from her mother to relieve her embarrassment. "My brothers can be so rude. I apologize."

"So you are the famous Blake sister. I heard you were like some type of mythological creature," Trevonte teased.

She giggled. "No, I'm no unicorn. I'm also no Blake, but that's a rather long story."

"Well, I would love to hear about it over dinner, perhaps?"

"Perhaps we can go out," she chuckled, "but *that* won't be the topic of discussion."

"Whatever words choose to spill from those lovely lips, I'm sure I will be just as interested," he replied, joining in on her chuckle.

****

Later that evening, Mr. Rose exited his office to meet three men in his warehouse. It was a huge factory-sized place, filled with everything from foreign cars to expensive paintings and sculptures.

"How are you gentlemen today?" Mr. Rose greeted, a huge smile spread across his face.

"Good, but not as good as you, my friend," the leader of the group answered.

Mr. Rose laughed and accepted the briefcase filled with money from the man. Cracking it open briefly, he beamed brightly at the many blue faces that he could see.

"Chase, I can already see that this is going to be the beginning of a beautiful relationship. Tell Mr. Drummond that he is greatly appreciated."

"Will do. May we?" Chase inquired, spotting the three vehicles they were there to pick up.

Mr. Rose nodded. "Go right ahead!"

"Filipe! Paul! Check them out!" Chase ordered, heading to one of the cars himself.

Each of the men piled into the foreign whips and pushed certain areas to make the hidden compartments open up. Chase viewed the boss's heroin and fentanyl supplies and was satisfied. Exiting the vehicle, Chase looked to Filipe and Paul, who both nodded their heads, signaling that their product was good as well.

"Pleasure doing business with you, my friend!" Chase exclaimed, preparing to leave.

Mr. Rose waved as he spun on his heels and headed back to his office. His eyes almost jumped out of his skull when he spotted Harold seated in his chair.

"Mr. Blake?"

Harold's eyes narrowed. "Insubordination will *not* be tolerated, Mr. Rose. Now, you had to know that I wouldn't let Mr. Lombardi rest before getting the details of your little plans with the Drummonds."

Raising a semiautomatic at Mr. Rose, Harold stood from his seat and backed him out of his own office. Suddenly, the sounds of rapid gunfire rang out within the warehouse. Chase sat down in the low Lamborghini and shut the door. Out the corner of his eye, he spotted a figure emerge from behind a huge box.

He gasped. "What the fuck?"

Geronimo ran directly up to Filipe's unsuspecting frame as he tried to start up his Aston Martin. He unloaded one hundred rounds from his Draco into the side of the vehicle. Filipe died instantly. Afraid, Paul reached for his firearm and pointed it toward Geronimo, but never saw Teague rise from his blind side. The same fate as Filipe grasped his soul, and he never got a shot off.

Witnessing Julian with his weapon aimed directly in front of him, Chase threw both his hands in the air. Amused, the younger of the Blake boys motioned for him to get out of the car. At that moment, Harold ushered in Mr. Rose at gunpoint. The terrified owner of the warehouse could see from a distance the bloody bodies in the bullet-riddled cars. He began to piss in his pants.

"Time for you to learn a valuable lesson, Mr. Rose," Harold said, hitting him in the head with the butt of his gun.

Mr. Rose fell to the cold pavement with blood trickling from the back of his scalp. Geronimo grabbed Chase by his neck and forced him over to Julian.

"Please, spare me. I was just following my boss's orders," Chase pleaded.

"Shut the fuck up, coward!" Julian snapped, punching him in the stomach.

The surprise blow knocked all of the wind out of Chase, and he dropped to his knees. Tossing his chopper on the ground, Julian unleashed his hunting knife.

"Hold that muthafucka steady for me, brother," he insisted.

As Geronimo lifted his head, Teague dragged Mr. Rose right over in his line of vision. Without hesitation, Julian began to stab Chase in his neck repeatedly. Blood gushed out over Mr. Rose, causing him to vomit all over himself. Julian carved into Chase until Geronimo was able to snatch his head off of his neck.

Satisfied with his point proven, Harold smiled at Mr. Rose. "And I assure you, I want the Drummonds to know that this is my declaration of war. They are not wanted in this city. Make sure you deliver that message for me," the elder instructed.

Shivering in blood, urine, and vomit, Mr. Rose was petrified. "Let's go, boys," Harold said, leaving the bloody scene.

Initiated

6

Over the next few months, a bloody war ensued between the Blakes and the Drummonds. However, although there was so much craziness going on, Trevonte and Bethany were light-years away from it all. They were in their own little world of romance. Day by day, the couple grew closer and closer.

Bethany only saw her brothers when her mother threw events like her previous shindig, and she liked it that way. She despised the Blakes. They were the very reason that she missed out on growing up with her mother. She often viewed it as a blessing, though. She found optimism in the fact that she didn't have to grow up around such wicked men.

The only person that knew how close she had gotten to Trevonte was her mother. Misti liked him and felt he was making her daughter happy. That was good enough for her.

After lying in bed and sharing one of their pillow-talk sessions, Bethany revealed to her beau that the war between the two factions was bearing a great toll on the Blakes. The fact that the family had lost a third of their army was great news to Trevonte. He figured they would be desperate for a few good men, so he decided to play his cards.

He phoned a few of his hittas back in Atlanta and put together a master plan that would gain him favor and access to the nucleus of the Blakes. Suited up, Trevonte looked around at all of his friends from back home.

"Listen, the intel I got says that this nigga is at the club celebrating his birthday against his family's wishes. With that being said, they'll have extra security on him, so everybody has to die except Antonio. No half stepping!" Trevonte ordered.

His boys nodded their heads, indicating they understood clearly.

"Here, pass this around." Travonte passed around the photo of Antonio. "That's the target. Remember, he lives and is brought to me," Travonte repeated as the men took in his face to commit it to memory.

After he felt confident everyone knew the play, Trevonte called for the men to move out.

****

Spud watched Antonio from a dark corner as the latter popped bottles with some of his hoes. Plans were going smoothly. His phone buzzed in his hand.

They're en route, the text message said.

Spud was alerted into action. He rose from his table, walked past the VIP section, and left.

Vikki had her cue. It was time for Lollipop and her to do their thing. Leaning over, Vikki slipped her tongue into Lollipop's mouth—directly in Antonio's face—while she caressed his dick through his jeans.

High and drunk, he laughed at the freaky women and tossed back more liquor.

"Daddy, we need you to come in the back and give both of us that birthday dick," Vikki purred.

"Yea, let me show you why they call me Lollipop," the other female whispered.

In two seconds flat, Antonio was on his feet with both women, heading to the back bathroom.

"Boss, where are you headed? I don't think you should—" was all his minion could utter before he was slapped and ordered to step aside.

Embarrassed, the underling obliged. The pair of prostitutes giggled as they led the way for Antonio.

Seated in the car with the rest of Travonte's souljahs, Spud saw one of his other girls exit and approach.

"What's good, baby?" he asked.

"They been in the back about five minutes now," she answered.

Spud looked at the men. Without a word, they fell out of four back-to-back vehicles in all black with ski masks. Unleashing their artillery, the men rushed the club.

Antonio was deep into Lollipop from the back. He smiled at Vikki as she faced him, seated on the sink with her legs spread wide. Vikki was enjoying Lollipop's mouth on her clit as Antonio pounded her friend's anus. Sprinkling cocaine on her breasts, Vikki welcomed Antonio to treat himself. Taking long strokes, he leaned forward to snort and lick away the white dust from her bountiful bosom. As the trio played, gunfire began to ring out in the club. Screams accompanied the shots.

"What the fuck?" Antonio yelped, hearing the madness.

Backing out of Lollipop, he attempted to pull his pants up. Vikki jumped from the sink countertop and viciously kicked him in the nuts. In anguish, Antonio fell onto his side, clutching his balls. Lollipop then reached up and snatched the face off of the napkin dispenser to retrieve the Taser that had been stashed there earlier. Before Antonio knew what hit him, he was out cold.

****

Awakening to the sight of two men in face masks, Antonio groggily looked around to find himself in a basement.

He realized he was tied to a chair. "Both of you muthafuckas are dead men!" he snapped.

Without so much as a concern for his threat, one of the men held up a cell phone.

"It's recording," Trevonte announced, holding it directly on Antonio.

Hidden behind the other mask, Spud reached in the tool bag around his waist and retrieved a power drill. He squeezed the trigger. As the tool bit began to spin, he stuck it directly into

Antonio's kneecap. Antonio screamed in pain as tears began to shed from his eyes like a baby.

"Noooo, please, stop! My family is rich. They'll pay you for my return," he pleaded.

Ignoring his sniffling, Spud stuck the drill in his other kneecap. Blood shot out and poured down his legs as he trembled in grief and pain. Trevonte stopped the recording as he watched Spud tie bandanas tightly around Antonio's wounds. Once Spud was done, he backed away and listened as Trevonte spoke.

"Now that you know we're not bullshitting, let's get down to business." Trevonte pulled out Antonio's phone and showed it to him. "Give me your unlock code, and tell me what your mother's name is saved in under your contacts," he demanded.

Antonio quickly obliged his kidnapper with the correct answers. Travonte pressed his mother's name and waited for her to answer.

"Hey, baby, how are you?" she asked.

"Mrs. Drummond, I have your son held hostage at gunpoint. If you don't do exactly what I say, then I will kill him. If you don't believe me . . ." Trevonte then ended the call. He forwarded the video from his phone to Antonio's, downloaded it, and sent it to Mrs. Drummond.

Instantly, she called back after viewing her son being tortured. "Please, spare my boy! What do you want? Money? Name your price!"

"I want two million dollars. Two duffle bags with a million dollars each in them. Have his two brothers, Domingo and Premo, come by themselves in separate vehicles to deliver."

"I'll need about an hour to get the money up, but where do they take it?"

"Once the money is in place, text this phone. I'll deliver the coordinates via text to them both once they get on I-75."

With no other choice but to comply, Mrs. Drummond agreed. Trevonte looked at Spud and nodded his head at him. Spud left the basement and went upstairs. He retrieved his phone and dialed up Julian.

"Hello?"

"It's me, bruh. I'm gonna need you to stop whatever you're doing, and get out to my place ASAP."

"What, you got a new bitch you want me to test out or something?" Julian beamed, excited about the prospect.

"Nah, but I'm sure I got something that you and Geronimo will be interested in. Make sure you bring him too."

Julian was curious. So curious that he called his brother and told him where they needed to meet.

The Truth

7

The Blake brothers approached Spud's front door with caution.

"What the fuck you got me out here for, bruh?" Geronimo inquired.

"This dude I know said he got something that'll interest both of us. I wanna see what it is," Julian admitted.

As the two approached the front door, it suddenly swung open.

"He's in the basement," Spud whispered, inviting them in.

"He?" Julian questioned.

Geronimo pulled out his pistol as they followed Spud into the lower level of the house. The first thing they saw was Trevonte in his mask. Once they looked down in front of him, that's when they laid eyes on Antonio. Trevonte turned to the brothers and removed his mask. The Blakes were speechless.

Trevonte smiled. "I told you that we'd see each other again in this business."

"That's one of the Drummond boys," Julian acknowledged.

"Correct. See, I heard from Bethany about the war between you two and the losses of people your family has taken. I figured that if I wanted in—which I do—then what better way to prove my worth and loyalty then by putting an end to this feud once and for all."

"This don't end shit. If anything, this will make them cocksuckers come at us even harder!" Geronimo reasoned.

"He is but one man," Julian agreed.

"Actually, he's one man that is the key to their heroin and fentanyl manufacturers. Without him, seventy-five percent of their business goes up in smoke! Also, I'm not just offering him. His brothers are en route to pick him up. They have two million in cash on them, are alone, and make up the muscle behind the

Drummonds. Kill them, and their army abandons them. Plus, that leaves nothing but an old man and woman to mourn their dead babies. Most importantly, that restores the balance of power once and for all," Trevonte informed the brothers.

The Blakes looked at each other and realized that he was speaking the truth.

Following Trevonte's plan to the letter, the Blakes killed all three Drummond boys that night and put an end to their ongoing war. Receiving a video of their sons' heads being decapitated sealed the deal for the Drummonds. Brokenhearted, they packed their belongings and escaped back to their hometown, fearing a similar fate would meet them in Macon, Georgia.

Trevonte was inducted into the Blake family with open arms. Over the next few months, he and Spud accompanied the brothers and their cousin Teague everywhere and became recognized as equals. Although things were looking up for Trevonte, it didn't appear as such for Bethany. The fact that her lover was cozying up to the two worst people in the world in her eyes left a disgusting taste in her mouth. Tired of holding back her true feelings, she decided to let it all out.

"What's on your mind, baby?" he asked.

"I don't like you being close to those men," she admitted.

"Your brothers? Don't worry about that."

"Don't tell me not to worry! They're dangerous and evil. Why would you even want to be a part of what they have going on? They're nothing but devils in human form."

Trevonte turned to study his woman. He was silent as he looked at her.

"Why are you staring at me like that?" she questioned.

"Because for the very first time, I'm really taking notice of how much you truly despise them. I mean, you've always shown a disdain for them, but this is interesting," he said, pulling her near. He looked into her eyes and waited for her story.

She knew she had to come clean, so she began to spill her truth to the man she had hopelessly fallen in love with. "As a girl, I always wanted brothers. I grew up alone. I never felt as if I truly belonged anywhere."

Trevonte listened attentively while holding her tightly.

"I never knew my mother or father, and then one day Misti comes along. She told me who she was and about my father, but never who he was. I was so happy to have her. It made me feel partially whole for once in my life," Bethany confessed.

Trevonte was finding it hard to figure out what any of that had to do with her brothers.

"Then one day, she thought it would be a good idea to introduce me to my siblings. They were horrible! They hated me and were jealous. They told Misti that they would tell Harold if she ever saw me again . . . so she didn't. Not until I was grown. She explained everything to me then, and although I hold her somewhat responsible, her fear of them hurting me is what kept her away. I understood that," she finished, tears streaming down her cheek.

Trevonte stroked her hair and felt her pain.

"I hate them. I just wish they never existed."

Trevonte raised her chin so her eyes could meet his. "Do you love me, Bethany?"

"More than anything! I love you with all of my heart," she confessed.

"So if you had to choose between them or me, what would your choice be?"

"Are you insane? *You!* A million times over!"

"Good. Now get dressed."

"Where are we going?"

He smiled. "To a party."

****

As they pulled up to a house, the first thing that Bethany took notice of was the huge moon bounce in the backyard.

"We're here," Trevonte announced.

"Tre, whose party is this?"

"My baby cousin. C'mon, let's go greet her!"

Hearing her doorbell chime, Brenda opened up and was happy to see Trevonte. Ever since the passing of Jamar, he had stepped up and been there for her and her daughter every step of the way.

"Brenda, I'd like you to meet the love of my life, Bethany," he beamed.

Blushing, Bethany hugged Brenda and entered with her man.

"Where's the birthday girl?" he asked.

"Chile, outside jumping around where she need to be. Giving me a much-needed break," Brenda teased.

Both Trevonte and Bethany chuckled.

"I'm gonna go and holla at her. Catch you before we leave," he said, taking Bethany out back.

Trevonte walked up to the moon bounce and spotted Boopie jumping as high as she could with the other children.

"Come give big cuz some suga-dooga!" Boopie heard Trevonte and turned to his voice. Ecstatic, she ran over to him and jumped into his arms. Bethany smiled wide as she watched them embrace. "My big girl turned five today, huh?"

"Yep! I'm a whole hand now," Boopie replied, waving at Bethany.

"That's right, girl, you tell 'em." She smiled, giving the child a high five.

"You're pretty," Boopie said.

"Awww, thanks, and so are you!"

The couple stayed with Boopie for another thirty minutes before heading back out.

"I'm 'bout to bounce. Need anything you just call," Trevonte announced.

Brenda walked him and his lady to the door and thanked him.

"You don't have to thank me. We're family, Brenda."

At that moment, tears began to fall from Brenda's eyes. Bethany was taken aback. She didn't know what was going on. Trevonte hugged Brenda tightly and wiped away her tears.

"Come on now, don't do that," he said.

"I'm sorry. I just miss him so much every single day."

"I miss him, too, but he watching over me, you, and definitely Boopie."

Brenda began to giggle. "Yea, definitely Boopie. He loved that little girl to death."

"Yes, he did."

"Well, I will let you two go'ne about your day. Thank you for stopping by, Trevonte, and nice to meet you, Bethany."

"Same here, Brenda."

Once the couple was in Travonte's car, Bethany looked into her man's eyes. "What happened to Boopie's dad?"

Taking a deep breath, Trevonte looked at his woman and sighed. "Your brothers happened to him."

Bethany sat up in her seat in disbelief.

"Them niggas shot my cousin in his face while he was holding her," he revealed, tears swelling in his eyes.

"Oh, baby," she said, caressing his shoulder.

Trevonte stroked her hand with his before continuing. "Baby, that's why I brought you here today. To make everything make sense."

"Talk to me, Tre. Make what make sense?"

"The fact that I'm hanging out with your family. I'm going to kill them, Bethany. They destroyed that little innocent girl's family. Destroyed your family. Now, I'm going to destroy theirs."

Bethany looked into his eyes and saw the sincerity. He meant business. Seated in Brenda's driveway for another half hour, he explained everything to her. She soaked it all in in silence.

After a long pause, she spoke. "They deserve everything you're going to give them. But not Misti. You can't harm my mother," she reasoned.

"She's as much a victim as the rest of you," he said.

"Exactly. She wants out of that family just as badly, but is trapped."

Taking her hand in his, Trevonte said, "She won't be trapped for much longer. I promise you that."

He Who Laughs Last

8

Trevonte looked in his rearview mirror at Teague seated in the backseat. He was busy checking his clip to make sure it was full. Tired of waiting, Trevonte honked his horn in order to speed up the pace.

"That nigga stay in some pussy. We might gotta go in there and scuba dive in that ho to pull him out," Teague joked.

"He got 'bout two minutes, and that's what's gon' happen!" Trevonte exclaimed.

Suddenly, the front door opened with Julian emerging from it, accompanied by Charlotte. The pair were kissing like schoolkids.

Teague chuckled. "Look at this shit."

Trevonte was definitely looking at it. He was glad to see that Charlotte had the man wrapped around her seductive snatch. Spud had definitely picked the right girl for the job. She knew her role and played it with proficiency. So much so that Julian had even purchased her a home to stay in away from the rest of Spud's stable. He wanted to be able to get to her whenever he wanted. Julian thought he was slick by controlling her living arrangements, but instead, made himself easy prey for revenge.

Breaking their liplock, Julian smacked her on the ass and raced over to the car.

"If I ain't know any better, I would say you really got a thing for that chick," Teague said.

"Mind ya business, cousin. Time to get in beast mode!" Julian replied, pulling out his gun.

Teague reached up front to pass him a silencer. Both men then screwed the accessories to the nose of their weapons. Trevonte pulled away from the curb and sped into traffic as Julian began to talk.

"This is how it's going down. Geronimo is already waiting in a rental at the end of the block where this snitch laying at. When you pull up to him, Tre, me and Teague will get out and walk. Now, Teague, his officers are stationed outside the house watching it on opposite sides of the street."

Julian paused to pull out surveillance photos of the unmarked vehicles that they had to be on the lookout for. "When we start walking, you see either of those cars, pull up and dome call the pussy in there," Julian ordered.

"And you'll get the other one across the street, right?" Teague inquired.

"Right! Once they taken care of, we follow Geronimo inside the house and do what we do to snitches. Once we come out, you pull up, Tre, and drop us off at my spot," Julian finished.

Trevonte nodded his head in compliance, but still had to ask questions. "Who this nigga snitch on, and why cops outside his place?"

Teague filled him in. "He testified against Geronimo a few years ago. Of course, Beeman ate the case like a shark, so Geronimo got off, but the fact that he even tried to rat is enough to get him exterminated."

"And they put that nigga in witness protection with his family after it was all over. We just now finding out where he located, so now, he gotta face Karma," Julian added.

With it all making sense, Trevonte hit *play* on his sound system to guide the convo where he really wanted to take it. The minute Julian heard Jamar aka Hotspitta blaring from the speakers, he flipped.

"Nigga, cut that trash off!"

Trevonte looked at his passenger as if he were crazy. "Fuck you mean? That nigga was raw before he got slumped!" Trevonte insisted.

"Man, that nigga was a traitor. Let the hip-hop hype gas him up, and he forgot who the fuck we are," Julian said.

"Oh shit, y'all had beef with that nigga?" Trevonte asked, playing naive.

"Yea, but we cooked that beef," Teague laughed.

Julian had to burst into laughter as well. "Nah, we flame-broiled that beef!" he added in an uproar.

Not amused, Trevonte probed further. "Y'all killed him?"

"Sure did. Caught that nigga lackin' with his baby girl in his arms. Pussy was begging for us to let him put her down. That's when Teague shot that nigga dead in the face. That little girl came down all right," Julian snickered.

Trevonte was disgusted. He wanted to kill them both right there but didn't want to be selfish. He had selfless intentions to manifest.

"But when you got outta the car and emptied ya clip in that nigga face, Julian, that shit was wild! I ain't gon' lie. I felt a little bad for the little girl at that point. How she was all screaming and shit," Teague chuckled.

"Man, fuck that little brat. Should've killed her, too! Li'l bitch lucky I used all my bullets on her weak-ass daddy."

Trevonte gripped the steering wheel and fought to maintain his composure as he turned the corner. He now knew who did what, and that's all he wanted to know. Now, it was his turn to laugh last—and the hardest.

****

Terrance Beeman was swamped with paperwork as he sat in his office going over legal motions. The sound of his assistant knocking at his door distracted him.

"What is it?" he called out.

Opening the door, she stepped inside and spoke. "I apologize for disturbing you, sir, but you have a walk-in."

"A walk-in? Listen, if they don't have an appointment, then I *definitely* don't want to see them," he declined.

Before the assistant could turn around, the young woman barged in on her own.

"Mr. Beeman, you will want to hear me out. This is urgent and dire," she insisted.

Beeman looked at the woman in disbelief.

"Ma'am, you're going to have to set up an appointment—" the assistant tried to finish, but the young woman strolled right past her and politely took a seat in front of Beeman's desk.

"It's all right. Leave us," he said, realizing that she wasn't going to give up.

Leaving the two alone, Beeman's assistant retired to her desk.

"Now, what seems to be your situation, young lady?"

"Hypothetically speaking, let's say that if a man was sleeping with a much more dangerous man's wife, what would you advise that woman to tell the man she's cheating with, who is in fear for his life?"

Beeman was totally confused. "Lady, I don't have time for hypothetical nonsense. Get a marriage counselor. I deal with litigation and provide legal representation. Sorry, but I can't help you."

"I think you're confused, Mr. Beeman. I'm here to help *you*," she said, pulling out a manila envelope and tossing it on his desk.

Opening the contents, Mr. Beeman nearly had a heart attack from the pictures. The woman had several photos of him with Misti in compromising positions.

"How did you get these?" he demanded to know.

"All that matters is how you make them disappear. Now, would you like to know how that happens?"

Beeman stood silently in shock. Sweat rolled down his forehead.

"Guess not. See you around, Mr. Beeman," she said, turning to leave.

"No! Tell me how we can fix this," he said, racing around his desk to catch her.

The woman looked him up and down before speaking. "Mr. Beeman, all you have to do is take Misti to dinner tonight. The venue, time you will arrive, and leave are all on a note in that envelope. Do this, and all will be forgiven. Tootles." She waved, exiting his office.

Beeman found the note in the envelope and dropped down into his chair. He realized that life as he knew it was no more.

****

Spotting his brother's rental, Julian made Trevonte pull over and park. They exited the vehicle and began to travel down opposite sides of the street as planned. As he crossed the street, Julian walked past Geronimo seated in the rental and spotted the first unmarked car. He casually looked across at Teague, who had also spotted the other officer. Nodding his head, Julian signaled for both of them to spring into action.

Brandishing their firearms, Teague and Julian both fired shots into the driver-side windows of the cars. Both officers were killed instantly.

Julian waved for his big brother as he placed his gun away in his pants. Geronimo leaped from his car and ran to meet his family so that they could charge into the house.

Darryl lay with his wife on the sofa when the sound of his front door bursting open caused him alarm.

"Oh my God!" Darryl cried out once he saw Geronimo.

Teague quickly shut the door behind them while Julian snatched Darryl's wife up by her throat.

"Don't touch her!" Darryl cried out, attempting to play the hero.

Instantly, Geronimo clocked him in the back of his head with his gun. Fighting for her life, the woman scratched Julian his neck. Furious, he began to beat her mercilessly in the face with his weapon. Blood and teeth flew from the gashes he caused.

"Please, stop! Don't hurt her!" Darryl pleaded.

"This is *your* fault, you piece of shit, so watch what you've wrought."

With a pistol to the back of his head, Darryl was forced to watch Julian rape his wife as she cried, his palm muffling her voice.

Suddenly, their eight-year-old son came into the room, wiping his eyes. "What's going on? I can't sleep—" The child froze, viewing the scene.

Before the boy could say another word, Geronimo raised his gun and shot him right between the eyes.

"Noooo!" Darryl screamed, crawling to his son's corpse.

Rising from his fun, Julian allowed the mother also to cradle her baby boy's head. Tears flowed as they held their child.

Looking from Teague to his brother, Julian shot the woman in the back of her head. No sooner than Darryl turned to Julian, Geronimo shot him in the back of his head.

Then Teague opened the door, and the trio casually exited the home. A few seconds later, the youngest of the house had awakened from all the commotion as well. Carrying her baby doll, the little girl walked into the living room and stopped in her tracks. Looking at her family slain, the child couldn't do anything but stare in shock.

****

Misti was desperately trying to enjoy herself at dinner, but Terrance Beeman was preoccupied with his thoughts.

"Terrance, you seem nervous. Are you all right?" she wondered.

Trying to mask his concerns, Beeman decided just to come clean. "Misti, somebody knows about us."

"What are you talking about?"

"I was approached today at my office by a woman with photos of us."

She was stunned. "Photos of us?"

"Yes! Of us, together, *intimately!*" he exclaimed.

"Calm your damn nerves right this second and lower your voice," Misti demanded. She raised her champagne flute to her lips and took a swallow.

"What are you thinking? Who could be behind this?"

"Harold," she said simply. "It's got to be my husband."

Terrance almost defecated on himself from the mere thought. On the other hand, Misti was convinced and coming to terms with facing death.

"Misti, after we leave here, I'm boarding a plane and never coming back. You'll never see me again."

Misti looked the coward in his eyes and wondered what it was that she ever saw in such a weakling.

He checked his watch. Noticing it was time to depart, he said, "I'm gonna miss you." He leaned in for a kiss.

Misti turned her lips away from his. Feeling the coolness of her cold shoulder, Beeman tossed a few bills on the table and said his final good-bye. Completely shaken to her core, Misti walked out of the restaurant by her lonesome and headed to the parking lot. As soon as she went to stick her key in the door, a figure emerged from the shadows, and covered her mouth and nose with a rag soaked in chloroform,knocking her unconscious. Like a thief in the night, both bodies vanished without leaving a trace.

The Big Payback

9

"Hi, my name is Tasha, and I'll be your waitress today. Will you ladies be needing menus, or are you ready to order?"

Charlotte studied the woman. She was still beautiful, but it was written all over her face how life had beat her down. "Nah, sweetheart. We don't need no menus. We came here to see you."

Tasha was confused. She looked from Charlotte . . . to Vikki . . . and finally, to Lollipop. Figuring that the women were either strippers or streetwalkers, Tasha didn't want to have anything to do with them.

"Listen, I'm just a single mother trying her best to make it in this world. I don't want no drama in my life," the waitress admitted.

"No drama, dear. We're bringing you an opportunity. How much do you make here?" Vikki questioned.

"It pays the bills."

"Barely making it isn't a good way of saying struggling last I checked," Lollipop added.

Tasha didn't want to stand and listen to the women patronize her. "Look, if you're not here to eat, then I'm going to have to ask you all to leave. These tables are reserved for paying customers only."

Charlotte pulled a brown paper bag from between her and Vikki. "Oh, we're paying," she said, tossing it to Tasha.

Hesitant, she opened the bag, and the large stacks of money made her eyes bulge.

"That's a quarter mill in all hundreds. All just for you," Lollipop informed her.

"Why for me? Who sent y'all?"

"Our employer wants to do right by you," Charlotte answered.

Tasha examined the money but pushed the cash away. "I mean no disrespect, but I've traveled down this road before, and it wasn't good for me."

Charlotte looked her square in the eyes and said, "No, Julian wasn't good for you. And now, we're offering you the chance to not be good for him."

Sliding the money back to the waitress, Charlotte had finally gotten Tasha's full attention.

****

Geronimo was surprised to find an envelope on the windshield of his truck. "What the fuck is this?" he said, removing it.

It read: *FROM A FRIEND* across it in a bold black marker. Tearing it open, a bunch of photos spilled out onto the pavement. Irritated, the large man bent down to retrieve them. Stunned, he didn't want to believe the images displayed all over the photographs. There she was, Evelyn Monroe . . . in bed with another. Each picture contained a different man between her thighs, suckling her breast, and penetrating her wanting mouth to make matters worse. Fury began to run its course through his veins as a note fell from the envelope.

Geronimo quickly began to read it. *"My friend, follow this address to catch her in the act. Do not allow her to play you for a fool any longer . . ."* he read, viewing the address attached. With his blood boiling, Geronimo jumped into his truck and hastily sped away.

****

Bound to a chair, Misti was in total darkness. As she heard the door open, she was determined not to die a coward. "Kill me and get it over with, you bastard!"

Trevonte removed her blindfold and stood before her. Shocked, Misti didn't know what to believe.

"First off, you're not in any danger. Bethany knows that I have you, and in case you were wondering, Harold *doesn't* know about you and Beeman. I had to leverage him with those photos so I could get you away long enough to bring you here," he revealed.

"But why go to all of this trouble? What are you up to?"

"Me and your daughter have grown close. So close that she opened up to me about your family history. I returned the favor and told her about mines. It appears that the Blake men have been as much a curse to you two as they have to my family."

"I'm not following you, Tre. I thought you and my boys were together in y'all activities. Hell, you helped end the war with the Drummonds," Misti reasoned.

"To get close to them. You see, Jamar was my cousin, but more so like my brother. They killed him because they wanted to own him. Harold made you give up Bethany, and your sons made you stay away from Bethany because they all think they own you."

Trevonte's words stung deep, only because she knew them to be true.

"Misti, I'm offering you your freedom, but you gotta accept the fact that I'm going to kill your boys."

A tear rolled down her face. "What kind of mother would I be to agree to such things?"

Suddenly, the door opened, and Mr. Lewis walked in.

Misti's lips began to tremble as she called his name. "Calvin?"

"I've missed you for far too long, Misti," he replied.

At that moment, Trevonte walked over and cut her free from the chair. Rising to her feet, Misti walked over to Mr. Lewis and stared passionately into his eyes.

Caressing her cheek, he began to speak. "Baby, they each made you sacrifice our daughter for their own jealous purposes. I had to stay away from her myself just to keep you both safe. Now, it's time for you to make your own choice to sacrifice them. I love you too much even to ask you to. I've always loved you too much," he confessed.

Misti looked from him to Trevonte and back.

"Will you help us end them once and for all?" Trevonte asked.

Without a word, Misti looked him in his eyes and nodded her head in agreement. The monsters had to go.

"It's time for us to be a family," Mr. Lewis said, grabbing her into his arms and kissing her passionately.

Spud and Lady Shyne walked in with bright smiles.

"It's amazing how God works. When Mr. Lewis showed us those pics, I wondered how he had a photo of the only daughter of Misti Blake. Then it all made sense. I had to bring her back to him," Trevonte admitted.

"Unc has always had secrets," Spud added.

"Glad to see them reunited, but we gotta roll," Lady Shyne reminded everyone.

"You ready for this?" Trevonte questioned.

"This is for Jamar. I've been ready since they took him from me," she replied.

Spud watched as they left and then looked to see Misti and his uncle still making out. "I'm just gonna let you two catch up," he said, exiting the room.

****

Arriving at the address on the note, Geronimo was in a blind fury. He hopped out and saw Evelyn's car parked on the street, which further infuriated him. He felt his heart breaking with each step he stomped toward the residence. Without hesitation, he marched up the porch steps and kicked in the door.

"I'm going to kill you both with my bare hands!" he promised at the top of his lungs.

Suddenly, Lady Shyne came from the kitchen and leaned over on the wall.

Geronimo recognized her. "What are you doing here, and where is Evelyn?"

"Look around, Geronimo. Do you *really* think that your slut of a woman is here?"

Geronimo looked around at the large empty space. There was no furniture. Plastic lined the walls and floors, with blinds over the windows.

"This is where you'll die, Geronimo," she promised.

He looked into her eyes and smirked.

"I remember the day you called into the station. How you taunted and threatened. How you vowed to take him from me," she said.

The big ogre attempted to reach for his gun, but it was to no avail. Trevonte walked in with his gun aimed directly at the back of his head.

"What the fuck is this?" Geronimo said, raising his hands above his head.

"You fucked up, Georgie Boy," she teased.

"You killed my cousin, Jamar. And you gotta answer for that," Trevonte promised.

Making his way alongside Lady Shyne, he handed her the gun.

Dropping his hands to his side, Geronimo began to laugh. "Do it, you little bitch. I'll be waiting in hell to fuck you while your little boyfriend watches," he snarled.

Lady Shyne held the gun before her with both hands. Tears streamed down her cheeks as she prepared to squeeze the trigger. "Get on your knees," she ordered.

"Fuck you," he retorted.

"Get on your knees!" she repeated, words accompanied by bullets this time.

Two shots landed in Geronimo's kneecap, causing him to stumble backward.

Fighting to stand tall, he leaned against the wall to brace himself. "Aaaghh," he cried as drool spilled from his lips. "You fucking bitch!"

"On your knees!" she hissed, shooting him in his other kneecap.

Geronimo fell to the floor and screamed out in agonizing pain. Trevonte smiled as Lady Shyne made her way over to him. Reaching for his gun, Geronimo caught more slugs in both of his hands. Bleeding out, Lady Shyne became a blur as she towered over the man's burly frame.

"So many men have fallen to your gun. Did you ever think your story would end like this?" Trevonte questioned from the near distance.

Paralyzed, Geronimo lay with his final words being a faint . . . "Fuck you."

Lady Shyne put a bullet right between his eyes and stared at his corpse with satisfaction.

****

"Did you hear that?" Evelyn asked, unlocking her car door to get inside.

"Hear what?" Bethany questioned.

"I could've sworn I heard gunshots," Evelyn stated.

Bethany laughed. "Not in this neighborhood."

Evelyn figured she was right.

"Thanks again for personally delivering those clothes to me from your boutique. I just love your shop."

"You're family, Bethany. No worries," Evelyn said, loading herself into her car.

As she sped out of view, Bethany headed over to her home to lock it up. Next, she raced across the street to her second apartment to help her man and Lady Shyne clean up their mess.

Death to Dynasty   **10**

Trevonte and Teague stood before Harold as the old man sat frustrated by his instincts.

"I knew something was wrong. When she didn't come home last night, I knew things weren't right," Harold said.

Holding his uncle's phone, Teague studied the image of his aunt bound and gagged. "I ain't never seen this place before. Think this Macon?" Teague asked, showing Trevonte the pic.

Trevonte played it smooth as he looked closer. "Nah, man, you see that?" he asked, pointing to a cross hanging in the background.

"What is it?"

"It's a long shot, but I think she being held in Atlanta. I ain't seen that type of cross but one place in my whole life. That black Jesus is unforgettable!" Trevonte exclaimed.

Overzealous, Harold stood to his feet. "Who in the hell could have taken her to Atlanta?" he wondered.

"We can figure that shit out in the car. Teague, call Geronimo and Julian and tell them we need them," Trevonte ordered.

"Man, I've been calling them all morning. Them niggas ain't picking up for shit."

"Fuck it! Try once more, but let's move 'cause every second count."

Harold looked at Trevonte and was glad to have him in the family. He had taken to him like another son and smiled as they headed out.

Calling Julian's phone, Teague still didn't get an answer.

****

Charlotte was on her knees sucking the life out of Julian's manhood as his phone repeatedly went straight to voicemail. She had convinced him to put it on DO NOT DISTURB while they did their thing.

"Suck that dick," he moaned as she bobbed her head up and down between his thighs. Spilling saliva down his length, Charlotte gently squeezed on his balls for additional comfort. Gripping the back of her head, Julian felt himself nearing a climax. "Come on . . . uggghhhh!" he groaned, spilling down her warm throat. Charlotte sucked up every drop and swallowed him whole. Sinking into the bed, Julian was in heaven. "My goodness! I gotta return the favor now," he cooed.

Charlotte beamed and got at the head of the bed. Spreading her legs wide, she invited his tongue inside. Julian lapped away at Charlotte's swollen clit like a thirsty dog. Caressing the back of his scalp, she ground her drenched pussy into his mouth as Tasha made her way into the bedroom. Clutching an aluminum baseball bat in her hand, the woman stood directly behind his bobbing head. Charlotte smiled at her and then yanked his head up to face her.

"Nothing personal. All business," she said. Pulling a knife from underneath her pillow, Charlotte stabbed Julian in his eye.

Rolling backward and onto the floor in excruciating pain, he snatched the blade from his eye. Tasha raised her bat and swung it across his face, breaking his jaw on contact.

"You remember me, you bitch-ass nigga?!" she screamed, now beating him in his dick with the bat.

Howling in pain, Julian could barely see his attacker. He threw up his hands as he pleaded for the woman to stop. Without hesitation, she swung the bat and broke both his thumbs and index fingers. Soon after, he crawled into the corner and looked at the woman. He recognized her face.

"Lucky Charms?" he asked, in total amazement.

"Yea! *Now* you remember me," she spat, cracking him in the head once more.

With his nuts and dick swollen, fingers broken, and blinded in one eye, Julian lay nearly unconscious as Charlotte brought out a duffle bag.

"Everything you asked me for is in there," she said.

"Good," Tasha replied, unzipping it.

Pulling out a mask and 12-inch dildo, Tasha put them both on. Charlotte pulled out her phone and started to record. Taking the bat, Tasha slapped him across his already broken jaw. Julian fell over onto the floor. Removing two steel nail stakes and a mallet, she lay Julian on his stomach and stretched his arm out. She took one of the stakes and held it over his fist. Taking the mallet, she struck it with all of her might. Julian screamed in horrific pain as the stake tore through his skin, bones, and the floor.

Unable to move his hand, he pulled the stake, but it wouldn't budge. Charlotte continued recording as he begged her for mercy. Without remorse, Tasha stretched his other arm out and repeated the same thing with the other steel nail stake. Pinned to the floor on his belly, Julian cried like a baby.

Tasha reached into the bag, pulling out a bottle of lighter fluid, and made her way around to face him. "It's *my* turn to make *you* feel the burn, Julian," she said, holding onto her 12-inch strap-on.

He cried and pleaded as she squirted lighter fluid all over the rubber penis. Then Tasha walked over and straddled his back.

"I want you to beg me to stop," she taunted.

Aiming for his anus, she shoved her fake dick up his ass repeatedly as he whimpered for her mercy. Charlotte sat on the bed making sure the camera caught his face. As his bloody eye socket spewed crimson, he seemed to be in a state of limbo. Tasha fucked him for nearly twenty minutes before she grew weary.

Unstrapping the fake dick from her waist, she stood up and left it buried in his rectum. It rested within him soaked in blood and lighter fluid. Tasha spit on him and then went back to the bag. Retrieving a lighter, she brought it to his ass and set the strap-on ablaze. Charlotte recorded as he sizzled, screamed, and squirmed.

Satisfied, Tasha signaled for Charlotte to stop filming. They left the house as Julian shook and burned to a crisp, followed by the entire house coming down on top of him.

Julian Blake trembled until his final breath was engulfed by smoke.

****

As Trevonte parked their car, Harold and Teague couldn't believe where they had stopped.

"A church?" Teague inquired.

"Shit, it's been closed down forever, but I recognize that cross anywhere. Misti's in there," Trevonte promised.

Harold didn't give a damn. He was ready to get his wife. The trio drew their pistols as they raced inside the run-down building. Moving carefully, they inched themselves into open view when Teague spotted his aunt. Harold looked as his wife sat seemingly bound to a chair on the church stage.

"Misti!" he exclaimed.

Looking up, she saw them all.

From behind ragged curtains, Mr. Lewis appeared and stood beside Misti.

"Hello, old friend," he taunted.

"You? *You* kidnapped my wife?" Harold questioned in surprise.

Suddenly, Lady Shyne, Spud, and Bethany emerged from behind the curtains as well.

"No. I reclaimed my love," Mr. Lewis replied.

Spotting Spud and Bethany at his side, Teague knew that Trevonte was part of the double cross. He focused his attention on him, but it was too late. Trevonte was already aiming at his temple. Right then, a series of men appeared all over the abandoned church with their guns drawn.

"Yea, these my niggas," Trevonte spoke.

Brokenhearted, Harold turned around and faced him. Misti stood to her feet and ordered the Blakes to throw down their weapons. Harold and Teague couldn't believe it.

"We fucking came to rescue you!" Teague snapped.

"Which makes you the fools. Now put down the fucking guns!" Mr. Lewis ordered.

Harold and Teague both tossed their pistols in front of them. Walking from the stage hand-in-hand, Mr. Lewis and Misti approached the men. Venom filled their eyes. Mr. Lewis looked from Harold and spoke to Trevonte.

"Now, avenge your cousin."

Handing Mr. Lewis his gun, Trevonte turned to Teague and gave him a stiff jab to the nose, breaking it instantly. As blood spilled from his nostrils, everything became blurry.

"You wanna brag about shooting people in the face while they holding their kid? You piece of shit!" Trevonte barked, kicking Teague in the side of his head.

Harold looked on as his nephew got the shit beat out of him. Mr. Lewis smiled as Trevonte stomped his cousin's killer into the gravel and dust of the run-down building. Bethany and Lady Shyne held each other's hands while viewing the last remnants of a fallen empire.

Coughing up blood, Teague was finished. Both his eyes were swollen shut, and he kept drifting in and out of consciousness. Tears filled his eyes as Trevonte thought about Jamar. He walked over to Mr. Lewis to retrieve his pistol.

"You piece of shit!" Trevonte snapped, placing the gun in Teague's mouth.

Bethany turned her head as her man squeezed the trigger. Harold watched as his nephew's brains blasted from the back of his open scalp. Mr. Lewis took the gun from Trevonte and embraced him.

"Now, it's one last cross to bear, young brother. I got this one," he assured him.

Placing the pistol between Harold's eyes, Mr. Lewis asked, "Any final words?"

Fighting back the tears, Harold swallowed and looked at his wife. "No matter what you may believe, I've always loved you. Everything that I did was for our family," he said.

Mr. Lewis smashed the gun to his head, and just as he prepared to end his life, Misti screamed, "No!"

Bethany gasped.

Trevonte looked at her in disbelief.

Harold began to smile.

Confused, Mr. Lewis looked at her.

"This isn't how this is supposed to be. You can't do this," she said, taking the gun away from him.

Laughing, Harold was relieved. "That's right, baby. You're my wife," he boldly stated.

Mr. Lewis looked into her eyes as she said, "I've imagined this moment a million times over, and this is *always* how it ends." With those words, she pointed the gun at Harold and shot him right between his eyes.

"Oh shit!" Spud exclaimed.

Trevonte's lips formed into a smile as the old man's body dropped. Mr. Lewis held Misti close as Trevonte did her daughter. Relieved, they all looked at the final piece of a deadly puzzle as the last of the Blake men drifted off to hell. The dawning of a new family had just been born.

-END-

All Hail the Street Kings.

NEW TITLES FROM WAHIDA CLARK PRESENTS

Other Titles by
Author Hood Chronicles

B-MORE CAREFUL

THE PREQUEL | NETTA AND TONE'S STORY

THE KING OF URBAN LIT
SHANNON HOLMES